W9-BVD-726

PENGUIN CLASSICS

ELECTIVE AFFINITIES

JOHANN WOLFGANG VON GOETHE was born in Frankfurt-am-Main in 1749. He studied at Leipzig, where he showed interest in the occult, and in Strassburg, where Herder introduced him to Shakespeare's works and to folk poetry. He produced some essays and lyrical verse, and at twenty-four wrote *Goetz von Berlichingen*, a play which brought him national fame and established him in the current *Sturm und Drang* movement. *Werther*, a tragic romance, was an even greater success. Goethe began work on *Faust*, and *Egmont*, another tragedy, before being invited to join the government at Weimar. His interest in the classical world led him to leave suddenly for Italy in 1768, and the *Italian Journey* recounts his travels there. *Iphigenie auf Tauris* and *Torquato Tasso*, classical dramas, were begun at this time. Returning to Weimar, Goethe started the second part of *Faust*, encouraged by Schiller. During this late period he finished the series of *Wilhelm Meister* books and wrote many other works, including *The Oriental Divan* and *Elective Affinities*. He also directed the State Theatre and worked on scientific theories in evolutionary botany, anatomy and colour. Goethe was married in 1806. He finished *Faust* before he died in 1832.

R. J. HOLLINGDALE has translated eleven of Nietzsche's books and published two books about him. He has also translated works by, among others, Schopenhauer, Goethe, E. T. A. Hoffmann, Lichtenberg and Theodor Fontane, many of these for the Penguin Classics. He is Honorary President of the British Nietzsche Society, and was for the Australian academic year 1991 Visiting Fellow at Trinity College, Melbourne.

Johann Wolfgang von Goethe

ELECTIVE AFFINITIES

Translated with an introduction by
R. J. Hollingdale

Penguin Books

PENGUIN BOOKS

Published by the Penguin Group
Penguin Books Ltd, 27 Wrights Lane, London W8 5TZ, England
Penguin Books USA Inc., 375 Hudson Street, New York, New York 10014, USA
Penguin Books Australia Ltd, Ringwood, Victoria, Australia
Penguin Books Canada Ltd, 10 Alcorn Avenue, Toronto, Ontario, Canada M4V 3B2
Penguin Books (NZ) Ltd, 182–190 Wairau Road, Auckland 10, New Zealand

Penguin Books Ltd, Registered Offices: Harmondsworth, Middlesex, England

First published 1809
This translation first published 1971
11 13 15 17 19 20 18 16 14 12

Translation and introduction
copyright © R. J. Hollingdale, 1971
All rights reserved

Printed in England by Clays Ltd, St Ives plc
Set in Linotype Juliana

CONTENTS

INTRODUCTION

1

GOETHE had lived with Christiane Vulpius for more than eighteen years and had had five children by her before, on 19 October 1806, he married her in the sacristy of the Hofkirche at Weimar. He was fifty-seven, she was forty-one. To Weimar society marriage was a contract not a 'sacrament', and divorce was a normal element of civilized life; but, like any society which still has the will to survive in it, Weimar society preserved and valued the social forms, and Goethe's irregular household was an embarrassment. But he put an end to the irregularity only under external pressure. On 14 October the battle of Jena was fought and lost and was followed by the entry of the French army into Weimar: plundering and other inconveniences occurred, Goethe's house was invaded, and it appears that the author of *Faust* was saved from a manhandling only by the valiant interposition of his Gretchen, who drove the soldiers away. The following day Napoleon arrived in the town and regularized military occupation commenced. In these circumstances, and also no doubt inspired to renewed affection by Christiane's brave behaviour, Goethe at last decided he must give her the security of regular wifehood, and he put his decision into effect at once. There is no reason to think – on the contrary, there is every reason to doubt – that he would have taken any such step had he not been driven to it almost literally at the point of a bayonet.

But now that he was a married man, he discovered that he had all along harboured very stern moral principles with regard to the marriage tie, and he became an emphatic critic of the laxity displayed by the society in which he lived. Franz Volkmar Reinhard, who met him during the summer

7

'cure' at Karlsbad in 1807, records that he was taken aback at the vehemence of Goethe's utterances on the sanctity and indissolubility of marriage – and Reinhard was head court chaplain at Dresden. There is, of course, no logical inconsistency involved in holding marriage in high regard and at the same time 'living in sin', but the two things do not lie very comfortably together and feeling rebels at their juxtaposition. Until his journey to Italy of 1786–8, Goethe avoided not only marriage but any binding relationship with women, and it was not from any strictness of principle but because until this epoch there had been a good deal of Georgie Porgie in that great man. Within a month of his return to Weimar, however, he had taken Christiane into his home and was openly living with her, in imitation, one may think, not only of the artists and bohemians with whom he had mixed while in Italy, but also of the Roman poets whose style he now began to adopt as his own : one understands Goethe's 'classicism' better when one realizes that it meant not only writing like 'Amor's triumvirate' Propertius, Catullus and Tibullus but also living like them; that 'classicism' meant to Goethe, not coldness and rigidity and suppression of emotion, but exactly the reverse. Emotionally he was far more relaxed and happy than he had been, and he was quite content to live *as if* married without actually being so, which suggests that he had no very strong feelings at all on the subject of marriage, that he was 'pagan' in that matter. When he was finally propelled into matrimony, it is clear that the acquisition of this novel status had a far more powerful effect on him than he had thought possible; and the first effect seems to have been to make him critical of the easy wedding and divorcing and wedding again sanctioned by custom among the petty aristocracy and bourgeoisie among which he moved.

In the winter of 1807–8, however, a complication appeared in the person of a young lady with the lovely name of Minna Herzlieb. Minna was the foster-daughter of the printer and

8

publisher Karl Friedrich Frommann, at whose home in Jena Goethe had first met her in 1803; then she had been only a girl, but now she had reached the ripe old age of eighteen, and Goethe began to feel towards her an emotion which, while again not involving any logical inconsistency with a high regard for marriage, does not lie very comfortably beside it. He fell in love with Minna Herzlieb: the first of the affairs of his later life with women far younger than he which, because of the difference in ages, could come to nothing in the prosaic world and were for that reason sublimated into poetry. Its first product was the cycle of seventeen sonnets written as a duel with Minna's other admirer, the Romantic poet Zacharias Werner, who was nineteen years younger than Goethe and, having just dissolved his third marriage, once more a single man. The weapons were of Werner's choosing: he was a specialist in Italian sonnets, while to Goethe it was a strange form. But to challenge Goethe to a contest of verse-writing was a foolhardy and foredoomed undertaking, for he was and remains the heavyweight champion of the world in that sport. Schiller, who had to work hard at his poetry, has left on record his amazement at the ease with which Goethe could reel off poems in any and every form without any kind of effort or preparation: he could, if he wished, speak poems as other men speak slabs of prose, and the ability was clearly innate, in the way composing music was innate in Mozart. His sonnets to Fräulein Herzlieb are, as one could have expected, perfect imitations of the Italian model: very smooth-flowing rhythm, effortless rhyming, each poem the vehicle of one mildly ingenious idea. But they are not serious work, and were quite inadequate as a vehicle for his passion for Minna.

Of far greater weight is the drama *Pandora* which, although unfinished, must be counted among the most remarkable of his achievements: that it is comparatively unknown is due entirely to the existence of the second part of *Faust*, completed

9

a quarter of a century later, in which the poetical innovations of *Pandora* are employed with even greater virtuosity and at much greater length. Goethe made no secret of the fact that this glittering imitation of Greek tragedy owed its substance to his passion for a girl forty years his junior and that such a passion could find no expression except a sublimated one in the form of art. But this vehicle too was insufficient to carry all that was now weighing on his mind and heart; it was in particular altogether silent on the subject of the conflict, of which he was at just this time acutely aware, between his idea of marriage and his experience of the waywardness of passion; and so, simultaneously with *Pandora*, he began a story whose immediate theme is precisely this conflict and to which he gave the odd and, when correctly understood, provocative title *Die Wahlverwandtschaften* – *Elective Affinities*.

The first time the story is mentioned is in his diary entry for 11 April 1808, where the title occurs along with plans for stories to be inserted into the loosely constructed novel *Wilhelm Meister's Travels* to illustrate its sub-title *The Renouncers (Die Entsagenden)*: the entry records that on that day he was engaged in plotting the stories for the novel, especially *Elective Affinities* and *The Man of Fifty*. The latter story has certain affinities with *Elective Affinities*: the man of fifty is in love with his niece but gives her up when he discovers she is in love with his son. *Elective Affinities*, as a short story, was begun on 29 May 1808 and finished at the end of July. But in April 1809 Goethe decided to expand it, employing the existing story as an outline upon which to work. He devoted the spring and summer to its composition, and on 28 July he sent the opening chapters to the printer so that he would be compelled to proceed with the rest at a brisk pace. The work was completed on 4 October and published by Cotta in two volumes the same autumn.

I have called the original form of *Elective Affinities* a story: the German is *Novelle*, for which there is no exact English equivalent. It means first of all a fictional narrative longer than a story (*Erzählung*, French *conte*) but shorter than a novel (*Roman*, the same word in French), but as a rule too short to be called a short novel. A long story is, I suppose, the English expression. But the classic German *Novelle* possesses distinguishing characteristics other than its length which make it a distinct species of narrative. These characteristics are: strict economy, deliberate avoidance of the breadth and relaxed tempo of the *Roman*; emphasis on plot, so that the characters of the story are subordinate to it and their characteristics are functions of it; as a consequence, they are given only forenames or titles or the names of their professions or an ironic surname, but not naturalistic names; the milieu is not naturalistic, natural scenes possess a function beyond their function as the setting of the action; the action itself is not naturalistic, it proceeds in a more orderly fashion than everyday life or everyday life in a novel, there is a symmetry of action foreign to reality and often the outcome is prefigured, so that there is a sense of inevitability about it; finally, there is always an explicit or implied narrator, the story is supposed to be something the narrator has experienced or heard about and not something he has invented, his function is to reproduce an actual event as a conscious work of art, so that his manner will display a higher degree of artistry and artificiality than is normally found in a novel. These 'rules' were, of course, extracted from the practice of German writers and not invented in advance: but by the late eighteenth century German literature had become a very self-conscious affair, and *Novellen* were then deliberately framed so as to accord with the 'rules', the object being, as with all 'formalism', to impose shape and order upon the flux of experience. The outcome was a type of fictional narrative as immediately identifiable as a strict fugue or an Italian operatic aria: although the reader or listener (for the *Novelle* clearly originates in the *spoken* story) will not know in advance the details of what is coming he will know the kind of artistic experience to expect. Perhaps the best-known *Novelle* is Goethe's story called simply *Novelle* and intended, as its title (or rather lack of title) indicates, as a model of the form. *Elective Affinities* contains an inset *Novelle*, 'The Wayward Young Neighbours', which exhibits the characteristics of the form on a small scale, and the reader will notice the typical *Novelle* atmosphere: the absence of names, the strict economy of means, the unnaturalistic action, and so on, and also the fact that the story is narrated, that it is concerned with an event the narrator has heard about and not invented, and that it has implications of which he is unaware.

Now the point of expounding all this is to show that *Elective Affinities* not only began life as a *Novelle*, but remained one, that it differs from the classic *Novelle* only in respect of length. And the point of emphasizing that fact is to warn the reader in advance what kind of narrative to expect, so that when he finds it does not proceed as a novel usually proceeds he will not experience any discomfort or suppose the work to be an unsuccessful attempt at a form which is in fact not being attempted at all.

The narrative style is characterized by a strict economy; the characters are functions of the plot, and their characteristics are those demanded by the furtherance of the plot; they are given only forenames (Eduard, Ottilie, Charlotte), or titles (the Captain, the Count, the Baroness), or professional names (the schoolmaster, the architect, the gardener), or in one case an ironic surname (Mittler); the setting is not naturalistic and the scenes in which the action takes place (the mansion, the village, the moss-hut, the pavilion, the park, etc.) also possess a symbolic function; the action itself is not naturalistic, it contains elements not susceptible to rational explanation, and it proceeds in a more orderly and symmetrical way than one would expect in a novel. Most important of all, it is narrated, not directly by the author, but by a narrator who is also an invented character, although he never appears. It may well be that Goethe chose to tell his story in the form of an expanded *Novelle* precisely in order that the reader should assume the existence of a narrator who is repeating something he has learned of but does not necessarily fully understand – a technique which makes possible the mystery and ambiguity underlying the action and permits the employment of an ironical tone without committing the author himself to an ironical view of that action.

3

The term *Wahlverwandtschaft* was a technical term of eighteenth-century chemistry, the German translation of a coinage of the Swedish chemist Torbern Olof Bergmann (1735–84) in the title of his book *De attractionibus electivis* (1775), first put into German by Heinrich Tabor in 1785. The English form, elective affinity, is closer to the original Latin than the German form and, although not self-explanatory, probably cannot be improved upon. Its meaning is described in the fourth chapter of Part One of *Elective Affinities* and need not be repeated here. What should be emphasized here, though, is its extraordinariness as the title of a novel. It is as if a contemporary novelist should call his book *The Principle of Verifiability* or *E Equals MC Squared*. The emotional and romantic connotations which the term subsequently acquired derived from the novel to which it was attached : at the time of the novel's publication, *Wahlverwandtschaft* was a term used solely in chemistry.

Goethe was conscious of the risk involved in prefixing such

a title to the book, and in an advertisement published in Cotta's *Morgenblatt* on 4 September 1809 he sought to explain that 'this strange title', which 'it seems was suggested to the author by his continuing work in the field of physics', was a 'metaphor in chemistry' whose 'spiritual origin' the novel would demonstrate. But this statement was altogether inadequate and was subsequently forgotten or frankly disbelieved: the almost universal view being that the book was intended to demonstrate the chemical origin of love. Such a thesis would, of course, be an immoral one, and *Elective Affinities* was generally charged with being an immoral book. Goethe was no stranger to such charges, but he was especially annoyed that they should be levelled at this particular work, for which he had an exceptional affection, and he angrily rejected every suggestion there was anything whatever in it that could be called reprehensible. Eventually he lost all patience with a stream of criticism that must to us today seem incredibly insensitive and pettifogging, and when his old friend Knebel started making moral objections to the novel he exploded: 'But I didn't write it for you, I wrote it for little girls!' – which I take to be an assertion that the book is altogether wholesome and romantic and that only a moralizing old man could find anything in it to object to.

4

The story's origin was clearly, as already suggested, the conflict between Goethe's idea of marriage, the currently accepted idea of it, and the passions with which neither idea seems able to cope. But when he expanded it to its present size, Goethe also took the opportunity to embody in it a criticism of more of current society than its marriage customs, so that *Elective Affinities* is often referred to as primarily the earliest German social novel. The ironic tone already bestowed upon the narrator proved very useful in this regard, enabling the author to paint a very unflattering portrait of his contemporaries without having to resort to explicit denunciation.

The society we meet in the novel is that of the German countryside at the beginning of the nineteenth century. Three-quarters of all Germans lived on and by the land, and towns were still small and far apart. In this milieu there were three social classes: the nobility, who owned the land and occupied the leading positions in the army and the civil service; the 'people', who were still for the most part peasants; and between these two extremes the 'middle class', i.e. the professions. The two latter classes were mainly engaged in working for the first. There was almost no social discontent: everyone knew his place and kept to it.

When the members of the landed nobility were not engaged in military or governmental activities they were idle, and it is in this state of idleness that the aristocrats of *Elective Affinities* are usually found. How they fill up their time is the subject of much of the narrative. Their activities vary very widely, but they are all characterized by the expenditure of a large amount of energy for what are at best inadequate results. The narrator leaves us in no doubt about what he thinks of Luciane and her crowd, and his sarcasm is particularly biting when he comes to describe their one attempt at artistic creativity: that this should be the reproduction of famous paintings as *tableaux vivants* speaks for the footling nature of their cultural interests. But it is a question whether he is very much more sympathetic towards the indubitably more useful occupations of the leading characters. What comes through, I think, is that, even when engaged in landscape gardening, the design and construction of a new building, or the improvement of the village, they are for the most part playing amateurishly at these things without any real objective except the consumption of time and the avoidance of boredom. The influence on these occupations of the periodical celebration of birthdays, and the very considerable additional effort and expenditure devoted to these celebrations, would give the game away if it had not been given away already.

The worst effect of this comfortable idleness in which they exist is, however, that which it exercises on their emotional lives: the emotional turmoil into which Eduard and Charlotte are thrown by the introduction into their home of two fresh faces is, according to contemporary testimony, in no sense a figment of the novelist's imagination but, on the contrary, almost the normal thing. It is not only their hands and minds that are under-occupied, their nerves and vital spirits are so too, and any occasion for bringing them into activity is likely to be seized upon. It is at this point, where idleness undermines marriage, that Goethe's social criticism and his romantic plot join forces.

December 1969   R.J.H.

PART ONE

CHAPTER ONE

EDUARD was the name of a wealthy baron in the prime of life and he had been spending the best hour of an April afternoon in his orchard nursery grafting new shoots he had just obtained on to the young trees. He had just finished and he was putting the tools back in their case and looking with satisfaction at the work he had done when the gardener came up. He was very pleased to see how interested and busy the master was.

'Have you seen my wife about?' Eduard asked him, about to move off.

'She is over in the new park,' the gardener said. 'The moss-hut she has had built by the cliff-face over against the mansion will be finished today. It's all been beautifully done and you're bound to like it, my lord. You get a marvellous view: the village down below, just to the right the church, and over the church tower you can see for miles. Then opposite, the mansion and the gardens.'

'Quite so,' said Eduard. 'I could see the men at work.'

'Then,' the gardener went on, 'to the right the valley opens up and you can see across the meadows and trees and far into the distance. The path up the cliff is laid out very fine. Her ladyship understands these things. It is a pleasure to work under her.'

'Go to her,' said Eduard, 'and ask her to wait for me. Tell her I want to have the pleasure of seeing the new creation.'

The gardener hurried off and Eduard soon followed him.

He went down the terraces and inspected in passing the greenhouses and the hotbeds until he arrived at the water and then, crossing over a little wooden bridge, at the place where the path to the new park divided into two branches. He ignored the one leading directly to the cliff in a straightish line through the churchyard and took instead the other branch to the left, which wound gently up through undergrowth and thickets. Where the two branches met again he sat down for a moment on a convenient bench, then set out on the actual ascent and the narrow path, now steep, now less steep, led him over steps and ledges of every kind finally to the moss-hut.

Charlotte met her husband in the doorway and had him sit in such a position that he could at a single glance view the different aspects of the landscape through the door and windows as though they were pictures in a frame. He said he was pleased by the prospect and hoped that spring would soon render it even more animated than it was at present. 'The only thing I would say,' he said, 'is that the moss-hut seems to me a little too small.'

'And yet there is room for us two,' Charlotte replied.

'That is so, indeed,' said Eduard. 'And I do not doubt that there would be room for a third.'

'Why not?' Charlotte replied. 'And for a fourth too. And for any larger company we would want to use somewhere else.'

'As we are here quietly by ourselves,' said Eduard, 'and in an altogether cheerful and relaxed frame of mind, I have to confess I have had something weighing upon me for some time which I have to confide to you, and want to, but which I cannot bring myself to speak of.'

'I have noticed something of the kind,' Charlotte said.

'And I have to admit,' Eduard went on, 'that if I was not pressed by the post tomorrow morning, and we did not have to come to a decision today, I might still have kept silent.'

'Well,' Charlotte asked, smiling and meeting him halfway, 'what is the matter?'

'It concerns our friend the Captain,' Eduard answered. 'You know of the sad situation in which he, like so many others, has through no fault of his own been placed. It must be very painful for a man of his acquirements, of his talents and accomplishments, to find himself out of employment and – but I shall no longer keep back what it is I want for him. I should like us to have him here with us for a time.'

'That needs considering,' Charlotte replied, 'and looking at from more than one point of view.'

'Well, I am ready to tell you what I think,' Eduard said. 'His last letter was a silent expression of the profoundest despondency; not that he is lacking for anything, for he knows how to limit his wants and, as for real necessities, I have taken care of them; nor does it trouble him to have to accept them from me, for we have during our lifetime become so much indebted to one another we can no longer compute how our credit and debit stand – that he is without occupation, that is what really torments him. His only pleasure – indeed, it is his passion – is daily and hourly to employ for the benefit of others the many abilities he has developed in himself. And now to sit idly with arms folded, or to go on studying and acquiring further skills because he cannot employ those he already possesses in full measure – in short, my dear, it is a painful situation, and he feels it doubly and trebly being all alone.'

'But I thought he had received offers from various quarters,' said Charlotte. 'I myself have written on his behalf to many active friends of mine and so far as I know not without effect.'

'Quite so,' Eduard replied; 'but even these opportunities, these offers, bring him fresh torment and discontent. None of the positions is suited to him. He would not be productive; he would have to sacrifice himself, his time, his convictions, his whole way of life, and that he finds impossible. The more I think about all this, and the more I feel it, the stronger grows my desire to see him here with us.'

'It is very good and kind of you,' Charlotte replied, 'to consider your friend's position with so much sympathy; only let me invite you to consider your own position, our own position.'

'I have done so,' Eduard said. 'His presence would promise nothing but profit and pleasantness for us. I will not speak of the expense, which will in any case be slight, especially when I consider his presence will not inconvenience us in the slightest. He can live in the right wing of the house and we shall easily see to everything else. Think how this will help him, and how much pleasure we shall have from his company ! Indeed, we shall profit from it. For a long time now I have wanted to have the estate and the neighbourhood surveyed; he will take care of that. You intend to administer the estate yourself in the future, as soon as the leases of the present tenants have expired. That is a hazardous undertaking ! We should benefit very much from his instruction ! I feel only too well how I lack a man of his sort. The country people possess the knowledge, but the information they give is confused and not honest. The people from the town who have studied the subject are clear and straightforward, but they lack direct discernment in this particular business. I promise myself both from our friend; and I can imagine a hundred other circumstances which will then arise which will concern you too and from which I anticipate much good. You have listened very patiently; now tell me what you have to say, don't be afraid to speak freely and to the purpose : I shan't interrupt.'

'Very well then,' Charlotte replied, 'I will begin with a general observation. Men think more of individual and present things, and rightly, because they are called upon to be active, while women, on the other hand, think more of what is continuous in life, and they are equally right, because their fate and the fate of their families is tied to this continuity and it is precisely this feeling for continuity that is demanded of them. So let us take a look at our present and past life; you will then grant me that to call the Captain here does not coincide so closely with our intentions, our plans or our arrangements as you have maintained.

'I like so very much to think back to when we first knew one another! When we were young we loved very dearly. We were parted: you from me, because your father, from an insatiable craving for possessions, married you to a somewhat older wealthy woman; I from you, because having no special prospects, I had to give my hand to a well-to-do man I did not love, though he had my respect. We became free again; you earlier, when your little mother left you in possession of a considerable fortune; I later, just at the time you came back from your travels. And so we found one another again. We rejoiced at what we remembered, loved what we remembered, and there was nothing to hinder our living together. You urged marriage; I did not consent at once for, since we are about the same age, I have grown older as a woman, you have not grown older as a man. In the end I would not refuse you what you seemed to consider your only happiness. You wanted to recover at my side from all the distresses you had experienced at court, in the army, on your travels; to come to yourself again, to enjoy life; but to do this with me alone. I sent my only daughter off to a boarding-school, where she is, to be sure, developing in many more directions than she would have if she had stayed in the country; and not her alone, I also sent there my dear niece Ottilie, who might perhaps have grown up into a domestic companion more suitably under my own guidance. All this took place with your agreement, simply so that we ourselves might live and enjoy undisturbed the happiness we had earlier longed for so intensely and later at last attained. Thus did we enter upon our sojourn in the country. I took charge of affairs indoors, you of affairs outdoors and of whatever affected us as a whole. I have ordered my life to meet your wishes in all things, to live only for you; let us try, at least for a time, to see whether we cannot in this way suffice one another.'

'Since, as you say, continuity is your real element,' Eduard replied, 'we ought not to pay attention to you when you call upon individual instances, nor give in to you without argument, though you may have been right before today. The foundation we have laid for our existence is a good one; but are we to build nothing more on it? Is nothing else to develop from it? What I have achieved in the garden, and you in the park – shall we have done that only for hermits?'

'That is all very true,' Charlotte replied; 'only do not let us bring in any impediment. Remember that our pleasures too were intended to a certain extent to depend on our being alone together. You wanted first of all to show me your travel journals in correct sequence and in so doing to reduce to order all the papers that belong with them, and with my support and assistance to assemble out of these invaluable but muddled leaves and notebooks a whole which we and others might enjoy. I promised to help you copy them out, and we thought to travel in memory, and in comfortable seclusion, through the world we were unable to see together. Indeed, we have already made a start. Then you have taken up your flute again in the evenings and I join you at the piano; and we do not lack visitors or people to visit. I at least have made for myself out of all this the first truly happy summer of my life, as happy as any I thought to enjoy.'

'That is very loving and sensible,' Eduard replied, rubbing his forehead, 'and I would agree with it were it not for the thought that the Captain's presence will disturb nothing, but rather expedite and enliven everything. He was with me on some of my travels, and he too noticed many things and in his own way: only if we employed his recollections with mine would it become a proper whole.'

'In that case,' Charlotte said, somewhat impatiently, 'let

me confess in all sincerity that this proposal goes against my feelings. I have a premonition that no good will come of it.'

'Granted this fashion of argument,' Eduard replied, 'you women would be invincible: first sensible, so that one cannot contradict; affectionate, so that one is glad to give in; sensitive, so that one does not want to hurt you; full of premonitions, so that one is frightened.'

'I am not superstitious,' Charlotte replied, 'and would pay no attention to these obscure stirrings if that was all they were; but mostly they are instinctive recollections of the happy or unhappy consequences of our own or other people's past actions. There is nothing of more significance in any situation than the intervention of a third party. I have known friends, brothers and sisters, lovers, married couples, whose relationship has been altogether changed, whose life has been turned upside down, by the chance or intended arrival of another person.'

'That might well happen with people who live with their eyes shut,' Eduard replied, 'not with those who, educated by experience, are more aware of themselves.'

'Awareness, my dear,' Charlotte rejoined, 'is no sufficient weapon for him who wields it; it is often, indeed, a dangerous one; and this much at least emerges from all our talk, that we should not be precipitate. Give it a few days more: do not decide now!'

'As matters stand,' Eduard answered, 'we should still be precipitate if we decided after a few weeks more. We have argued back and forth the reasons for and against; it is time for a decision, and now the best thing would really be to leave the decision to chance.'

'I know that when you cannot make up your mind you like to act on a throw of the dice,' Charlotte replied, 'but in so serious a matter as this I would regard such a proceeding as wicked.'

25

'But what am I to write to the Captain?' Eduard exclaimed, 'for I have to set about it right away.'

'A calm, sensible, soothing letter,' said Charlotte.

'That is as good as no letter at all,' Eduard replied.

'And yet,' said Charlotte, 'in many instances it is better and kinder to write nothing than not to write.'

CHAPTER TWO

EDUARD was alone in his room. Charlotte's rehearsal of the vicissitudes of his life, together with the lively realization of their mutual position and prospects, had in truth aroused his naturally genial spirits in a very pleasant manner. He had felt so very contented when he was with her he had already begun composing in his head a friendly and sympathetic but soothing and non-committal letter to the Captain. But when he went to his desk and took up his friend's letter to read it through again he was instantly overcome once more by the mournful position in which that good man found himself. The painful sensations of which he had been the victim during the past few days came to life again. It seemed impossible he should abandon his friend to so distressing a situation.

Eduard was not used to denying himself anything. He was an only boy, and pampered, and his wealthy parents had doted on him. They had persuaded him to marry a woman far older than himself, an unconventional but very advantageous match. His wife had in turn indulged him in every way, she had tried by a limitless liberality to requite his gallant conduct towards her. After her death, which was not long delayed, he was his own master. He could travel wherever he liked, he could do whatever he liked. His desires were moderate, but he had an appetite for many and various things. He was candid, amiable, stout-hearted, he was even valiant if he had to be. What was there in all the world that could stand in his way!

To that present moment he had had everything he wanted. He had even got Charlotte, he had at long last won her through an obstinate constancy which bordered on the fabulous. But now, just as he was also going to get the friend of his youth and thus so to speak round off his whole existence, he felt himself for the first time contradicted and crossed. He was filled with annoyance and impatience. He took up his pen several times and laid it down again because he could not make up his mind what he ought to write. He did not want to oppose his wife's wishes, but he was unable to do what she wanted him to do. Agitated as he was, he found it quite impossible to compose a tranquil letter. The most natural thing would be for him to try for a postponement. In a few words he begged his friend's forgiveness for not having written to him of late and for not writing at length that day, and promised to send him shortly a more informative letter that would set his mind at rest.

Charlotte employed the opportunity on the following day, while they were strolling towards the same spot, to resume their conversation, perhaps in the conviction there is no surer way of blunting an intention than talking it over as often as possible.

This reiteration suited Eduard very well. He was affable and engaging. That was his way. Being susceptible he easily flared up, and he could press you too hard when there was something he wanted, and you could get impatient with him for his obstinacy; but then too he was always so thoughtful of other people and always so considerate you had to like him even when he was being a burden.

That was his way, and it was in that way he first got Charlotte into a good mood and then charmed her into confusion, so that she said finally: 'I do believe you want me to grant my lover what I refused my husband !'

And then she went on: 'In any event, my dear, you shall know that your wishes and the spirited way you urge them do not leave me entirely unmoved or untouched. They compel me to make a confession. I too have been keeping something back. I find myself in a similar situation to you. I have been imposing the same restraint upon myself as I now require you to exercise.'

'I am delighted to hear it,' said Eduard. 'I see it is a good thing for husband and wife to have the occasional disagreement, since they thereby come to learn things about one another.'

'Well then,' said Charlotte, 'you shall now come to learn that my sentiments towards Ottilie are the same as yours towards the Captain. I do not like to think of the dear child at the boarding-school. She finds conditions there grievously oppressive. My daughter Luciane was born to live in the world and there she is learning to live in the world. She takes in her languages and her history, and whatever else they teach her, as easily as her piano-playing. With her vivacious nature and lively memory she can, one might almost say, forget everything one minute and remember it again the next. She excels all the others in the freedom of her deportment, the gracefulness of her dancing, the becoming ease of her conversation, and through an innately commanding personality she has made herself queen of her little circle. The headmistress of the establishment regards her as a little goddess who is blossoming only now under her care and who will bring her credit and the confidence of others, which will produce an influx of more young ladies into her school. The opening pages of her letters and monthly reports are never anything but hymns to the excellence of such a child, which I of course know how to translate into my own prose. But when she finally comes to speak of Ottilie there is only excuse upon excuse that a girl otherwise evolving so well should have no wish to develop her talents or display any accomplishments. The little she adds to this is likewise no puzzle to me, since I perceive in the dear child the entire character of her mother, who was my closest friend and grew up beside me and whose daughter I would certainly have made into a lovely creature if I could have had her care and education in my charge.

'But since that does not accord with our plans, and one ought not to be for ever chopping and changing and introducing novelties, I prefer to endure the present state of affairs, and I even overcome the unpleasant feeling it gives me when my daughter, who knows very well that poor Ottilie is totally dependent upon us, haughtily parades her advantages before her, and so to some extent nullifies our kindness.

'Yet who is sufficiently cultivated not to make his superiority over another sometimes cruelly evident? Who is sufficiently elevated not to have to suffer sometimes under such behaviour? These trials only enhance Ottilie's worth; but since I have come clearly to see the painful position she is in, I have been making efforts to have her transferred somewhere else. I expect a reply hourly, and when it comes I shall not delay. So that, my love, is how I am placed. We both, you see, bear similar sorrows in a kind and loyal heart. Let us bear them together since they do not cancel one another out.'

'What strange creatures we are,' Eduard said, smiling. 'If we can only banish from our sight whatever gives us sorrow we believe we have abolished it. In big affairs we are capable of great sacrifice, but to give way on some single issue is a demand we are seldom equal to. That is how my mother was. As long as I lived with her as a boy or a youth she was never free of apprehensions. If I was late home, I must have met with an accident; if I got soaked in a shower, I was certain to catch a fever. And when I journeyed away from her it was as if I scarcely belonged to her any more.

'If we consider it more closely,' he went on, 'we are both acting in a highly irresponsible and foolish manner to leave in misery and oppression two of the noblest natures on earth, who are moreover so close to our hearts, merely so as not to expose ourselves to danger. If this should not be called selfishness I know not what should! Take Ottilie, let me have the Captain, and in God's name let us make a trial of it!'

'We might well venture to do so,' Charlotte said doubtfully, 'if the danger were to us alone. But do you consider it advisable to have the Captain and Ottilie sharing the same roof, a man of about your age, of the age – I may flatter you with this only because we are quite alone – at which a man first becomes capable of love and worthy of love, and a girl with Ottilie's advantages?'

'I really cannot see why you have so high an opinion of Ottilie!' Eduard replied. 'I can explain it only by supposing she has inherited your affection for her mother. It is true she is pretty, and I recall that the Captain pointed her out to me when we came back a year ago and met her with you at your aunt's. She is pretty, she possesses in particular lovely eyes; yet I cannot say she made the least impression on me.'

'That is very commendable in you,' said Charlotte, 'for I was there too, was I not? Although she is far younger than I, yet the presence of your more elderly friend charmed you so thoroughly you overlooked the beauty that was yet in bud. This too is part of what you are like and why I am so happy to share my life with you.'

Charlotte gave the impression of talking very frankly and openly, but she was keeping something concealed, and that was that she had deliberately produced Ottilie in front of Eduard when he came back so as to throw so advantageous a match in the way of her foster-daughter. At that time she no longer thought of Eduard in connection with herself. The Captain too had been suborned to draw Eduard's attention to Ottilie, but Eduard had been obstinately mindful of his youthful love for Charlotte, and he had looked neither to right nor left, but was thinking only that he might now be going to find it possible to seize at last the possession he wanted so much but which events seemed to have put beyond his reach for ever.

31

The couple were about to go down to the mansion across the new park when a servant came clambering up towards them laughing, and called out from below: 'Come along quick, sir! Come along quick, madam! Herr Mittler has just come bursting in. He has roused us all up and told us to go and look for you and ask you if you need him. "Ask if they need me, d'you hear!" was his words. "And make haste, make haste!"'

'The strange fellow!' Eduard exclaimed. 'Has he not arrived at just the right moment, Charlotte?' Turning to the servant, he said: 'Go back quickly! Tell him we do need him, very much! Ask him to dismount, take care of his horse, invite him in and offer him some breakfast. We are just coming.

'Let us take the shortest way back,' he said to his wife, and went off down the path through the churchyard which he usually avoided. He was very surprised when he discovered that here too Charlotte had provided for the demands of sensibility. With every consideration for the ancient monuments she had managed to level and arrange everything in such a way as to create a pleasant place which was nice to look at and which set the imagination working.

The oldest memorial of all had been put in a place of suitable honour. In the order of their antiquity the gravestones were erected against the wall, inserted into it, or lodged in some other way. The base of the church itself was ornamented and augmented by this arrangement. Eduard felt very moved when, entering through the little gateway, he saw the place. He pressed Charlotte's hand and tears came into his eyes.

But they went out of them the next instant when the eccentric guest appeared. Incapable of sitting quietly in the mansion he had ridden at full gallop through the village up to the churchyard gate, where he drew rein and shouted out: 'You're not pulling my leg, eh? If you really do need me I'll stay until lunchtime. But don't detain me. I've a lot still to do today.'

'Since you've taken the trouble to come so far,' Eduard called up to him, 'you might as well ride all the way in. We meet in a solemn place. See how Charlotte has beautified this funeral-ground.'

'Into that place,' replied the mounted man, 'I enter neither on horse, nor by carriage, nor on foot. The people in there are at peace, with them I have no business. You'll never find me joining them until they drag me in feet first. So you're serious, then?'

'Yes,' Charlotte cried, 'quite serious! It is the first time we newly-weds have found ourselves in a difficulty we don't know how to get out of.'

'You don't look as if you are in any difficulty,' he replied, 'but I'll believe you. If you're leading me on I'll leave you in the lurch another time. Follow me back. Make haste! My horse could do with a rest.'

The three were soon back home and in the dining-room. They ate and Mittler said what he had done and what he was going to do that day. This singular gentleman was in earlier years a minister of religion. Unflagging in his office, he had distinguished himself by his capacity for settling and silencing all disputes, domestic and communal, first between individual people, then between landowners, and then between whole parishes. There were no divorces and the local judiciary was not pestered by a single suit or contention during the whole period of his incumbency. He recognized early on how essential a knowledge of law was to him, he threw himself into a study of this science, and he soon felt a match for the best lawyers. The sphere of his activities expanded wondrously and he was on the point of being called to the Residenz so that he might complete from on high what he had begun among the lowly when he won a big prize in a lottery. He bought a modest estate, farmed it out and made it into the central point of his life, with the firm intention, or rather according to his fixed habit and inclination, never to enter

any house where there was not a dispute to settle or difficulties to put right. People superstitious about the significance
of names say it was the name Mittler, which means mediator,
which compelled him to adopt this oddest of vocations.

As a sweet was being served the guest earnestly admonished
his hosts to hold back their disclosures no longer, as he
would have to leave as soon as he had had coffee. The couple
made their confessions in some detail, but no sooner had he
grasped the point of it all than he leapt up from the table in
vexation, sprang to the window and commanded his horse
be saddled.

'Either you don't know me,' he cried, 'or don't understand
me, or this is some malicious joke. Is there any contention
here? Is assistance needed here? Do you think I exist to hand
out advice? That's the most preposterous trade a man can ply.
Let each advise himself and do what he can't help doing. If it
turns out well, let him congratulate himself on his wisdom
and good fortune; if it goes ill, he can always turn to me. He
who wants to rid himself of an evil always knows what he
wants, but he who wants something better than he already
has is night-blind – yes, you can laugh ! – he's playing blind-
man's buff. He will catch something, perhaps – but what? Do
what you wish : it's all one ! Invite your friends, don't invite
them : it's all one ! I've seen the most judicious plans miscarry, the absurdest succeed. Don't go racking your brains
over it, and if it goes ill, in one way or the other, still don't
go racking 'em. Just send for me and I'll come to your assistance. Till then, your servant !'

And with that he swung himself onto his horse without
waiting for the coffee.

'Here you see.' said Charlotte, 'how little it profits to bring
in a third party when two intimates are not entirely in accord.
We are now surely even more confused and undecided than
we were before, if that be possible.'

They would both no doubt have continued to vacillate if a

34

letter had not arrived from the Captain in reply to Eduard's. He said he had decided to accept one of the posts offered him, although it was in no way suited to him. He was to participate in the boredom of an aristocratic and wealthy circle on the understanding he would know how to dissipate it.

Eduard saw the whole situation very clearly and painted it in vivid colours. 'Are we to sit back and witness our friend reduced to such circumstances?' he exclaimed. 'You cannot be so inhuman, Charlotte!'

'Our singular friend Mittler is right after all,' Charlotte replied. 'All such undertakings are perilous adventures. No one can foresee what will come of them. Such new arrangements can produce happiness or unhappiness without our venturing to ascribe to ourselves any particular merit or blame. I do not feel strong enough to oppose you any longer. Let us make a trial of it. The sole thing I ask is that it should be for only a short while. Allow me to stir myself more on his behalf and make zealous use of my influence and connections to procure for him a place which will in his own way afford him some contentment.'

Eduard certified his gratitude in the most charming possible manner and hastened, with light and happy heart, to write to his friend and tell him what they proposed. Charlotte had to append her approval in her own hand and to join her own cordial invitation to his. Her words were kind and courteous, and she wrote with a nimble pen, yet with a kind of haste not usual with her and, an uncommon thing for her to do, she disfigured the sheet with a blot, which annoyed her and only became bigger when she tried to rub it out.

Eduard made a joke of it, and because there was still room he added a second postscript, saying his friend should see from this sign with what impatience he was awaited and pattern the speed of his journey on that with which the letter had been written.

The carrier went off and Eduard thought he could not express his gratitude more convincingly than by insisting again and again that Charlotte should at once have Ottilie taken out of school and brought home.

She asked him not to press her at present over that matter, and in the evening she managed to arouse his interest in a musical diversion. Charlotte played the piano very well, Eduard played the flute less well. He sometimes made great efforts but he had not been granted the patience and perseverance needed for the cultivation of a talent of this sort. He played very unevenly: some passages he played well, only perhaps too fast, while at others he would halt and hesitate, so that it would have been difficult for anyone else to get through a duet with him. But Charlotte knew how to manage it. She would halt and then let him draw her along again and thus she discharged the double duty of proficient conductor and prudent housewife: both know how to keep the whole thing to the correct measure, even if individual passages may not always be in tempo.

CHAPTER THREE

THE Captain arrived. He had sent ahead of him a very judicious letter which altogether calmed down any fears Charlotte may have had. She thought that so great an insight into himself and so clear a perception of his own position and that of his friends was a good sign.

Conversation during their first hours together was lively, almost exhausting, as it usually is among friends who have not seen one another for some time. Towards evening Charlotte took them for a walk in the new park. The Captain was very pleased with it and noticed every beautiful sight and spot which the new paths had for the first time opened up. He had a practised eye but it was one that was easily pleased. He recognized very well what shortcomings there were but he refrained (many do not refrain) from making those who were conducting him round ill-humoured by demanding more than circumstances allowed or (which is worse) by recalling something more perfect he had seen somewhere else.

When they reached the moss-hut they discovered it very gaily decked out. The materials were, to be sure, only artificial flowers and evergreens, but fine sheaves of natural wheat and other products of field and tree were mixed with them and the arrangement did credit to the artistic sense of whoever had carried it out. 'Although my husband hates to have any fuss made over his birthday or nameday, I know he will not take it amiss if today I dedicate these few garlands to a threefold celebration,' Charlotte said.

'A threefold celebration?' Eduard exclaimed. 'Yes indeed!' Charlotte said. 'We may fairly treat our friend's arrival as an occasion for celebration; and then, has it occurred to neither of you that today is your nameday? Are you not both called Otto?'

The two friends took hands across the little table. 'You bring back to my mind,' said Eduard, 'that youthful deed of friendship. As children we both bore that fine, laconic name; but when we were at school together and confusion arose, I voluntarily resigned it to him.'

'In doing which you were not actuated entirely by generosity,' said the Captain. 'For I recall quite well you preferred the name Eduard, which does indeed sound uncommonly pleasing when uttered by fair lips.'

The three were now sitting around the little table at which Charlotte had exclaimed so passionately against the guest's coming. Contented as he was, Eduard had no wish to remind his wife of that occasion, but he could not refrain from saying: 'I do not doubt there would be room for a fourth too.'

At that moment there came from the mansion the sound of horns. It was like a confirmation that our friends were right to be together like this, and they listened to the sound in silence and each of them was sunk into himself and was doubly conscious of his own happiness in being together with the others.

Eduard first interrupted the interval by getting up and stepping out in front of the moss-hut. 'Let us take our friend right to the top of the hill,' he said to Charlotte, 'in case he should think this narrow valley comprises our whole home and estate. Up there the view is more open and there is more room to breathe.'

'Then we shall still have to clamber up the old footpath,' Charlotte replied. 'It is rather hard going, but I hope the steps and paths I am having constructed will very soon make an easy way right to the top.'

By this route, over rocks and through brushwood and thickets, they reached the top of the hill, which was not a plateau but a continuous fertile ridge. Village and mansion to the rearward could no more be seen. Ahead and far below lay a chain of lakes. Beyond them lay tree-covered hills with the lakes stretching towards them. Finally, steep cliffs cut off the farthest of the lakes perpendicularly and threw their massive image down onto the water's surface. Across in the ravine, where a rushing stream fell down into the lakes, stood a half-hidden mill which, together with the ground surrounding it, appeared to be a good resting-place. The whole visible semi-circle was filled with a great variety of hills and gullies and of woods and thickets whose early greenery promised a luxuriant prospect later in the year. In many places there stood out isolated clumps of trees, and in particular a mass of poplars and plane-trees, green and full-grown, their branches striving up and outward, on the edge of the middle lake at the feet of our friends as they stood gazing down.

Eduard drew special attention to these trees. 'I planted those myself in my youth,' he said. ' I rescued them as young shoots when my father had them uprooted while he was laying out a new section of the big walled garden one midsummer. They are clearly going to show their gratitude again this year by putting out more buds !'

They went back home feeling very happy and contented. The guest was given cheerful roomy quarters in the right wing of the mansion. He soon set up his books, papers and instruments so as to carry on with his normal life. But during the first few days Eduard would not leave him in peace. He showed him around everywhere, on horseback and on foot, and familiarized him with the neighbourhood and the estate. While doing so he confided to him that he had for a long time wanted to get to know it better himself and learn how to make better use of it.

'The first thing we ought to do,' said the Captain, 'would be for me to make a compass survey of the area. It is a simple and pleasant job, and if it doesn't ensure absolute accuracy it is always useful and makes a good beginning; moreover, you can do it without much assistance and you know you'll get through it. Should you later think of making a more exact survey it would always be possible to take advice on that.'

The Captain was very experienced in this sort of surveying. He had brought with him the necessary instruments and he started on it at once. He instructed Eduard and some of the local trappers and peasants who were to assist him. The days went very well. He spent the evenings and early mornings on his map, drawing the contours and hatching the heights. Soon everything was shaded and coloured and Eduard saw his possessions taking shape on the paper like a new creation. It seemed to him that only now was he coming to know them, only now did they really belong to him.

Occasions for discussing the neighbourhood and the grounds can be created much more readily after a review like this than if you are merely trying out individual chance ideas on the spot, he thought.

'We must make that clear to my wife,' said Eduard.

'No, don't do that!' replied the Captain, who did not like crossing other people's convictions with his own. Experience had taught him that human opinion is much too various to be unanimous on so much as a single point even in regard to the most reasonable proposition. 'Don't do that!' he said. 'She could easily become confused. Like all who engage in such things only for amusement she is more concerned to do something than that something should be done. This sort of person fumbles with nature, prefers this little spot or that, dares not venture to remove this or that obstacle, isn't bold enough to sacrifice anything, cannot imagine in advance what is supposed to be created, experiments – it may work out, it may not – makes changes and changes perhaps what ought to be left alone; and so in the end it remains nothing but a hotch-potch that may turn out pleasing and stimulating but can never fully satisfy.'

'Confess it honestly,' said Eduard; 'you don't like the way she has laid out the park, do you?'

'If the conception, which is very fine, had been realized in the execution, there would be nothing to criticize. But she has laboriously toiled her way through the rocks and now, if I may so put it, everyone she conducts up there also has to toil. Neither side by side nor in file can you walk with any real comfort. You have to break step every other minute; and there are many more objections that might be raised.'

'Would it have been easy to do it any other way?' Eduard asked.

'Quite easy,' the Captain replied. 'All she had to do was cut away the angle of cliff which juts out there; the thing is in any case insignificant-looking, since it is composed of small segments; then she would have acquired a fine curving ascent, and at the same time a quantity of superfluous stone for building up the path where it would have been broken and narrow. But let this be in strictest confidence between us or it will confuse and upset her. And what has been done must be left alone. If you want to expend more money and effort, there are still plenty of pleasant things to do above the moss-hut and over the high ground.'

So the two friends kept themselves occupied with present affairs, but they also found plenty of material for lively discussion of the past too, and in this latter pursuit Charlotte usually also took part. They also proposed, as soon as the most immediate tasks were disposed of, to set to work on the travel journals and relive the past through them too.

Moreover, Eduard now had less to talk about with Charlotte alone, especially since he had taken to heart the Captain's criticism of her park lay-out, which seemed to him quite just. For a long time he said nothing of what the Captain had confided to him; but when eventually he saw his wife again occupied in labouring her way up from the moss-hut to the high ground with little steps and paths he held back no longer, but after some irrelevant preamble told her what he now thought.

Charlotte was confounded. She could see at once the Captain was right, but what she had done contradicted him. It existed, and she had found it right and good. Even what was criticized was dear to her in every part and particular. She resisted conviction, she defended her little creation, she chided the men with flying off into the vast and grandiose, with wanting to turn a pastime into a labour, with failing to think of what a more ambitious plan would cost. She was agitated, hurt, upset. She could not relinquish the old ideas nor entirely reject the new. But she was a resolute woman and she had the work stopped at once and gave herself time to reflect and let the thing mature within her.

Since she was no longer engaged in this entertaining pastime and the men went about their affairs in closer and closer companionship (they were in particular taking great care of the nursery gardens and glasshouses and also going on with their usual pursuits as horsemen, hunting and buying, exchanging, training and breaking-in horses), Charlotte began to feel more and more lonely as the days went by. She took a more lively interest in her correspondence, also on the Captain's behalf, but there were many lonely hours. So she found the reports from the boarding-school all the more agreeable and amusing when she received them.

A long letter from the headmistress, which expatiated as usual on the progress her daughter was making, had appended to it a brief postscript and was accompanied by an enclosure in the hand of one of the young schoolmasters. We here reproduce these two documents.

The Headmistress's Postscript

As for Ottilie, Madam, I can only reiterate what is contained in my previous reports. I know of no reason for reproaching her, and yet I cannot be satisfied with her. She remains, as heretofore, modest and agreeable to others; but I do not find this retirement and humbleness altogether pleasing. Your Ladyship recently sent her money and a variety of material. She has not touched the former, and the material too is still lying undisturbed. It is true she keeps her things very clean and fine, but she seems to change her clothes only for cleanliness' sake. Neither can I commend her great moderation in eating and drinking. There is no superfluity at our table; but there is nothing I would rather see than the children eating their fill of tasty and nourishing food. What has been prepared and served with care and thought ought to be eaten up. This I can never induce Ottilie to do. Indeed, when there is sometimes an interval in the meal because the maids have been delayed, she invents some task or other to do simply to avoid one of the courses or the dessert. We must, however, take into consideration that, as I have only recently discovered, she sometimes suffers from a headache on the left side, which goes away, it is true, but may nonetheless be painful and significant. So much on this otherwise so dear and lovely child.

The Schoolmaster's Letter

Our good headmistress usually lets me read the letters in which she communicates her observations on her pupils to their parents and guardians. I always read those directed to your Ladyship with double attention and double pleasure: for while we have to congratulate you on possessing a daughter who unites all those brilliant qualities through which one rises in the world, I at least must think you no less fortunate in having had bestowed upon you in your foster-daughter a child born to promote the well-being and contentment of others, and also surely her own happiness. Ottilie is almost our only pupil over whom our esteemed headmistress and I are not in agreement. I do not in any way blame this industrious lady for wanting to see the fruits of her conscientiousness in clear and visible form; but there also exist hidden fruits which alone are the true substantial ones and which sooner or later develop into vigorous life. Your foster-daughter is undoubtedly of this kind. As long as I have been teaching her I have always seen her proceed at the same pace; slowly, slowly forwards, never back. If it is ever necessary to begin at the beginning with a child, then it certainly is in her case. She cannot understand what does not follow from what has gone before. She stands incapable, indeed obdurate, before something quite easy to grasp if it is not, for her, connected with anything else. But if one can discover the intermediate stages, she is able to understand the most difficult things.

With this slow rate of progress she remains behind her fellow-students who, endowed with quite different capabilities, are ever hurrying on, easily grasping, retaining and again applying everything they learn, even the most disconnected facts. If the teacher too hurries ahead she learns and is capable of nothing whatever, as is the case in certain classes taken by excellent but hasty and impatient teachers. Complaint has been made about her hand-writing and about her inability to grasp the rules of grammar. I have gone into these difficulties more closely: it is true her writing is slow and stiff, if you will, but not irresolute or clumsy. What I taught her stage by stage of the French language, which is to be sure not my subject, she easily understood. It is a strange thing, I admit: she knows much and knows it well; only when she is questioned she seems to know nothing.

If I may close with a general observation, I would say: she learns, not as one who is to be educated, but as one who wants to educate; not as a pupil, but as a future teacher. Perhaps your ladyship will think it odd that I, as an educator and teacher, should believe the only way to commend anyone is to declare her to be no different from me. Your Ladyship's better judgement and knowledge of men and the world will know how to place the best construction on my dull but well-meant words. You will see for yourself that from this child, too, much joy is to be hoped for. I commend myself to your Ladyship and ask that I be allowed to write again as soon as I believe I have something significant and agreeable to report.

Charlotte was very pleased with this note. Its contents agreed with the idea of Ottilie she herself had. But she could not repress a smile. The schoolmaster's interest seemed to be somewhat warmer than that usually aroused by seeing virtues in a pupil. But she was not one to get ruffled about such a thing and she resolved to let that situation, as she had so many others, evolve how it would. She knew how to appreciate the sensible man's sympathetic involvement with Ottilie. She had learned sufficiently in the course of her life how highly any true affection is to be esteemed in a world where indifference and antipathy are rightly at home.

CHAPTER FOUR

THE topographical map was soon finished. It represented, to a fairly large scale, the estate and its environs made palpable in their characteristic outlines by pen and paint and fixed by trigonometrical measurements the Captain had been making. Few men could manage with as little sleep as he could and he always devoted the day to the task in hand, so that each evening something had been done.

'Let us now,' he said to his friend, 'turn to what remains to be done, the inventory of the estate, for which sufficient preparatory work must be already to hand, and which will afterwards lead on to the tenancy deeds and other things of that sort. Only let us firmly determine on one thing: to separate everything that is actual business from living. Business demands seriousness and severity, living demands caprice; business requires consistency, living often requires inconsistency, for that is what makes life agreeable and exhilarating. If you are secure in the one, you can be all the more free in the other; whereas if you confound the two, your freedom uproots and destroys your security.'

Eduard heard in these suggestions a mild reproach. He was not disorderly by nature but he could never manage to arrange his papers according to subject. What also involved other people was not separated from what involved himself alone. He likewise did not adequately divide business from pursuits, entertainment from distractions. But now he found it easy to do so. His friend, a second self, was making the division the single self may not always want to make.

They installed in the Captain's wing a registry for current documents, an archive for those no longer current. They collected together all the papers and reports which lay scattered in containers, rooms, cupboards and boxes. With the greatest of speed the chaos was reduced to a gratifying order and lay captioned in named compartments. What was required was found in a more complete state than could have been hoped for, and in this regard an elderly copying-clerk, with whom Eduard had hitherto always been dissatisfied, proved very serviceable, never leaving his desk the whole day long and even working on into the night.

'I no longer recognize him,' said Eduard to his friend, 'he is so industrious and useful.'

'The reason for that,' the Captain replied, 'is, we never give him anything new to do before he has finished what he already has to do in his own time; and thus, as you see, he gets through a great deal. If you start pestering him, he dries up completely.'

The friends spent their days together but they did not neglect Charlotte in the evenings. If there were no visitors, and often there were none, they talked together and read, usually about useful subjects.

Charlotte, accustomed in any event to improving the hour, felt she could put the good mood her husband was evidently now in to her own advantage. Domestic improvements she had long wanted to make but had been unable to were now put in hand through the Captain. The domestic dispensary, which had consisted of only a few medicines and remedies, was enlarged. Charlotte was industrious and helpful by nature and through discussion and by reading comprehensible textbooks she was enabled to be so more effectively and more often.

They also thought about emergencies which might arise. Emergencies were really quite commonplace, nonetheless they too often took them by surprise. They bought everything they might need for lifesaving and this was all the more necessary in that, because there were so many lakes, watercourses and waterworks, accidents often occurred. The Captain took very detailed care of this department, and Eduard let fall the remark that a case of this sort had in the strangest way made an epoch in his friend's life. But when the Captain was silent and seemed to be finding the recollection of it unpleasant, Eduard checked himself and Charlotte too, who was in general no less informed about it, paid no attention to what he had said.

'We have done well to make all these arrangements,' the Captain said one evening, 'but we still lack what we need most, which is an able man who knows how to use them. I can suggest for this post a field-surgeon I know who can be had on tolerable terms, an excellent man in his trade and one who has oftentimes treated me for serious internal troubles too, and better than a specialist might have done; and immediate aid is, after all, what is most seriously missed in the country.'

The man was immediately written to and Eduard and Charlotte were glad to have been enabled to use so well so much money they might otherwise have frittered away.

Thus Charlotte too exploited the Captain and she began to be very content he should be there and not at all worried about any consequences that might ensue. When she met him she usually had a number of questions in her head to ask him. She liked being alive and so she sought to do away with anything that might be harmful or deadly: the lead-glazing on the earthenware crockery and the verdigris that formed on copper pots had worried her for a long time and she had him instruct her about this and the instruction had naturally to begin with the fundamental principles of physics and chemistry.

Chance but welcome opportunity for talking about these things was offered by Eduard's taste for reading aloud. He had a very melodious deep voice and had in earlier days been well-received and well-known for his lively and sensitive recitation of oratory and poetry. Now it was other subjects that engaged him and other books from which he read, and as it happened these had for some time been principally works on physics, chemistry and technical matters.

A particular trait of his, but one which perhaps he was not alone in, was that he could not bear someone else looking over at a book when he was reading from it. In earlier times, when he read poems, plays and stories, it was the natural consequence of the desire, possessed as much by a reciter as by a poet, an actor or a story-teller, to evoke surprise, to vary the pace, to arouse tension; and it militates very greatly against these intended effects if a third party is already looking ahead and knows what is coming. This was one reason it was his practice when reading before company to sit so that he had no one behind him. Now that there was only the three of them this precaution was unnecessary, and since his objective was no longer to stir the emotions or startle the imagination he did not think about being particularly careful.

Only, one evening when he had sat down without thinking about where, he noticed Charlotte was reading over his shoulder. His old impatience came to life again and he rebuked her for it rather roughly, saying bad habits of that kind, like so many others that were an annoyance to society, ought to be broken once and for all. 'If I read aloud to someone,' he said, 'is it not as if I were speaking to him and telling him something? What has been written down and printed takes the place of my own mind and my own heart; and would I ever take the trouble to speak at all if a window were constructed in my forehead or in my chest, so that he to whom I want to expound my thoughts one by one, or convey my feelings one by one, could always know long in advance what I was getting at? Whenever anyone reads over my shoulder it is as if I were being torn in two.'

Charlotte, whose address in great or intimate society was revealed especially in her ability to circumvent any unpleasant, forcible, or even merely lively remark and to interrupt a conversation that was going on too long and stimulate one in danger of breaking down, was quite equal to this occasion. 'You will forgive me, I know,' she said, 'when I confess the reason for my error. I heard you speak of "affinity", and straightway there came into my mind my own affinity, a pair of cousins who happen to be troubling me at this very moment. I attend again to your reading; I hear that what is being spoken of is quite inanimate things, and I look over your shoulder to find out where I am.'

'It is a metaphor which has misled and confused you,' said Eduard. 'Here, to be sure, it is only a question of soil and minerals; but man is a true Narcissus: he makes the whole world his mirror.'

'Very true,' the Captain continued: 'that is how he treats everything he discovers outside himself; his wisdom and his folly, his will and his caprices, he lends to the beasts, the plants, the elements and the gods.'

'As I do not wish to lead you too far away from the present subject,' Charlotte said, 'I wonder if you would tell me just briefly what is actually meant here by affinities?'

'Very gladly,' replied the Captain, to whom Charlotte had directed the question, 'as well as I can from what I learned from reading about it some ten years ago. Whether the scientific world still thinks of it in the same way, or whether it agrees with the latest theories, I cannot say.'

'It is a great annoyance,' cried Eduard, 'that one can no longer learn anything once and for all. Our ancestors observed their whole life long the instruction they received in their youth; but we have to learn anew every five years if we do not want to fall completely out of fashion.'

'We women are not so particular about that,' said Charlotte; 'and, to be frank, all I am really interested in is knowing what the word means; for nothing makes you look so silly in society as to misapply an unfamiliar coinage. That is why all I want to know is in what sense this expression is employed in the present context. Let us leave what its scientific status may be to the scientists, who are in any case, as I have been able to observe, hardly ever in agreement.'

'But where shall we begin, so as to get to the point with the least delay?' Eduard asked the Captain after a pause. The Captain, having thought it over, replied : 'If I may be allowed to go what will seem a long way back, we shall soon get to the point.'

'I am all attention, you may be sure,' said Charlotte, laying aside her work.

And the Captain began : 'In all the phenomena of nature of which we are aware, the first thing we observe is that they adhere to themselves. It sounds odd, I know, to expound something that goes without saying; but it is only when we have fully comprehended what is already known that we can go forward together into the unknown.'

'I should think,' Eduard interrupted, 'that examples will make the matter clearer to her, and to us. If you think of water, or oil, or quicksilver, you will find a unity and coherence of their parts. They will not relinquish this unified state except through the action or force of some other agent. If this is removed, they immediately come together again.'

'Unquestionably,' Charlotte said, agreeing. 'Raindrops like to join together into streams. And even as children we play with quicksilver, and see in amazement how we can separate it into little balls and then let it run together again.'

'And therefore I may mention in passing this significant point,' the Captain added, 'that this unalloyed adherence made possible by liquidity is always definitely distinguished by the spherical form. The falling water-drop is round; you yourself have spoken of little balls of quicksilver; indeed, a falling drop of molten lead, if it has time completely to solidify, arrives in the form of a ball.'

'Let me hurry on,' said Charlotte, 'and see whether I have

guessed aright what you are coming to. Just as each thing has an adherence to itself, so it must also have a relationship to other things.'

'And that will differ according to the difference between them,' Eduard hurriedly went on. 'Sometimes they will meet as friends and old acquaintances who hasten together and unite without changing one another in any way, as wine mixes with water. On the other hand, there are others who will remain obdurate strangers to one another and refuse to unite in any way even through mechanical mixing and grinding, as oil and water shaken together will a moment later separate again.'

'It needs little imagination,' said Charlotte, 'to see in these elementary forms people one has known; what they especially suggest is the social circles in which we live. But most similar of all to these inanimate things are the masses which stand over against one another in the world : the classes, the professions, the nobility and the third estate, the soldier and the civilian.'

'And yet,' Eduard replied, 'just as these can be unified through laws and customs, so in our chemical world too there exist intermediaries for combining together those things which repulse one another.'

'Thus,' the Captain interposed, 'we combine oil with water by means of alkaline salt.'

'Not too fast with your lecture,' said Charlotte. 'Let me show that I am keeping up. Have we not already arrived at the affinities?'

'Quite right,' the Captain replied; 'and we shall straightway go on to see exactly what they are and what their force consists in. Those natures which, when they meet, quickly lay hold on and mutually affect one another we call affined. This affinity is sufficiently striking in the case of alkalis and acids which, although they are mutually antithetical, and perhaps precisely because they are so, most decidedly seek and embrace one another, modify one another, and together form a new substance. Think only of lime, which evidences a great inclination, a decided desire for union with acids of every kind. As soon as our cabinet of chemicals arrives we will show you some very entertaining experiments which will give you a better idea of all this than words, names and technical terms.'

'Let me confess,' said Charlotte, 'that when you call all these curious entities of yours affined, they appear to me to possess not so much an affinity of blood as an affinity of mind and soul. It is in just this way that truly meaningful friendships can arise among human beings: for antithetical qualities make possible a closer and more intimate union. And so I shall wait to see how much of these mysterious effects you are going to reveal. Now I will not interrupt your reading further,' she said, turning to Eduard, 'and, being so much better instructed, I shall be listening to you with attention.'

'Now you have summoned us up,' Eduard said, 'you cannot get away as easily as that: for the most complicated cases are in fact the most interesting. It is only when you consider these that you get to know the degrees of affinity, the closer and stronger, the more distant and weaker relationships; the affinities become interesting only when they bring about divorces.'

'Does that doleful word, which one unhappily hears so often in society these days, also occur in natural science?' Charlotte exclaimed.

'To be sure,' Eduard replied. 'It even used to be a title of honour to chemists to call them artists in divorcing one thing from another.'*

'Then it is not so any longer,' Charlotte said, 'and a very good thing too. Uniting is a greater art and a greater merit. An artist in unification in any subject would be welcomed the

*The pun vanishes in translation: Scheidung = divorce, Scheidekünstler = analytical chemist.

53

world over. – But now you are in the vein for once, let me hear of a few such cases.'

'Let us then go straight ahead,' said the Captain, 'and connect this idea with what we have already defined and discussed. For example: what we call limestone is more or less pure calcium oxide intimately united with a thin acid known to us in a gaseous state. If you put a piece of this limestone into dilute sulphuric acid, the latter will seize on the lime and join with it to form calcium sulphate, or gypsum; that thin gaseous acid, on the other hand, escapes. Here there has occurred a separation and a new combination, and one then feels justified even in employing the term "elective affinity", because it really does look as if one relationship was preferred to another and chosen instead of it.'

'Forgive me,' said Charlotte, 'as I forgive the scientist, but I would never see a choice here but rather a natural necessity and indeed hardly that; for in the last resort it is perhaps only a matter of opportunity. Opportunity makes relationships just as much as it makes thieves; and where your natural substances are concerned, the choice seems to me to lie entirely in the hands of the chemist who brings these substances together. Once they have been brought together, though, God help them! In the present case I only feel sorry for the poor gaseous acid, which has to go off and drift around again in the void.'

'All it has to do,' the Captain replied, 'is to join up with water and it will then, as a mineral spring, serve as a source of refreshment to sick and healthy alike.'

'It is all very well for the gypsum to talk,' said Charlotte; 'the gypsum is now complete, a finished body, it has been taken care of; whereas that expelled substance may go through a very hard time before it again finds refuge.'

'Unless I am much mistaken,' said Eduard with a smile, 'your remarks carry a double meaning. Confess it now! When all is said, I am in your eyes the lime which the Captain, as a sulphuric acid, has seized on, withdrawn from your charming company, and transformed into a stubborn gypsum.'

'If your conscience prompts you to such reflections,' Charlotte replied, 'I have no need to worry. These figures of speech are pretty and amusing, and who does not like to play with analogies? But man is so very much elevated above those elements, and if he has in this instance been somewhat liberal with the fine words "choice" and "elective affinity", it is well for him to turn and look within himself, and then consider truly what validity such expressions possess. I know, alas, of all too many cases in which an intimate and apparently indissoluble union between two beings has been broken up by a chance association with a third and one of the couple at first so fairly united driven out into the unknown.'

'Chemists are far more gallant in this matter,' said Eduard : 'they introduce a fourth, so that no one shall go empty away.'

'Yes indeed !' the Captain added : 'these cases are in fact the most significant and noteworthy of all; in them one can actually demonstrate attraction and relatedness, this as it were crosswise parting and uniting : where four entities, previously joined together in two pairs, are brought into contact, abandon their previous union, and join together afresh. In this relinquishment and seizing, in this fleeing and seeking, one really can believe one is witnessing a higher determination; one credits such entities with a species of will and choice, and regards the technical term "elective affinities" as entirely justified.'

'Describe to me such a case,' said Charlotte.

'Description is inadequate,' the Captain replied. 'As I have already said, everything will become clearer and more acceptable once I can show you the experiments themselves. At present I should have to put you off with dreadful technical terms which would still give you no idea of what is happening. One has to have these entities before one's eyes, and see how, although they appear to be lifeless, they are in fact perpetually ready to spring into activity; one has to watch sympathetically how they seek one another out, attract, seize, destroy, devour, consume one another, and then emerge again from this most intimate union in renewed, novel and unexpected shape: it is only then that one credits them with an eternal life, yes, with possessing mind and reason, because our own minds seem scarcely adequate to observing them properly and our understanding scarcely sufficient to comprehend them.'

'I do not deny,' said Eduard, 'that anyone who has not become reconciled to it through immediate physical observation and comprehension must find the strange jargon troublesome, indeed ludicrous. Yet in the meantime we could easily express what we have been talking about by means of letters.'

'Provided it does not seem pedantic,' the Captain said, 'I think I can briefly sum up in the language of signs. Imagine an A intimately united with a B, so that no force is able to sunder them; imagine a C likewise related to a D; now bring the two couples into contact: A will throw itself at D, C at B, without our being able to say which first deserted its partner, which first embraced the other's partner.'

'Now then!' Eduard interposed: 'until we see all this with our own eyes, let us look on this formula as a metaphor from which we may extract a lesson we can apply immediately to ourselves. You, Charlotte, represent the A, and I represent your B; for in fact I do depend altogether on you and follow you as A follows B. The C is quite obviously the Captain, who for the moment is to some extent drawing me away from you. Now it is only fair that, if you are not to vanish into the limitless air, you must be provided with a D, and this D is unquestionably the charming little lady Ottilie, whose approaching presence you may no longer resist.'

'Very well,' Charlotte replied. 'Even if, as I think, this

example does not precisely fit our case, I still consider it a good thing that today we are for once fully in agreement, and that these natural and elective affinities should hasten me to tell you something in confidence. Let me confess, then, that this afternoon I decided to send for Ottilie : for my housekeeper, who has been loyal to me till now, is leaving to get married. This is why for my own sake and convenience I want Ottilie to come; but I also want her to come for her own sake, and why that should be so you shall read aloud to us. I shall refrain from looking over your shoulder, although it cannot matter whether I do so or not, for I already know the contents. However, do read it to us !' With these words she drew out a letter and handed it to Eduard.

CHAPTER FIVE

The Headmistress's Letter

Your Ladyship will forgive me if I write quite briefly today : for the examinations are now over, and I have to report to all our parents and guardians what we have achieved with our pupils during the course of the past year; and brevity is also quite in order here, since I can say much in few words. Your daughter has proved herself the first girl in the school in every respect. The enclosed certificates, and her own letter describing the prizes she has won and expressing the pleasure she feels at so successful an achievement, will bring you reassurance, and indeed joy. Mine is to some extent diminished when I foresee that we shall not for very much longer have any cause to detain with us a lady who has made such vast progress. I commend myself to your Ladyship and will take the liberty in the near future of communicating to you what I consider will be the most advantageous course for her to take now. My assistant has been good enough to write to you on the subject of Ottilie.

The Schoolmaster's Letter

Our revered headmistress would have me write on the subject of Ottilie, in part because it would, to her way of thinking, be painful to tell what has to be told, but in part too because she herself owes an apology which she would prefer me to make in her stead.

As I know all too well how little our good Ottilie is able to express what lies within her and what she is capable of, I was somewhat fearful of the examination, the more so since no preparation for it is possible, and, if it were to be conducted in the usual fashion, Ottilie could not even be prepared for making a show of knowledge. The event proved my fears to be only too justified : she received no prize, and she is also one of those who have been awarded no certificate. There is no point in expatiating on this. In writing, the others hardly had such well-rounded letters, but they wrote much more fluently; in arithmetic everyone else was faster, and the test did not involve the more difficult problems which she is better able to cope with. In French she excelled many in both the oral and written exercises; in history she could not remember names and dates; in geography she failed to pay attention to political divisions. At the musical recital there was neither time nor leisure for her few modest melodies. In drawing she would certainly have carried off the prize: her outlines were clear and the execution of the picture careful and gifted. Unfortunately she attempted something too big and was unable to complete it.

When the pupils had withdrawn and the examiners took counsel together and granted at any rate a few words to us teachers, I soon noticed that Ottilie was not mentioned at all, or if she was, it was with disapproval or indifference. I hoped I might inspire some goodwill for her by describing her nature and character to them, and I ventured on this with a twofold fervour, firstly because I could speak according to my own conviction, then because in earlier years I had found myself in precisely the same sad case. I was listened to with attention; but when I had finished the chairman of examiners said to me, in an affable but nonetheless laconic manner: 'Ability is presumed, the point is to turn it into performance. This is the purpose of all education, this is the clearly expressed intention of the parents and guardians, the unexpressed, only half-conscious intention of the children themselves. This is also the object of the examination, whereby both pupil and teacher are judged together. From what we have heard from you we may hope well of the child, and it is in any event to your credit that you pay such exact attention to the abilities of your pupils. Should you succeed in the course of the year in transforming such abilities into performance, you and your favoured pupil shall not lack our applause.'

I resigned myself to the consequences of this, but I did not anticipate a worse thing that happened not long afterwards. When the gentlemen had departed, our good headmistress who, like a good shepherd, does not like to see even one of her sheep go astray – or, as was here the case, undecorated – could not conceal her displeasure, and said to Ottilie, who was standing quietly beside the window while the others were rejoicing over their prizes: 'For Heaven's sake, girl! Tell me how it is possible to appear so stupid, when one is not stupid!' Ottilie replied quite composedly: 'You must excuse me, dear mother, but today I happen to have another of my headaches, and quite a bad one.' 'How could I be expected to know that!' replied the headmistress, who is usually so sympathetic, and turned away in irritation.

It is true no one could be expected to know, for Ottilie does not alter her expression, nor have I noticed her once raise a hand to her brow.

But that was not all. Your Ladyship's daughter, who is always very frank and lively, became under the influence of her triumphs of that day arrogant and exuberant. She ran around the room with her prizes and certificates and waved them in front of Ottilie's face. 'You've done badly today!' she exclaimed. Ottilie replied quite composedly: 'We have not yet sat the last examination.' 'Even so you'll always be last!' the girl cried, and ran off again.

To everyone else Ottilie appeared composed, but not to me. When she is resisting a violent and unpleasant inner agitation, the fact betrays itself in an unequal colouring of her face: the left cheek suddenly becomes red, the right one pale. I observed this symptom and was unable to restrain my sympathy. I took our headmistress to one side and spoke earnestly with her. The good lady recognized her error. We took counsel together, we discussed the matter at length and, not to be more prolix than I have been already, I should like to put our decision and our request before your Ladyship at once: it is that you should for a while take Ottilie back to live with you. The reasons for this will best become apparent to you yourself. If you do decide to do this, I shall say more about how the good child should be managed. If your Ladyship's daughter does then leave us, as is to be expected, we should be delighted to see Ottilie return to us.

One thing more, which I might later forget: I have never seen Ottilie ask for anything, not to speak of demanding or pleading for it. On the other hand, there are instances, albeit rare ones, when she tries to refuse to do something she is being asked to do.

She signifies this refusal with a gesture which, once you have grasped what it means, is irresistible. She presses the palms of her hands together and, raising them in the air, carries them to her breast, at the same time bowing very slightly and bestowing on whoever has made this urgent request such a glance that he is glad to desist. If your Ladyship should ever observe this gesture – which, in view of the way you will manage her, is not very probable – remember what I have said and spare Ottilie.

Eduard had to smile and shake his head as he read these letters to them and he could not help commenting on the people mentioned and on the state of things which became apparent.

'Enough!' he said when he had finished. 'It is decided, she is coming! You will then be taken care of, my love, and we can now also venture to produce a proposal we have in mind. It is most necessary that I should move over to the Captain in the right wing. The best time for working together is the evening and the morning. You, for your part, will get on your side the finest room in the house for yourself and Ottilie.'

Charlotte did not object and Eduard went on to describe how they were going to live in future.

'It is really most obliging of your niece to have a headache now and then on the left side,' he said. 'I sometimes have one on the right. If they come at the same time and we sit opposite one another, I leaning on my right elbow and she on her left, with our head on our hand on different sides, it will make a nice pair of contrasting pictures.'

The Captain said there might be danger in that, but Eduard exclaimed: 'You just be careful of the D, my friend! What would B do if C were torn from him?'

'I would have thought the answer to that was obvious,' Charlotte replied.

'It is!' cried Eduard: 'It would return to its A, to its A and O, its alpha and omega!' he cried, leaping up and pressing Charlotte hard against his breast.

CHAPTER SIX

A CARRIAGE bringing Ottilie had driven up. Charlotte went out to meet her. The dear child hurried towards her, threw herself at her feet and embraced her knees.

'Why this humility?' said Charlotte, who was somewhat confused by it and tried to raise her up. 'It is not meant to be so very humble,' Ottilie replied without moving. 'It is only that I want to remind myself of the time when I reached no higher than your knees and was already so certain of your love.'

She stood up and Charlotte embraced her. She was introduced to the men and was at once, as a guest, treated with especial respect. Beauty is everywhere a very welcome guest. She seemed attentive to the conversation although she took no part in it.

The following morning Eduard said to Charlotte: 'She is a pleasant amusing girl.'

'Amusing?' Charlotte replied with a smile: 'she has not yet opened her mouth.'

'Oh?' Eduard said, apparently trying to recall whether she had spoken or not: 'what a remarkable thing!'

Charlotte needed to give Ottilie only a few indications of how the household was run. Ottilie quickly understood the whole order of things. She felt them intuitively. She easily grasped what she was supposed to take care of on behalf of them all and on behalf of each individual. Everything was done punctually. She knew how to give directions without seeming to be giving orders and if anyone was lax she saw to the thing herself.

When she realized how much spare time she had she asked to be allowed to allot specific hours to specific duties, and this routine was thenceforth punctiliously observed. She worked at what she had to do in a way Charlotte had anticipated from what the schoolmaster had told her and she let her alone to carry on in her own fashion. Only now and then she would try to stimulate her in some fresh direction. She would slip worn-down pens into her room so as to induce her to write with a more fluent hand, but soon they were cut sharp again like her own pens.

The women had decided always to talk in French when they were alone. Charlotte stuck to this resolve the more firmly since Ottilie was more communicative in the foreign tongue. It had been suggested to her that practising it was a duty. Under these circumstances she often said more than she apparently intended. Charlotte particularly enjoyed her occasional closely-observed but affectionate descriptions of the whole boarding-school institution. Ottilie became a treasured companion and Charlotte hoped some day to find a dependable friend in her.

In the meantime, Charlotte took out again all the old letters and reports referring to Ottilie and refreshed her memory of how the headmistress and the schoolmaster had judged the dear child, so as to compare these opinions with the girl herself. Charlotte believed you could not get to know the character of the people you had to live with too quickly, so as to know what could be expected of them and cultivated in them or what you had once and for all to allow and forgive them.

This research revealed nothing fresh, it is true, but much that she already knew became more significant and striking. Ottilie's moderation in eating and drinking, for example, was now a source of real anxiety.

The next thing to engage the women was the question of dress. Charlotte demanded of Ottilie that she should be better dressed. The industrious child at once set to and cut up the material she had earlier been given and with only a little assistance was quickly able to make it into something very elegant. The more fashionable dresses improved her figure. Since what is pleasant about you extends even to your clothes, your good qualities seem to appear in a new and more charming light if you provide them with a new background.

And so she became for the men more and more what she had been from the first, which was (to call things by their right names) a feast for the eyes. For if the emerald is through its loveliness a pleasure to the sight, and indeed exerts a certain healing power on that noble sense, human beauty acts with far greater force on both inner and outer senses, so that he who beholds it is exempt from evil and feels in harmony with himself and with the world.

The company had thus profited in several ways from Ottilie's arrival. The two friends broke up their solitary meetings more punctually, even to the minute, and at mealtimes, or for tea, or for walks, they did not keep the women waiting longer than was reasonable. They did not hurry so quickly away from the table, especially in the evenings. Charlotte noticed all this and kept both men under observation. She wanted to know which one was the instigator of this change of behaviour, but could see no distinction between them. Both of them were being altogether more sociable. When talking together they seemed to bear in mind what subjects might engage Ottilie's interest and about which she might know and understand something. When reading aloud they broke off until she returned. They became gentler and on the whole more communicative.

In response, Ottilie's eagerness to make herself useful increased with every day that passed. The better she got to know the circumstances of the house and of the people in it, the more spiritedly did she go about her work and the more promptly did she understand the meaning of every glance, of every gesture, of a mere half-word, of a mere sound. She had at all times the same quiet attentiveness and the same unruffled alertness. And so her sitting and standing, her coming and going, her fetching and carrying and sitting again without any appearance of restlessness, was a perpetual change, perpetual exquisite motion. And you could not hear her when she walked, she walked so softly.

This proper zeal of Ottilie's to be serviceable gave Charlotte much pleasure. But she did not hide one thing which seemed to her not quite right. 'One of the most laudable attentions we can show to other people,' she said to her one day, 'is to stoop down if they should drop something and try to pick it up quickly. We thus as it were acknowledge that we are at their service; but in wider society one has to consider to whom one displays such submissiveness. I do not want to prescribe rules with respect to women. You are young. Towards older women and those in a more exalted station it is a duty, towards your equals it is politeness, towards younger women and those in a lower station it demonstrates kindness and human-feeling; only it is not quite seemly for a woman to display service and submission of this sort to a man.'

'I will try to break myself of the habit,' Ottilie replied. 'In the meantime, I know you will forgive me when I tell you how I came by it. We were taught history; I have not retained as much of it as I no doubt should have, for I could not see what use it would be to me. Only individual incidents made a great impression on me, and this is one of them:

'When Charles I of England was standing before his so-called judges, the gold knob at the end of the stick he was carrying came off and fell to the floor. Accustomed to everyone's springing to his assistance when such things happened, he seemed to be looking about him and expecting someone to come forward this time too and perform this small service for him. Nobody stirred; he himself bent down to pick up the knob. I found that so sad – whether rightly or not I cannot say – that from that moment on whenever I have seen anyone drop anything I have felt compelled to bend down after it. But since, I know, it may not always be proper to do so, and since,' she went on with a smile, 'I cannot be repeating my story every time it happens, I will restrain myself more in future.'

In the meantime, the good work to which the two friends felt themselves called went on without interruption. No day passed without they found a fresh occasion for planning and undertaking something.

As they were one day walking together through the village they noticed with displeasure how much less clean and tidy it was than those villages whose inhabitants have to pay attention to such things because they do not have much room to be untidy in.

'You will remember,' said the Captain, 'how when we were travelling through Switzerland we expressed the desire to adorn a country park, as such things are called, by instituting in a village lying just as this one does, not Swiss architecture but Swiss cleanliness and tidiness, which make a place so much more usable.'

'That would be feasible here, for example,' Eduard said. 'The mansion hill runs down to form a salient; the village is built in a fairly regular semicircle over against it; in between flows the stream, and to guard against flooding from it one villager erects stones, another stakes, a third beams, and his neighbour planks – none helps the other, but rather harms and obstructs him. And the road, too, follows its clumsy way now uphill, now down, now through the water, now over the rocks. If the people were willing to lend a hand, it would not cost very much to put up a semicircular wall here, to raise the road behind it to the level of the houses, to produce a fine open space and clear the way for the production of cleanliness; and by rearranging things on a large scale to do away once and for all with every petty inadequacy.'

'Let's try it,' said the Captain. He looked the locality over and quickly took stock of the situation.

'I do not like having anything to do with peasants or townspeople unless I am in a position to give them direct orders,' Eduard replied.

'That point of view is not so far wrong,' the Captain said, 'for I too have experienced a great deal of irritation in my life from jobs of this kind. How hard it is for a man to weigh aright what must be sacrificed against what is to be gained! How hard to will the end and not despise the means! Many even go so far as to confuse the means with the end, and take pleasure in the former without keeping the latter in view. It is supposed that each evil should be cured at the spot where it breaks out, and no thought is taken for the place where it actually originates and whence it spreads its influence. That is why it is so hard to work through consultation, especially with the crowd, which is quite judicious with respect to day-to-day affairs but seldom sees further than tomorrow. And if, in addition, one man is going to gain by a communal project and another lose, then compromise will achieve nothing. Anything which really promotes the common good can be attained only through unlimited sovereignty.'

While they were standing and talking a man who looked more insolent than needy came up and begged from them. Eduard was annoyed at being interrupted and, after having several times tried in vain to send him away politely, started reprimanding him, and when the man made off one slow step at a time, grumbling and even answering back, and said that beggars too had rights, and while they might be refused alms they ought not to be insulted, since they stood as much under the protection of God and the Authorities as anyone else, Eduard lost his temper entirely.

To calm him again afterwards, the Captain said: 'Let us regard this incident as a challenge to us to extend our country-side regulations to cover this sort of thing as well. Certainly one has to give alms, but it is better not to give them in person, especially when one is at home. At home one should be moderate and consistent, even in giving. Too great generosity entices beggars instead of dispatching them; on the other hand, when you are travelling abroad you might well, as you are sailing by, appear before a poor man in the street as an angel of fortune and cast him a surprisingly bountiful gift. The situation of the village and the mansion makes very easy an arrangement I have already been thinking over.

'At one end of the village there lies the inn, at the other there lives a benevolent old couple; you must lay down a small sum of money in both places. Not he who is coming into the village but he who is leaving it shall receive something; and since both houses also stand on the roads leading up to the mansion, anyone thinking of coming up there will be directed to them instead.'

'Come,' said Eduard, 'let's arrange it right away; we can always see to the details later.'

They visited the innkeeper and the elderly couple, and the thing was done.

'I know very well,' said Eduard as they were going back up to the mansion, 'that everything in the world depends on an intelligent idea and a firm decision. Thus you very justly criticized my wife's layout of her park and gave me a hint how it might be improved, which I will not attempt to deny I passed on to her straight away.'

'I could have realized you would,' the Captain replied, 'but I could not have approved. You have made her confused; she is now doing nothing there, and it is the only thing about which she is at odds with us : for she never talks about it, and she has never invited us to the moss-hut again, although she goes up there with Ottilie from time to time.'

'We must not allow ourselves to be deterred by that,' Eduard replied. 'When I am convinced of something good that could and should be done, I cannot rest until I can see it has been done. We find no difficulty in introducing innovations in other quarters, do we? So let us this evening take out the English books giving descriptions of parks with copper-plates and then your plans of the estate. We must first treat it as if it were merely a pleasant way of passing the time; before we know it we shall be discussing the matter seriously.'

In accordance with this conspiracy the books were brought out and opened up. They presented an outline of each region and a view of the landscape in its original natural condition, then on other pages the changes art had made upon it so as to take advantage of and enhance every existing good feature.

From this it was very simple to pass over to their own property, to their own environs, and to what might be made of them.

It was now a pleasant job to set to work using the map the Captain had drafted. They could not entirely escape from the original conception on the basis of which Charlotte had begun, but they managed to work out an easier ascent up the hill. They decided to build a pavilion before a pleasant little copse on the upper slope. This pavilion was to stand in a significant relation to the mansion; it was to be overlooked by the mansion's windows and its own windows were to give a sweeping view of the mansion and the gardens.

The Captain had carefully considered everything and he again brought up for discussion the village road, the wall beside the stream and the question of building it up. 'By making an easy path up to the height,' he said, 'I shall gain exactly the amount of stone I need for that wall. When you coordinate one project with another both can be effected more cheaply and more quickly.'

'But now comes my worry,' said Charlotte. 'We have to set aside a definite sum for this; and when you know how much such plans as these are going to cost, you can divide up this amount, if not into so much a week, at any rate into so much a month. The money-box is in my custody; I shall pay the bills and keep the accounts myself.'

'You do not seem to trust us overmuch,' said Eduard.

'Not when it comes to caprices like this,' Charlotte replied. 'We know better than you how to govern our caprices.'

Arrangements were made, work was quickly begun and the Captain was to be seen everywhere. Charlotte had almost daily evidence of how serious and determined he was. He too learned to know her better and they found it easy to work together and get something done.

Working together is like dancing together: if you keep in step you become indispensable to one another. Mutual good-will must necessarily develop. A sure proof that, since she had got to know him better, Charlotte felt genuine goodwill towards the Captain was that she let him destroy a fine resting-place, which in her original designs for the park she had specially chosen and decked out but which now got in the way of his plans, without the slightest feeling of resentment.

CHAPTER SEVEN

As Charlotte and the Captain had now found a common occupation Eduard was thrown more into the company of Ottilie. A quiet affection had in any case for some time been her advocate in his heart. She was polite and obliging towards everyone; his self-esteem would have had it appear that she was most so towards him. But now the fact was unquestionable: she had noticed minutely what food he liked and how he liked it, how much sugar he took in his tea, and other details of that sort. She was especially careful to shield him from draughts, towards which he showed an exaggerated sensitivity and as a result often came into conflict with his wife, who could never have too much fresh air. She also knew her way about the orchard and the flower-garden. What he wanted she tried to provide, what might provoke his impatience she sought to prevent. She quickly became, like a guardian spirit, indispensable to him, and he began to notice it when she was absent. She seemed to grow more communicative and candid as soon as they found themselves alone.

Despite his advancing years Eduard had retained something childlike to which Ottilie's youth was particularly congenial. They liked to recall together earlier occasions on which they had seen one another. These recollections went back as far as the time Eduard was first attracted to Charlotte. Ottilie claimed to remember them as being the handsomest couple at court, and when Eduard denied she could remember anything so early she asserted she could still perfectly well recall how once, when Eduard had come into the room, she had hidden her face in Charlotte's lap, not because she was afraid but out of childish confusion. She could have added:

71

because he had made so lively an impression upon her, because she liked him so well.

Under these circumstances much of the business the two friends had been doing together was beginning to come to a halt. They found it necessary to take renewed stock of the situation, draft memoranda, write letters. They arranged to meet in their office, where they found their ancient copy-clerk idling his time away. They set to work and soon had him active again, although they failed to notice they were burdening him with many things they had previously been used to taking care of themselves. The Captain's very first memorandum, Eduard's very first letter both failed to come right, and they toiled about for a time with drafting and copying, until Eduard, who was making the least headway of the two, at length asked what the time was.

It then transpired that the Captain had, for the first time for many years, forgotten to wind his watch. They seemed, if not to realize clearly, at any rate to suspect that time was beginning to be a matter of indifference to them.

While the men were to some extent neglecting their business the women were becoming more industrious. As a rule the ordinary life of a family, which has its origin in the nature of the people and the circumstances involved, assimilates an extraordinary inclination, a growing passion, like a vat, and quite a long time may elapse before this new ingredient causes any perceptible fermentation and finally comes foaming over the edge.

The mutual affections which had developed were having the pleasantest effect upon our friends. Their hearts were opened and a general feeling of goodwill evolved from the particular. Each one was happy and did not envy the other his happiness.

A condition like this, by opening the heart elevates the mind, and everything we do or undertake to do tends towards the immeasurable. Our friends no longer confined themselves to the house. They went for longer walks and when Eduard hurried ahead with Ottilie to find out new paths and to break new ground the Captain and Charlotte quietly followed talking seriously and taking an interest in many newly-discovered spots and many unexpected vistas.

One day their walk took them through the gate of the right wing of the mansion down to the inn over the bridge towards the lake. They walked along the lakeshore as far as they could, up to the place where the bank became enclosed by a bush-covered hill, and further along by cliffs, and ceased to be passable.

But Eduard, who was familiar with the region from when he had hunted there, pressed further on with Ottilie up to an overgrown path, knowing the old mill hidden among the cliffs could not lie far off from there. But the rarely frequented path soon disappeared and they found themselves lost amid thick undergrowth and moss-covered rocks. But it was not for long. The roaring of the mill-wheel soon told them the place they were looking for was near at hand.

Advancing on to a crag they saw the curious old black wooden structure in the declivity before them, overshadowed by steep cliffs and tall trees. They at once made up their minds to clamber down over the moss and broken rocks. Eduard went first and when he looked back up the way he had come and saw Ottilie following fearlessly behind him, stepping lightly from stone to stone with untroubled poise, he thought it must be a creature from heaven hovering there above him. But when she stepped on insecure places and had to take his outstretched hand or lean against his shoulder he could not doubt that what touched him then was the tenderest female creature. He almost wished she would stumble or slip so that he could catch her in his arms and press her to his heart. But this he would on no condition have done, and for more than one reason. He feared he might offend or injure her.

What this last remark is intended to mean we shall straightway discover. As soon as they had arrived at the bottom, and he had sent the friendly miller's wife off to fetch milk and the welcoming miller off to meet Charlotte and the Captain and he was sitting opposite Ottilie at the rustic table under the tall trees, Eduard said to her after some hesitation: 'I have a request to make, my dear Ottilie: I hope you will excuse it, even if you have to refuse it. You make no secret of the fact – as indeed there is no need to – that you wear on your breast, beneath your dress, a miniature. It is a picture of your father, that worthy man whom you hardly knew and who deserves, in every sense of the term, a place near your heart. Now forgive me, but the picture is uncomfortably large, and this glass and metal give me a thousand anxieties whenever you pick up a child, or carry anything in front of you, or the carriage sways, or when we battle through the undergrowth, or just now, as we were clambering down from the cliff. I dread that if you should stumble or fall or be jolted you may be hurt or injured. For my sake do please remove that picture – not from your thoughts or from your room – indeed, give it the finest and most sacred spot in your dwelling – no, remove it from your breast, remove something whose proximity seems to me, perhaps from an exaggerated anxiety, so dangerous to you.'

Ottilie sat looking in front of her while he was speaking. She was silent for a time. Then, without haste or hesitation and with her eyes turned to heaven rather than to Eduard, she unfastened the chain, drew out the picture, pressed it to her forehead and handed it to Eduard with the words: 'Keep it for me until we get home. I have no better way of showing how much I appreciate your friendly solicitude.'

Eduard did not dare to press the picture to his lips. He grasped her hand and pressed it to his eyes. It was perhaps the loveliest pair of hands that had ever been clasped together. He felt as if a stone had fallen from his heart, as if a wall between him and Ottilie had been broken down.

Guided by the miller, Charlotte and the Captain came down

by an easier path. They greeted one another and sat and took refreshment. They did not want to go back by the same route and Eduard suggested a cliff-path on the other side of the stream from which you could have another view of the lakes, although some effort was needed to go up it. They now made their way through intermittent woodland and looking towards the open country saw villages, plots and dairy farms in green fertile fields. They came to a farmstead lying hidden among the trees on the hillside. The opulence of the region before and behind them could be seen at its best from the gently rising hill. From there they made their way to a pleasant little coppice and when they came out of it they found themselves on the heights facing the mansion.

This prospect, at which they had as it were arrived unexpectedly, gave them great pleasure. They had walked around a little world and were standing on what was to be the site of the new building and looking again into the windows of their own house.

They climbed down to the moss-hut and for the first time all four sat in there together. It was natural they should all want the route they had that day walked slowly and with difficulty built up so that it could be walked in companionable ease and comfort. Everyone offered suggestions and it was calculated the path which had taken them several hours must, if properly laid down, lead back to the mansion in no more than one hour. They were already in their minds constructing a bridge below the mill, where the stream flows into the lakes, to shorten the route and add beauty to the landscape when Charlotte called a halt by reminding them of the cost such an undertaking would involve.

'There is a way of meeting that,' Eduard replied. 'We only have to sell that farmstead in the wood that looks so well situated and brings in so little and employ the proceeds on this new enterprise: thus we shall have the pleasure of enjoying on an incomparable walk the interest from well-invested capital from which, when we come to reckon up at the end of the year, we now discontentedly draw a very meagre income.'

Charlotte could not as a good housekeeper find much to say against this proposal. The matter had been spoken of before. Now the Captain wanted to draw up a plan for parcelling out the ground among the peasantry but Eduard thought he knew a quicker and more convenient way of disposing of it. The present tenant, who had already produced ideas for improving it, ought to keep it and pay for it by instalments and they would undertake the new project also by instalments, one stage at a time.

So reasonable and cautious an arrangement could not be objected to, and they all were already seeing the new paths in their mind's eye and thinking of the agreeable resting-places and vantage-points they would discover along it and near it.

To picture it all in more detail, at home that evening they straightway took out the new map. They inspected the route they had covered and considered how it might perhaps in this or that spot be redirected to better advantage. Their earlier ideas were discussed again and coordinated with the latest ideas, the site of the new pavilion over against the mansion was again approved and the circle of paths leading to it settled on.

Ottilie had stayed silent during all this. Eduard finally moved the plan, which had been lying in front of Charlotte, over to her and invited her to offer her opinions, and when she hesitated, gently encouraged her to say whatever she had to say, for the whole thing, he said, was still only at the stage of discussion.

'I would build the pavilion here,' said Ottilie, laying her finger on the highest level place on the hill. 'You could not see the mansion, I know, for it is concealed by the little wood; but to make up for that you would find yourself in a new and different world, since the village and all the houses would also be hidden. The view of the lakes, of the mill, of the heights, and out towards the mountains and the countryside is extraordinarily fine; I noticed it when we went past.'

'She is right!' cried Eduard: 'How is it we did not think of that? This is where you mean, isn't it, Ottilie?' – and he took a pencil and drew a thick black rectangle on the hill.

The Captain felt a stab of pain when he saw this. He did not like to see a carefully and neatly drawn plan disfigured in that way. But he contented himself with a mild expression of disapproval and acquiesced in the idea. 'Ottilie is right,' he said. 'Food and drink taste better after a long walk than they would have tasted at home. We want variety and unfamiliar things. It was right for your forefathers to build the house over here, for it is sheltered from the wind and within easy reach of all our daily requirements; on the other hand, a building intended more for pleasure trips than as a house would be very well placed over there and during the fine seasons would afford us the most agreeable hours.'

The more they talked the matter over the better it seemed and Eduard could not hide his elation that the idea had been Ottilie's. He was as proud of it as if it had been his own.

CHAPTER EIGHT

THE first thing the next morning the Captain inspected the site and sketched out a rough plan and then, when they had all again agreed on the spot, a detailed one together with an estimate and everything else necessary. There was no lack of preparation. The business of selling the farmstead was taken up again straight away. The men found fresh opportunity for being busy together.

The Captain suggested to Eduard it would be courteous – that it was virtually their duty – to celebrate Charlotte's birthday by the laying of the foundation-stone. It did not need much effort to overcome Eduard's old aversion to such celebrations because it came into his mind that Ottilie's birthday, which was later in the year, could be celebrated in a similar solemn manner.

Charlotte, who took the new arrangements with the utmost seriousness, and was indeed almost suspicious of the facility with which they were being carried through, busied herself with checking the estimates and the apportionment of time and money on her own account. They saw one another less often during the day, so they sought one another out with the greater eagerness in the evening.

Ottilie had meanwhile become altogether mistress of the household. With her quiet and confident manner it could hardly have been otherwise. All her thoughts were directed towards the house and the domestic life rather than towards the world outside and the outdoor life. Eduard soon noticed that it was only to oblige them that she went with them on their walks, that it was only out of a sense of social duty that she lingered with them outside in the evenings, and then she often found some household task as an excuse for going in. He was therefore very soon able to arrange their excursions so that they got back home before sunset. He took up again (what he had for long let drop) the reading of poems aloud, especially poems whose recitation permitted the expression of a pure but passionate love.

In the evenings they usually sat about a small table on seats they had pulled up to it. Charlotte sat on the sofa, Ottilie in an easy chair opposite her, and the men sat on the other two sides of the table. Ottilie sat to the right of Eduard and it was in this direction he turned the light when he read. Ottilie then used to draw nearer so as to see the book, for she too trusted her own eyes more than someone else's mouth, and Eduard also used to draw nearer so as to make it easier for her and he even paused in his reading longer than he needed to so as not to turn the page before she too had reached the end of it.

Charlotte and the Captain did not fail to notice all this and they often looked at one another and smiled. But another sign which chanced to reveal the quiet affection Ottilie had developed for Eduard took them by surprise.

One evening, which had been partly ruined for the little group by the presence of tedious visitors, Eduard suggested staying together for a little longer than usual. He felt inclined to take out his flute, which instrument had not been on the agenda for a long time. Charlotte looked for the sonatas they usually played together, and when she could not find them Ottilie admitted with some hesitation that she had taken them up to her room.

'And you can and you want to accompany me at the piano?' Eduard exclaimed. His eyes shone with pleasure. 'I think I might manage it,' Ottilie replied. She fetched the scores and sat down at the keyboard. Their audience heard with surprise how completely she had mastered the music by herself, but with greater surprise how she had learned to adapt it to Eduard's mode of performance. 'Learned to adapt' is not the right expression : if Charlotte held back at one point and hurried along at another in response to her husband's hesitations and precipitancies it was because she was skilled enough and willing to do so, but Ottilie, who had heard them play the sonata once or twice, seemed to have taken it in only in the manner in which Eduard played it. She had made his shortcomings so much her own that a new living whole had evolved which, if it did not keep to the original measure, at any rate managed to sound very pleasant and agreeable. The composer himself would have enjoyed hearing his work distorted in so charming a manner.

The Captain and Charlotte looked silently upon this strange unexpected event with the feeling with which you often regard the behaviour of children which, because of its consequences, you cannot exactly approve of but cannot reprove either but must perhaps even envy. For the fact was that an affection was growing up between Charlotte and the Captain just as much as between Ottilie and Eduard and perhaps, since Charlotte and the Captain were more serious-minded, more sure of themselves, more capable of self-control, it was an even more dangerous affection.

The Captain was already beginning to feel that, because she was always near him, he was becoming attached to her irresistibly. He made himself avoid appearing during the hours Charlotte was usually in the park. He got up early in the morning, took care of everything, and then retired to work in his wing of the mansion. The first days on which this happened Charlotte thought his absence was accidental and looked for him everywhere. Then she believed she understood him, and on that account esteemed him all the more highly.

If the Captain avoided being alone with Charlotte he was all the more diligent in hastening the brilliant celebration of her approaching birthday. While he drove the easy ascending path up from behind the village he at the same time started on a descending path from the top, ostensibly so as to acquire the stone thus broken out, and had so organized things that the two sections would meet on the last night. The cellar for the new pavilion on the hill had been dug out rather than properly excavated and a handsome foundation-stone, with panels and covering slabs, had been hewn out.

This activity, these little secret designs, combined with feelings more or less repressed, placed a constraint on the liveliness of the company when they were together, so that Eduard, who sensed that something was missing, one evening called on the Captain to bring out his violin and play something with Charlotte at the piano. The Captain could not resist the general desire that he should comply with this suggestion and the two performed together a very difficult piece of music with sensitivity, ease and lack of constraint, so that they and the couple who formed their audience were overcome with pleasure. They promised themselves they would play more often and practise more together.

'They can do it better than we can, Ottilie !' said Eduard. 'Let us admire them, but let us go on enjoying our own playing too.'

CHAPTER NINE

THE birthday had arrived and everything was ready. The wall which raised the village street and protected it from the water was finished and so was the pathway, which now ran past the church, following for a stretch the path already laid out by Charlotte, then wound up the cliff and passed the moss-hut, where it turned and so gradually made its way to the top of the hill.

A crowd of visitors had come on this day. They all went along to the church, where they found the local community assembled in festive dress. As had been arranged, the boys and youths and men left first after the service was over, then the ladies and gentlemen with their visitors and retinue left, and the girls and women left last of all.

A raised rock-platform had been set up where the path turned; here the Captain conducted Charlotte and the guests. From this place they overlooked the entire pathway, the troop of men walking further along up and the women following them who were now passing by. It made a glorious sight in the sunshine. Charlotte was surprised and moved by the spectacle and she warmly pressed the Captain's hand.

They followed the slowly advancing crowd which had by now formed a circle round the site of the new building. Its owner and his party and the most prominent of his guests were invited to step down to where the foundation-stone stood supported on one side ready to be laid. A mason dressed in his best suit and carrying a trowel in one hand and a hammer in the other now delivered a well-turned address in verse which we are able to reproduce only imperfectly in prose.

'Three things,' he began, 'have to be taken into account

when erecting a building: that it is standing on the right spot, that the foundations are sound, that it is well constructed. The first is properly a matter for the owner: for as in a town only the prince and the municipality can decide where a building is to be erected, so in the country it is the privilege of the landowner to say: Here and nowhere else shall my house stand.'

Eduard and Ottilie avoided looking at one another during these words although they were standing quite close together.

'The third, the completion of the building, is in the care of very many crafts; there are few indeed which have no part in it. But the second, the foundation, is the mason's business and, if we may make so bold as to say so, it is the chief business in the entire undertaking. It is an earnest labour, and our summons to you is earnest: for this ceremony is dedicated to the depths. Here within this narrow excavated space you do us the honour of appearing as witnesses of our secret labour. Soon we shall lay this well-hewn stone, soon these earthen walls, now adorned with so many fair and worthy persons, will be inaccessible, they will be buried.

'This foundation-stone, whose firm corner denotes the firm corner of the building, whose square-cut form denotes the regularity of the building, whose perpendicular and horizontal position denotes the trueness of the walls without and within – this stone we might now lay without further ado: for by its own weight it would rest firm. Yet here too there must be lime and cement: for, as men who are naturally inclined to one another hold together better when they are cemented by the law, so too bricks whose shapes are already well matched are better united by this binding force; and since it is not fitting to be idle while others are working, you will not disdain to become one of us on this occasion.'

At this he handed his trowel to Charlotte, who threw a trowelful of lime under the stone. Others were asked to do so too and the stone was then lowered. Then Charlotte and the others were handed the hammer and with a threefold blow blessed the union of the stone and the ground.

'Although the mason's work continues above ground,' the speaker went on, 'it is still hidden, or where not hidden is done for the sake of what is hidden. The square-cut foundation is choked with earth, and even the walls we build in the light of day in the end almost disappear from mind. The work of the stone-cutter and the sculptor are most visible to view, and we are even compelled to approve when the decorator obliterates the traces of our labour altogether and appropriates our work to himself by overlaying, smoothing and painting it.

'Who then must be more concerned than the mason to make well so that he may appear well in his own eyes? Who has more cause than he to nourish his assurance of his own worth? When the house is built, the floor flattened and plastered, the exterior decorated, he can still always see through this covering and recognize still those well-proportioned painstaking joints which the whole has to thank for its existence and stability.

'But as he who has done evil must fear that, in spite of all precaution, his deed will come to light, so he who has done good in secret must expect that, counter to his will, his deed too will be revealed. That is why this foundation-stone is to be a memorial-stone also. Here in these hollow spaces we shall place various objects as witnesses to a distant posterity. These sealed metal containers hold written messages; on these metal plates have been engraven all sorts of inscriptions; in these handsome glass bottles we bury the best of our wine with a designation of its vintage; likewise coins of various kinds minted this year: all this we have received through the munificence of the owner. And there is still plenty of room left if any guest or spectator would also like to bequeath something to posterity.'

The workman paused and looked around. But, as usual on such occasions, no one was prepared, everyone was taken by surprise, until at length a young officer took the lead and said: 'If I am to contribute anything to this storehouse that has not been put in there already I will have to cut a couple of buttons off my uniform. I think they too deserve to go down to posterity.' No sooner said than done. And then many others had similar ideas. The ladies offered their hair-combs, and smelling-bottles and other trinkets went in. Ottilie alone, sunk in contemplation of the offerings, failed to give anything, until a word from Eduard brought her back and then she unfastened from around her neck the gold chain from which her father's picture had hung and laid it gently on top of the other treasures, and after she had done that Eduard hastily had the covering slab put on and fixed at once.

The young workman, who had been busier than anyone during all this, now took up his oratorical posture again and continued: 'We found this stone for eternity, to ensure the enjoyment of this house to its present and future possessors for the longest possible time. But while we here as it were bury a treasure and are occupied with the most fundamental of all tasks, we think at the same time of the transitoriness of human things: we think of the possibility that this firm-sealed lid may one day be opened again, which could not happen unless that which has not yet even been built were all to be destroyed again.

'But let us bring our thoughts back from the future, let us return to the present, so that this building may be accomplished. As soon as this ceremony is done let us straightway get on with our task, so that none of the guilds at work on our site need stand idle, that this structure may rapidly rise upward and be completed, and that, through those windows which do not yet exist, the master of the house, his family and his guests, may happily enjoy the view of the region round; to whom, and to all here present, let us herewith drink a health!'

And with that he emptied at a single draught a shining crystal cup and threw it into the air: for to destroy the vessel you have used on a happy occasion is a sign of overflowing joy. But on this occasion something else happened: the glass did not come back to earth and yet there was no miracle involved.

So as to get ahead with the building the foundations at the opposite corner had already been dug out, and a start had even been made on the walls, and for the purpose of building the walls a scaffold had been put up.

For the benefit of the work-people the scaffold had been fitted with planks and a crowd of spectators allowed up on it. The glass sailed up as high as these planks and one of the spectators caught it. He took it for a sign of luck and without letting it go he showed it around and everyone could see that there had been cut into it the letters E and O entwined. It was a glass of Eduard's made for him as a boy.

When the spectators had got down from the scaffold the nimblest among the guests climbed up on it and were loud in praise of the beautiful view on every side: for you can see much more if you stand higher, even if it is only one storey higher. Towards the country they could see several new villages that had not been visible before, the silver streak of the river was clearly visible, one of them even said he could see the towers of the capital. Rearwards behind the wood-covered hill rose the blue peaks of a distant mountain range and the immediate neighbourhood could be viewed overall. 'What wants doing now,' one of them said, 'is to join the three lakes together into one great lake, then the view would have everything you could ask for.'

'That could be done,' said the Captain. 'They were at one time a single mountain lake.'

'Only let my group of plane-trees and poplars alone,' said

Eduard. 'They look very fine beside the middle lake. Look' –
turning to Ottilie and leading her a few steps forward and
pointing down – 'I planted those trees myself.'

'How long have they stood there?' she asked. 'About as
long as you have been on earth,' Eduard replied. 'Yes, dear
child, I was already planting trees while you were still in the
cradle.'

The company went back to the mansion. When they had
eaten they were invited to take a walk through the village so
as to see the new arrangements there too. At the Captain's
instigation the villagers had assembled in front of their
houses. They were not standing in line but grouped naturally
in families, some busy with evening tasks, some relaxing on
benches newly provided. It had become a pleasant duty for
them to keep the village clean and tidy at any rate on Sun-
days and holidays.

An intimate affectionate companionship such as had grown
up between our friends can only be unpleasantly disturbed
by the presence of a larger company. All four were glad when
they were back alone in the big drawing-room, but this cosy
feeling was somewhat broken into by the arrival of a letter
announcing that other guests would be coming next day.

'As we expected!' said Eduard, to whom the letter had
been handed, turning to Charlotte. 'The Count is not going to
fail us. He is coming tomorrow.'

'In that case the Baroness cannot be far away either,' Charlotte replied.

'She isn't!' Eduard answered. 'She's arriving tomorrow too.
They ask if they can stay overnight. They want to leave together the day after.'

'Then we will have to make arrangements in good time,
Ottilie!' said Charlotte.

'What do you want arranged?' Ottilie asked.

Charlotte said what she wanted arranged and Ottilie went
away.

The Captain inquired what the relationship was between these two. He knew about it only vaguely. Already married, they had fallen passionately in love. Two marriages were broken up, not without scandal. They thought of divorce; it was possible for the Baroness, for the Count not. They had to pretend to part but their relationship remained what it was; and if they could not be together in the winter in the Residenz, they made up for it in the summer on pleasure trips and taking the waters. They were both somewhat older than Eduard and Charlotte and in earlier days they had all been close friends at court. They had always remained on good terms, even if you could not always approve of everything about your friends. Only this time Charlotte found their arrival somewhat inopportune and if she had to say why she found it inopportune she would say it was on Ottilie's account. The good pure child ought not to have such an example put before her at so early an age.

'They could have left it for a couple of days,' said Eduard as Ottilie came back, 'until we have settled the farmstead sale. The contract is ready. I have one copy here but we need a second and our old clerk is ill.' The Captain offered to do it, Charlotte also offered; but he raised objections to their offers. 'Just give it to me!' Ottilie cried suddenly.

'You will not be able to get it finished,' said Charlotte.

'I would have to have it the day after tomorrow, first thing, and there is a lot to copy,' said Eduard. 'It shall be ready,' Ottilie cried. She already had the paper in her hands.

Next morning, as they were looking out of the upper floor windows so as not to miss seeing their guests arrive and going to meet them, Eduard said: 'Who is that riding so slowly down the road?' The Captain described the figure in more detail. 'Then it is him,' said Eduard. 'The details, which you can see better than I, accord with the general picture, which I can see very well. It is Mittler. But how does he come to be riding so slowly?'

88

The figure came closer and it was Mittler. They received him affably as he came slowly up the steps. 'Why didn't you come yesterday?' Eduard called to him.

'I do not like noisy festivities,' he replied. 'But today I come to celebrate my friend's birthday with you quietly.'

'But how can you manage to find time?' Eduard asked, joking.

'You owe my visit, for what it is worth, to a thought I had yesterday. I spent half the day very pleasantly in a home to which I had brought peace, and then I heard that birthday celebrations were going on over here. I thought to myself: it could be called selfish, when all's said and done, to enjoy yourself only among people to whom you have brought peace. Why don't you go for once and enjoy yourself with friends who have never needed peace brought to them because they keep it themselves! No sooner said than done! Here I am, as intended.'

'Yesterday you would have found a large company here,' said Charlotte, 'today you will find only a small one. You will find the Count and the Baroness, with whom you have already had some dealings.'

The strange gentleman the four were welcoming jumped away with the sudden celerity of irritation. He looked round for his hat and switch. 'An evil star unfailingly appears above me as soon as ever I decide to relax and do myself a favour! But why do I go against my own nature? I ought not to have come, and now I am being driven away. For I will not stay under one roof with that pair. And you watch out for yourselves too: they bring nothing but harm! They are like a leaven that spreads and propagates its own contagion.'

They tried to appease him but tried in vain. 'Whoever attacks marriage,' he cried, 'whoever undermines the basis of all moral society, because that is what it is, by word not to speak of by deed, has me to reckon with. Or if I cannot get the better of him I have nothing further to do with him. Marriage is the beginning and the pinnacle of all culture. It makes the savage gentle, and it gives the most cultivated the best occasion for demonstrating his gentleness. It has to be indissoluble : it brings so much happiness that individual instances of unhappiness do not come into account. And why speak of unhappiness at all? Impatience is what it really is, ever and again people are overcome by impatience, and then they like to think themselves unhappy. Let the moment pass, and you will count yourself happy that what has so long stood firm still stands. As for separation, there can be no adequate grounds for it. The human condition is compounded of so much joy and so much sorrow that it is impossible to reckon how much a husband owes a wife or a wife a husband. It is an infinite debt, it can be paid only in eternity. Marriage may sometimes be an uncomfortable state, I can well believe that, and that is as it should be. Are we not also married to our conscience, and would we not often like to be rid of it because it is more uncomfortable than a husband or a wife could ever be?'

He would probably have gone on talking in this energetic vein for a long time more if the sound of coach horns had not announced the arrival of the Count and the Baroness. They drove into the courtyard from either side at the same time as if it had been prearranged. Our friends hurried to meet them and Mittler hid himself and had his horse brought him and rode off in annoyance.

CHAPTER TEN

THE guests were welcomed and conducted in. They were very happy to be again in the house and the rooms where they had spent so many good days and which they had not seen for a long time. The Count and the Baroness were both of that tall well-formed type of person you almost prefer to see in middle age than in youth: if they have lost something of their first bloom, they now excite not only affection but a decided feeling of trust and confidence. This couple too were very easy to get along with. Their easy manner of accepting and dealing with life's circumstances, their cheerfulness, their apparent unaffectedness communicated themselves right away, and their whole deportment was characterized by a noble decorum untouched by any sense of constraint.

This effect made itself felt immediately. The new arrivals had come straight from the great world, as you could see from their dress, their effects and everything else about them, and they supplied a kind of contrast to our friends, with their country ways and their secluded passions. But this was soon dissipated as old memories and present interests mingled, and they were quickly united in lively conversation.

But before long they separated again. The ladies retired to their wing, where they found plenty of entertainment in exchanging confidences and criticizing the latest fashions. The men busied themselves with the coaches and horses and were soon horse-trading and horse-exchanging.

They first reassembled at table. They had dressed and in this too the new arrivals showed themselves to advantage. All they wore was new and so to speak unseen, and yet already tried out and therefore comfortable and familiar.

Conversation was lively and varied: when people such as

this are present everything and nothing seems to be of interest. They spoke French so as to exclude the servants, they chattered gaily about the affairs of the great world and the not so great. But on one point their talk stayed with a subject longer than might seem proper, and that was when Charlotte inquired after a friend of her youth and learned with some surprise she was about to be divorced.

'Disagreeable,' said Charlotte, 'to think your absent friends are safe, a friend you love is well taken care of, and before you know it to hear her fate is in the balance, to hear she is about to enter on to a new road and perhaps an uncertain one.'

'Actually, my dear,' replied the Count, 'it is our own fault if we are surprised in this fashion. We do so like to imagine that earthly things are so very permanent, and especially the marriage tie. And as to that, we are misled by all those comedies we see so much of into imaginings which are quite contrary to the way of the world. In a comedy we see a marriage as the final fulfilment of a desire which has been thwarted by the obstacles of several acts. The moment this desire is fulfilled the curtain falls, and this momentary satisfaction goes on echoing in our minds. Things are different in the real world. In the real world the play continues after the curtain has fallen, and when it is raised again there is not much pleasure to be gained by seeing or hearing what is going on.'

'It cannot be as bad as all that,' said Charlotte, smiling, 'since you see actors who have retired from this stage glad enough to get back on to it.'

'You cannot take objection to that,' said the Count. 'To assume a new role may be a very pleasant thing. When you know the world you see that in the case of marriage too it is only this fixed eternal duration amid so much change that has something inappropriate about it. A friend of mine whose humour usually takes the form of suggesting new laws used to say marriages ought to be contracted for only five years. He said this lovely odd and sacred number and the length of time measured by it would suffice for getting to know one another, producing a few children, separating and, what would be the best of it, becoming reconciled again. He used to say: What a happy time you would have at first! Two or three years at the least would be spent in contentment. Then one of the parties would be interested in seeing the relationship protracted, would grow more and more attentive as the end drew closer. The indifferent or even discontented party would be propitiated and won over by this behaviour. As you forget the time when in good company, so they too would forget the passage of time and would be most pleasantly surprised to notice after the term was up that it had already been silently prolonged.'

This was all very clever and merry, and Charlotte was not unaware the joke could be given a profound moral meaning, but she found such utterances unpleasant, especially on account of Ottilie. She knew well nothing is more dangerous than too free conversation in which a culpable or semiculpable situation is treated as normal, commonplace, or even praiseworthy; and anything that impugns the marriage tie certainly comes into this category. She tried with all her skill to turn the conversation elsewhere; she was unable to do so, and she was sorry Ottilie had arranged everything so well that she had no occasion to leave the table. The quietly observant child was directing the steward merely by glances and gestures and everything was going splendidly, even though a couple of the liveried servants were new and awkward.

And so, oblivious of Charlotte's effort to change the subject, the Count went on talking about marriage. As a rule he was in no way given to monopolizing the conversation, but this theme weighed too heavily on his heart, and the difficulties living apart from his wife involved him in had embittered him against everything connected with the marriage tie, although this did not prevent his very keenly desiring to marry the Baroness.

'That friend of mine,' he went on, 'made a further suggestion for a marriage law. He suggested a marriage should be regarded as indissoluble only if both parties or at any rate one of them marries a third time. A person who marries three times incontestably confesses that for him or her marriage is something indispensable. It would already be known from how he or she had behaved in previous marriages whether or not the party possessed those qualities which often give more cause for separation than do downright bad qualities. Reciprocal inquiries would have to be made. You would have to keep as close an eye on the married as on the unmarried, because you could never know how each case would turn out.'

'That would certainly make society more interested in us,' said Eduard. 'As things are now, once we are married no one bothers himself further about either our virtues or our shortcomings.'

'Under such an arrangement,' the Baroness interposed, smiling, 'our dear host and hostess would already have surmounted two stages with flying colours, and could be preparing for the third.'

'They have been fortunate,' said the Count. 'Death has done for them what the courts are usually reluctant to do.'

'Let us leave the dead alone,' said Charlotte, not altogether in jest.

'Why,' the Count replied, 'when we can think nothing but good of them? They were modest enough to content themselves with a few years of life in return for the manifold good things they left behind them.'

'Which would be very fine,' said the Baroness with a suppressed sigh, 'if it were not that in such cases it is the best years of life that have to be sacrificed.'

'True,' replied the Count; 'it would reduce you to despair

were it not that in this world in general so little turns out as you hope it will. Children do not fulfill their promise; young people do so very rarely, and when they do keep their word the world does not keep its word to them.'

Charlotte, who was glad the conversation had taken another direction, replied cheerfully : 'Well, we are in any case compelled soon enough to take the good things of life in bits and pieces and learn to enjoy them in that condition.'

'Certainly you two have enjoyed some good times,' the Count replied. 'When I think back to the years you and Eduard were the handsomest couple at court ! Such brilliant times and such fine people are a thing of the past now. When you danced together all eyes were on you. And how you were sought after, while you had eyes only for one another !'

'Since so much is changed,' said Charlotte, 'perhaps we can accept such compliments without immodesty.'

'I have often thought Eduard was to blame for not being more persistent,' said the Count. 'His eccentric parents would have given in in the end, and to gain ten years of youth is no small thing.'

'I must defend him,' the Baroness interposed. 'Charlotte was not entirely free from blame, not entirely innocent of looking elsewhere. And even though she was in love with Eduard and had secretly determined to make him her husband, yet I was myself a witness to how much she sometimes tormented him, so that it was not hard to persuade him to his unhappy decision to travel and get away and get used to being without her.'

Eduard nodded to the Baroness and seemed grateful she was speaking up for him.

'But I have to say one thing on Charlotte's side,' she went on. 'The man who was courting her at that time had long demonstrated his affection for her, and when you got to

95

know him better was certainly a nicer person than you others are willing to admit.'

'Well, my dear,' said the Count rather briskly, 'let us also admit that you were not totally indifferent to him, and that Charlotte had more to fear from you than from anyone else. It is a very attractive trait in women that once they have become attached to a man they retain that attachment for so long and do not allow any sort of separation from him to disturb or destroy it.'

'Perhaps men possess this fine quality to an even greater degree,' the Baroness replied. 'In any event, I have noticed in your case, dear Count, that no one has more power over you than a woman for whom you once felt an affection. I have seen you go to more trouble to accommodate such a woman than your friend of the moment could perhaps have persuaded you to do.'

'If that is a reproach it is one that can be borne lightly,' the Count replied. 'So far as Charlotte's first husband is concerned, the reason I did not like him was that he broke up that handsome couple, a couple truly predestined for each other who, once united, had no need to fear a five-year period or think about a second marriage, not to speak of a third.'

'We shall try to make up in the future for what we have neglected in the past,' said Charlotte.

'You must hold to that,' said the Count, 'because your first marriages,' he went on with some vehemence, 'were so completely marriages of the rotten sort, and unfortunately marriages in general have about them something – excuse the expression – doltish: they ruin the tenderest relationships and the only real reason they exist is so that at any rate one of the parties may pride himself on a crude sense of security. Everything is taken for granted and the people involved seem to have got married only so that they may thereafter go their own way.'

At this moment Charlotte, who was now determined to change the subject once and for all, broke in with a bold expression which had the desired effect. Conversation became more general, both couples and the Captain could now take part in it, even Ottilie was given occasion to speak, and the dessert was enjoyed in the best of moods, in the production of which the wealth of fruit in decorated baskets and the abundance of flowers in display vases made the principal contribution.

The new park also came in for discussion. After the meal they went to see it. Ottilie stayed behind, saying she had things to do in the house. What she really did was go and get on with her copying. The Count was entertained by the Captain; later Charlotte joined him. When they had reached the top of the hill and the Captain had obligingly hurried back to fetch the map, the Count said to Charlotte: 'I am extraordinarily impressed by that man. He is very well informed, in details and in the thing as a whole. He works very seriously and his work is very logically thought out. What he is doing here would, if performed in higher circles, be of great significance.'

This praise of the Captain gave Charlotte profound pleasure, which she concealed, calmly confirming what the Count had said. But she was overcome by surprise when the Count went on: 'I have met him at a very opportune moment. I know of a position which would suit him perfectly, and if I recommend him for it I shall not only be doing him a favour but doing a very good service for a highly-placed friend of mine.'

Charlotte felt as if she had been struck by a thunderbolt. The Count noticed nothing: accustomed to restraint at all times, ladies retain even on the most exceptional occasions the appearance of composure. But she was no longer hearing what the Count was saying as he went on: 'Once I have decided on something I do not delay. I have already put my letter together in my head and I am anxious to get it written down. Will you arrange for a courier who can be sent off this very evening?'

Charlotte was torn in two inside. Surprised by the Count's suggestions and surprised also by the way she was feeling, she was unable to utter a word. Fortunately the Count went on talking about his plans for the Captain and Charlotte could see only too clearly how advantageous they would be. The Captain came back up and unrolled his map for the Count to look at. But with what other eyes did she now look at him, now she was going to lose him! With a perfunctory bow she turned away and hurried down to the moss-hut. Before she was halfway there tears were starting up in her eyes. She threw herself into the little secluded house and gave herself over completely to a torment, a passion, a despair of whose possibility she had a few moments before not had the remotest presentiment.

On the other side of the hill Eduard had gone with the Baroness down to the lakes. This shrewd lady wanted to know about everything, and in the course of sounding him out she soon noticed that Eduard was very eloquent when it came to speaking of Ottilie and of how well she had done, and since she knew how to keep him talking in this vein without seeming to prompt him she was finally left in no doubt that here there was no growing passion but one already in full bloom.

Married women, even when they are not very fond of one another, maintain an unspoken alliance, especially against young girls. The consequences of such an attachment were all too quickly obvious to the Baroness's worldly-wise mind. And she had already spoken to Charlotte about Ottilie that morning: she had not approved of Ottilie's staying in the country, especially since she had such a quiet disposition already, and had suggested taking her to live with a friend in town who was devoting great care to the upbringing of her own daughter and was only looking for a suitable companion who would became a second child to her and enjoy all the advantages such a status would afford. Charlotte had undertaken to think it over.

Now her insight into Eduard's frame of mind turned this suggestion into a firm resolve. The more quickly this resolve hardened in the Baroness, the more eagerly did she appear to flatter Eduard's desires. No one had better control of herself than this lady had, and self-possession in exceptional circumstances habituates us to dissimulation even in unexceptional circumstances. Because we exercise constraint over ourselves we are inclined to extend this constraint over other people too, so that we can so to speak compensate ourselves for what we lose inwardly with what we gain outwardly.

Usually joined to this attitude is a kind of secret malicious pleasure in the blindness of others, in the unconsciousness with which they walk into a trap. We rejoice not only in the present success but also in the coming humiliation. And so the Baroness was malicious enough to invite Eduard to come with Charlotte to the vintage harvest on her estate and, when he asked if he might bring Ottilie as well, to answer in a way he could if he felt inclined interpret favourably.

Eduard was already enthusing over the wonderful countryside, the great river, the hills, the cliffs and the vineyards, the ancient castles, boat trips on the river, the harvest and grape-pressing festivities, and so forth; and in the innocency of his heart saying how he was already looking forward to the impression such scenes would make on Ottilie's unspoiled sensibilities – when Ottilie was seen approaching and the Baroness said quickly that Eduard was to say nothing about this prospective autumn trip because if you looked forward to something such a long time in advance it usually failed to come off. Eduard promised to say nothing but made her hasten more quickly towards Ottilie and finally hurried up to the dear child several paces ahead of her. His whole being radiated pleasure. He kissed her hands and pressed into them a bunch of wild flowers he had picked on his walk. The spectacle irritated, nearly incensed the Baroness: though she could not approve of what might be culpable in this affection of Eduard's, neither could she help envying this insignificant chit of a girl what was pleasant and desirable in it.

When they sat down for supper the mood of the company had changed altogether. The Count, who had already written his letter and sent it off by the courier, sat himself this evening beside the Captain and discreetly pumped him. The Baroness, sitting on the Count's right, got little entertainment from that direction and just as little from Eduard who, at first thirsty and then, when his thirst had been quenched, excited, helped himself liberally to the wine and engaged in very animated conversation with Ottilie, whom he had drawn to his side of the table. Charlotte, at the other side of the table next to the Captain, found it hard, nearly impossible to conceal her inner agitation.

So the Baroness had plenty of leisure to observe the others. She noticed how ill at ease Charlotte was and because she was thinking only of Eduard's relations with Ottilie she found no difficulty in convincing herself that Charlotte too suspected him and was vexed by her husband's behaviour, and she revolved in her mind what would be the best thing to do now.

When supper was over the company divided. The Count wanted to get to know everything about the Captain, but the Captain was a quiet man, not in the least vain, and in general laconic, and the Count had to try every turn and trick he knew to get anything out of him at all. They paced together up and down one side of the room while Eduard, excited by wine and hopeful anticipation, chattered gaily with Ottilie over beside the window. But Charlotte and the Baroness walked in silence side by side back and forth on the other side of the room. Their silence and idle loitering about eventually brought the party to a standstill. The women withdrew to their wing, the men withdrew to theirs, and so this day seemed to have come to an end.

CHAPTER ELEVEN

EDUARD accompanied the Count to his room and was happy to be induced to stay for a while and talk with him. The Count became lost in memories of earlier times. He reflected on the beauty of Charlotte, on which as a connoisseur he expatiated with much warmth : 'A beautiful foot is a great gift of nature. This charm is indestructible. I watched her walking today. She still makes you want to kiss her shoe and do as the Sarmatians do, who know of nothing better than to drink the health of someone they love and respect out of her shoe – a rather barbarous way of doing honour but a deeply felt one.'

The tip of the foot was not the only object these two intimates found to admire. From discussing Charlotte they went on to discussing past adventures and recalled the obstacles that used to be placed in the way of these lovers' meeting and what trouble they had taken and what artifices they had had to invent merely so as to be able to tell one another they loved one another.

'Do you remember,' the Count said, 'an occasion when our lords and masters paid a visit to their uncle and they all met together in the great rambling mansion, and how I then stood by you in a certain adventure and how very helpful and unselfish I was? The day had been spent in solemnities and ceremonial dress, and we were, if you remember, determined that at any rate part of the night was going to be spent in unbuttoned ease among more congenial company.'

'I remember you had made a note of the way to the quarters of the ladies-in-waiting,' said Eduard, 'and to my beloved we succeeded in finding our way.'

'Who,' said the Count, 'thought more about the proprieties

than she did about my comfort and had kept with her a chaperone of an extreme ugliness, so that while you two were billing and cooing together I was having a very unpleasant time of it.'

'It was only yesterday,' Eduard said, 'when we heard you were arriving, that I was talking with my wife about that escapade, and especially about what happened when we withdrew. We lost our way and came upon the guardroom. We now thought we could find our way out, having arrived here, and so we thought we could go straight past the guard as we had gone straight past all the others in the place. Do you remember our amazement when we opened the door? The floor was strewn with rows of mattresses and those giants were lying on them asleep. The only one awake in that guardroom looked at us in astonishment; but we, with the courage and wantonness of youth, strode quite calmly over the outstretched boots without waking even one of those snoring children of Enoch.'

'I had a strong urge to make a noise,' said the Count, 'and we should have seen a very strange resurrection then!'

At that moment the great clock struck twelve.

'It is full midnight,' said the Count, smiling, 'and the time is now ripe. I have to ask you a favour, my dear Baron: conduct me tonight as I conducted you that night we have been speaking of. I have promised the Baroness I would visit her again. We have not been alone together the whole day, we have not seen one another for so long, and nothing could be more natural than for us to want to spend an intimate hour together. Show me how to get there; I can find my own way back, and in any case there won't be any boots lying around to stumble over.'

'I shall be only too glad to do this favour for a guest,' Eduard replied. 'The only thing is, all three women are over in that wing: suppose we find them still together?'

'No need to fear that,' said the Count. 'The Baroness is

expecting me. By this time she is certain to be in her room, and alone.'

'There is no difficulty about it otherwise,' Eduard replied. He took a lamp and lighted the Count down a secret stairway into a long corridor. At the end of it Eduard opened a little door. They went up a spiral staircase. At the top they arrived at a narrow landing and, giving the Count the lamp, Eduard pointed out to him a door to the right papered over so as to look like the wall. The door opened at the first attempt and admitted the Count and left Eduard standing in the dark.

Another door to the left led into Charlotte's bedroom. He heard voices, and listened. Charlotte was speaking to her maid: 'Has Ottilie gone to bed yet?' – 'No,' the maid answered, 'she is still downstairs writing.' – 'Light the night-light then,' said Charlotte, 'and go off now. It is late. I will put out the candle myself and get myself ready for bed.'

Eduard was overjoyed to hear Ottilie was still writing. 'For me,' he thought exultantly, 'she is busying herself for me!' Closed in by the darkness, in imagination he saw her sitting there, writing. He stepped towards her, he saw her turn towards him. He felt an unconquerable desire to be close to her once more. But from here there was no way to the *entresol* where her room was. Now he found himself directly in front of his wife's door. There was a strange confusion in his soul. He tried to open the door, he found it was locked, he knocked softly, Charlotte did not hear.

She was walking agitatedly up and down her dressing-room. She was repeating to herself again and again what had been going round and round in her mind ever since the Count had brought out his unexpected proposal. She seemed to see the Captain standing before her. His spirit filled the house, his spirit enlivened their walks outside it, and he was to go away and all was to become empty! She told herself everything a woman can tell herself, she even looked ahead to the common but sorry consolation that time would heal even such torments as these. She cursed the time it would take to heal them; she cursed the dead time when they would be healed.

And then finally she sought refuge in tears and it was all the more welcome because she so rarely sought refuge in them. She threw herself on to the sofa and gave herself over to her torment completely. Eduard for his part found it impossible to go away from the door. He knocked again, and a third time more loudly, so that through the stillness of the night Charlotte heard it quite clearly and started up afraid. Her first thought was: it might be, it must be the Captain. Her second thought was: it cannot possibly be the Captain. She thought she must have imagined it; but she had heard it, she wanted to have heard it, she feared to have heard it. She went into the bedroom, she went softly up to the bolted door. She felt ashamed of her fear: it could easily be the Baroness, the Baroness could easily be wanting something! She pulled herself together and called in a firm voice: 'Is someone there?' A voice answered softly: 'It's me.' – 'Who?' Charlotte asked, unable to distingush the voice. She saw the Captain standing before the door. The voice came again, louder: 'Eduard!' She opened the door and her husband stood before her. He greeted her with a joke, and this vein was one she found it possible to continue in. His enigmatic visit he accounted for with enigmatic explanations. Finally he said: 'Why I have really come I must now confess. I have taken a vow that tonight I shall kiss your shoe.'

'It is a long time since it has occurred to you to want to do that,' said Charlotte. 'All the worse,' Eduard replied, 'and all the better!'

She had sat down in a chair so that he should not see how little she had on. He threw himself at her feet and she could not prevent him from kissing her shoe nor, when this came off in his hand, from seizing her foot and pressing it tenderly to his heart.

Charlotte was one of those women who, without intending

to and without being put to any effort, continue after they are married to act in the manner of lovers. She never provoked her husband, she hardly responded to his desire, but without coldness or repelling severity she continued to be like a loving bride who is secretly shy of doing even what is now permissible. And this is how Eduard found her to be this night, and in a double sense. She wished intensely her husband were not there: the figure of her friend seemed to stand and reproach her for his presence. But what should have driven Eduard away only attracted him more. A certain agitation was noticeable in her. She had been weeping, and if weak and gentle people usually lose some of their charm when they weep, those we usually know as strong and self-controlled gain infinitely. Eduard was so kind, so affectionate, so pressing. He begged her to let him stay with her, he did not demand, he tried seriously and then playfully to persuade her, he forgot he had rights here, he made no mention of them. Finally he put out the candle.

In the lamplit twilight inner inclination at once asserted its rights, imagination at once asserted its rights over reality. Eduard held Ottilie in his arms. The Captain hovered back and forth before the soul of Charlotte. The absent and the present were in a miraculous way entwined, seductively and blissfully, each with the other.

And yet the present will not be robbed of its daemonic right. They passed some of the night in chatter and pleasantry which was all the freer since unhappily the heart had no part in it. But when Eduard awoke beside his wife next morning the day seemed to be looking in upon him with ominous foreboding, the sun seemed to be lighting up a crime; he stole softly away from his wife and when she awoke she found herself, strangely enough, alone.

CHAPTER TWELVE

WHEN the company assembled again for breakfast an observant witness could have learned how each was feeling from how each behaved. The Count and the Baroness were cheerful and relaxed, as two lovers are when after enduring separation they have confirmed their mutual affection. On the other hand, Charlotte and Eduard encountered the Captain and Ottilie as if they were ashamed and contrite. For the nature of love is such that it believes it alone is in the right, that all other rights vanish before the rights of love. Ottilie was happy in the way a child is happy, you could have said she too was in her own fashion relaxed and open. The Captain appeared to be in a serious mood; his conversation with the Count had aroused in him what had for some time been dormant and quiet, and he had come to feel all too clearly that he was not really fulfilling his vocation here and was in effect only wasting his time in semi-active idleness. The two guests departed, and they were hardly gone before other visitors arrived. Charlotte was glad to see them because she wanted to get out of herself and be distracted; Eduard found them inconvenient because all he wanted to do was occupy himself with Ottilie; Ottilie also found them unwelcome because she had not yet finished her copying and it was going to have to be ready by the following morning. When the visitors left later in the day she hurried at once to her room.

The day passed, evening came. Eduard, Charlotte and the Captain walked the visitors to their coach and after they had gone decided not to go straight back to the house but to walk on to the lakes. Eduard had bought a small boat, it had cost quite a lot, and it had now arrived. They wanted to see how easy it was to row and whether it steered well.

The boat was tied up against the bank of the middle lake not far from a group of ancient oak-trees. These trees had already had a role assigned to them in the coming development of the lakes. A landing stage was going to be constructed there and under the oak-trees there was going to be a bench with an awning which would be a point for anyone steering over the newly-constructed great lake to steer towards.

'Now where would be the best place to put the landing stage on the other side?' Eduard asked. 'Beside my plane-trees, I should think.'

'They are a little too far to the right,' said the Captain. 'If you land further down you will be closer to the house. But it needs thinking about.'

The Captain was already standing at the stern of the boat with one of the oars in his hand. Charlotte got into the boat and Eduard also got in and took up the other oar. But as he was about to push off from the bank he thought of Ottilie and how this boating excursion would make him late back, because who knew what time they would get back from it, and he made up his mind at once and jumped back on to the bank, handed the oar to the Captain, and made a hasty excuse and hurried back to the house.

There he was told Ottilie had shut herself in her room and was writing. Although it gave him a pleasant feeling to know she was doing something for his sake he also felt an intense displeasure at not being able to see her at once. His impatience increased with every minute that passed. He paced up and down the drawing-room, he tried to interest himself in this or that, but nothing was able to hold his attention. He wanted to see her and see her alone before Charlotte came back with the Captain. Night came on and the candles were lit.

At last she came in. She looked radiant. The feeling of having done something for her friend had exalted her whole being. She laid her copy and the original on the table in front of Eduard. 'Shall we collate them?' she asked, smiling. Eduard did not know what to reply. He looked at her, he examined the copy. The first pages were written with the greatest care in a delicate feminine hand; then the characters seemed to change, to grow freer, easier. But he was astonished when he came to look at the last pages. 'My God!' he exclaimed, 'what's this! It is my handwriting!' He looked at Ottilie and again at the pages. The end of the copy especially was just as if he had written it himself. Ottilie stayed silent, but looked at him with an expression of the greatest satisfaction. Eduard flung up his arms. 'You love me!' he cried. 'Ottilie, you love me!' And they embraced one another and held one another embraced. And which first embraced the other you would not have been able to say.

From this moment the world was transformed for Eduard, he was no longer what he had been, the world was no longer what it had been. They stood face to face, he holding her hands, they looked into one another's eyes, they were about to embrace again.

Charlotte came in with the Captain. At their apologies for staying out so long Eduard smiled quietly to himself. 'Not at all, you have come back too soon, oh how much too soon!' he said to himself.

They sat down to supper. The people who had visited them that day were discussed and adjudged. Eduard, excited by love, spoke well of them all, indulgently and often approvingly. Charlotte, who was not altogether in agreement, noticed this mood of his and remarked jokingly that he usually let the judgement of his tongue fall very heavily on departing company but today he was being so gentle and forbearing.

With great warmth and heartfelt conviction Eduard exclaimed: 'If you love one person, love from the very heart, all other people seem lovable too!' Ottilie lowered her eyes and Charlotte looked straight ahead.

The Captain took up the conversation and said: 'It is somewhat the same with feelings of respect and admiration. You know how to recognize what is to be valued in society only when such sentiments have been aroused in you towards a single object.'

Charlotte went early to her bedroom so as to give herself up to the recollection of what had happened that evening between her and the Captain.

When Eduard, jumping on to the bank, had pushed the boat out from the land and had himself delivered up wife and friend to the uncertain element, Charlotte then had the man on whose account she had secretly suffered so much sitting before her in the twilight moving the boat on with the two oars in the direction he had decided to go. She felt very sad, she had seldom felt such a sensation of sadness. The circling of the boat, the splash of the oars, the chill breath of the wind across the surface of the water, the murmur of the reeds, the birds hovering over the water for the last time before the darkness came on, the first stars flashing and flashing again in the sky – these all had something spectral about them in that universal stillness. It seemed to her as if her friend was taking her a long way away to leave her in some distant place. There was a strange agitation inside her and she could not weep.

The Captain was describing how he intended the park should look. He said the boat was very good and that it was a sign of a good boat that one person with two oars could easily row and steer it by himself. She would discover that for herself, it was a nice feeling to float off across the water alone sometimes and be your own ferryman and steersman.

These words made the imminent separation weigh suddenly more heavily upon her heart. 'Is he saying it deliberately?' she asked herself. 'Does he know? Or suspect? Or is it only chance, does he unconsciously foretell me my fate?' She was seized by a terrible feeling of dejection and by a feeling of impatience. She begged him to go back to shore now, at once, and return with her to the mansion.

It was the first time the Captain had been on the lakes and although he had undertaken a general survey of their depth there were still places he was not familiar with. It began to get dark. He directed the boat to where he thought there might be a spot where it would be easy to disembark and where he knew the footpath to the mansion was not far off. But he went a little aside even from this course he felt fairly sure of when Charlotte repeated in a voice that had a kind of alarm in it that she wanted to get quickly to land. He rowed harder and got closer to the bank, but when he was still some way from it he felt a resistance and realized the boat had got stuck. He tried to force it free but it had stuck fast. What could he do now? There was nothing for it but to get out of the boat, the water was shallow enough, and carry Charlotte to land. He succeeded in taking the dear burden across without accident, he was strong enough to do it without tottering or giving her any cause for anxiety, but at the outset she had been anxious and had clasped her arms round his neck. He held her tight and pressed her to him. Not until he reached a grass slope did he put her down and when he did so it was not without a feeling of agitation and confusion. She was still clasping his neck. He put his arms around her again and kissed her violently on the mouth. But that same moment he was lying at her feet, pressing his lips to her hand and saying: 'Charlotte, will you forgive me?'

The kiss her friend had given her and which she had almost returned brought Charlotte to herself. She pressed his hand but did not lift him up from where he was lying. Instead she leaned down to him and laid a hand on his shoulder and said: 'We cannot help it if this moment is an epoch in our lives, but whether this moment shall be worthy of us does lie within our power. You must go, dear friend, and you will go. The Count is now making arrangements which will make a better life for you : I am very glad of it and very sorry. I wanted to keep quiet about it until it was certain, but this moment compels me to reveal this secret to you. I can forgive you, and forgive myself, only if we have the courage to alter our mode of life, since it does not lie within our power to alter our feelings.' She lifted him up and took his arm and supported herself on it, and they went back to the mansion in silence.

But now she was standing in her bedroom, where she had to feel and regard herself as Eduard's wife. In this confusion of contradictory feelings her sound character, disciplined and tested in a hundred ways through life's experiences, came to her aid. She was always accustomed to know herself, to exercise self-control, and even now she did not find it difficult, by giving serious thought to the matter, to come close to the equanimity she desired. She was even able to smile at the way she had acted when Eduard had paid his curious visit the previous night. And then she was suddenly seized by a strange presentiment, a joyful anxious shuddering went through her, and deeply affected she knelt down and repeated the vow she had made to Eduard at the altar. Friendship, affection, renunciation passed as vivid images before her mind. She felt inwardly restored. Soon she was taken by a sweet feeling of weariness, and she fell peacefully to sleep.

CHAPTER THIRTEEN

EDUARD is for his part in quite a different mood. He thinks so little of going to sleep it does not even occur to him to undress. He kisses the copy of the document a thousand times, he kisses the beginning of it in Ottilie's coy childish hand, he hardly dares to kiss the ending because it seems to be in his own hand. 'Oh if it were only another kind of document!' he whispers to himself, and yet even as it is he considers it the loveliest assurance that his dearest desire has been fulfilled. He will keep it and keep it close to his heart always, even though it is to be disfigured with the signature of a third!

The waning moon rises over the trees. The warm night lures Eduard out. He roams about, the most restless and the most happy of mortal men. He wanders through the gardens, they are too confined; he hurries into the field, it is too broad and distant. He is drawn back to the mansion, he finds himself under Ottilie's window. There he sits on one of the terrace steps. 'Walls and bolts divide us,' he says to himself, 'but our hearts are not divided. If she stood before me now she would fall into my arms and I would fall into hers, and being certain of this what more do I need!' All was silent around him, not a breath of air was stirring; it was so still he could hear the burrowing of the busy animals under the earth to whom day and night are one. He gave himself up wholly to happy dreaming, at length he fell asleep, and he did not awake until the sun rose in a splendour of light and dissolved the earliest morning mist.

He found he was the first to awake. The labourers seemed to be too long arriving. They came, and they seemed to be too few and the work proposed for the day too little. He asked

113

for more labourers; he was promised them and they were provided in the course of the day. But even these are not enough to see his plans carried out quickly. He no longer derives any pleasure from the work: he wants everything finished now, at once. And for whom? The paths are to be levelled so that Ottilie can walk in comfort, the seats in place so that Ottilie can rest. On the new pavilion too he does what work he can: it is to be got ready for Ottilie's birthday. Eduard's intentions are, like his actions, no longer ruled by moderation. The consciousness of loving and of being loved drives him beyond all bounds. His rooms, his surroundings have all changed, they all look different. He no longer knows his own house. Ottilie's presence consumes everything: he is utterly lost in her, he thinks of nothing else but only her, the voice of conscience no longer reaches him; everything in his nature that had been restrained, held back, now bursts forth, his whole being flows out towards Ottilie.

The Captain notices this passionate activity and wants to prevent the unhappy consequences that must follow from it. He had counted on all these new plans and arrangements going forward as part of their quiet amicable life together, now they are being pushed ahead in an unbalanced one-sided fashion. He had organized the sale of the farmstead, the first payment had been made, and in accordance with their agreement Charlotte had taken charge of it. But already in the first week she has need of all her patience and level-headedness: with the precipitate way things are going the amount set aside will not last very long.

Much had been started on and there was much to do. How can he leave Charlotte in this situation! They confer together and decide they would prefer to accelerate the work themselves. For this purpose they agree to take up additional money and to replace it with the money due from the instalments on the sale of the farmstead. This could be done almost without loss by ceding the title: they now had a freer hand, now everything was in motion and there were enough labourers available they could do more at once, and could proceed with certainty and speed. Eduard was glad to agree because these proposals accorded with his own intentions.

While this is going on Charlotte remains in her inmost heart faithful to what she has proposed for herself; and her friend, of the same mind as she, stands manfully by her. But this very act of renunciation only serves to make them more intimate. They discuss together Eduard's passion, they confer on what to do. Charlotte draws Ottilie closer to her, keeps a stricter watch on her, and the more she comes to know her own heart the deeper she sees into the girl's heart. She sees no way out except to send the child away.

It now seems providential that Luciane has received such exceptional commendation at the boarding-school: her great-aunt, informed of this, now wants to take her into her home for good, have her with her, introduce her into society. Ottilie could go back to the boarding-school, the Captain would depart well provided for, and everything would be as it was a few months before or even better. Charlotte hoped soon to restore her own relationship with Eduard, and she expounded all this to herself so reasonably she became more and more confirmed in the delusion you can return to an earlier, more circumscribed condition once you have left it, that forces you have once set free will let you tie them down again.

Eduard was in the meantime becoming very sensible of the obstacles being placed in his way. He noticed right away that he and Ottilie were being kept apart, that it was being made hard for him to talk with her alone, even to get near her except when others were present, and by growing annoyed about this he also grew annoyed about much else. When he could get in a hasty word with Ottilie he employed the occasion not only to assure her of his love but also to complain about his wife and the Captain. He had no sense that he himself was, through his impetuous activities, on the way to exhausting their funds; he bitterly blamed Charlotte and the Captain for departing from the terms of their original agreement on how the work was to proceed, yet he himself had consented to the subsequent agreement, it was he who had occasioned and necessitated this change.

Hatred is partisan but love is even more so. Ottilie too became somewhat estranged from Charlotte and the Captain. When on one occasion Eduard complained to Ottilie that the Captain did not always act as a friend and especially one in the position he was in ought to act, Ottilie replied without thinking: 'I have noticed before he has not been quite straightforward with you, and I found it unpleasant. I once heard him say to Charlotte: "I wish Eduard would give us less of his blessed flute-playing. He will never be able to play the thing properly, and it is so boring to listen to." You can imagine how upset I was, because I do so like accompanying you.'

She had hardly said it before her mind whispered to her she ought to have kept quiet; but it was too late. A change came over Eduard's expression. He had never been so annoyed by anything. The remark had assailed his dearest endeavours, in which he had been conscious only of a naïve aspiration, he was not in the least presumptuous about it. Surely your friends ought to show some consideration for what you found entertaining and gave you pleasure. He gave no thought to how fearful it is to have to sit and have your ears assaulted by an inadequate talent. He was insulted, furious, too insulted ever to forgive. He felt absolved from all obligations.

His need to be with Ottilie, to see her, to whisper something to her, to confide in her, grew with every day that passed. He resolved to write to her to ask her to conduct a secret correspondence with him. The slip of paper on which he had with all brevity written this request lay on his desk and was blown off by the draught when the valet came in to curl his hair. The valet needed a piece of paper to cool the tongs with and he usually bent down and picked up what he needed from the floor. On this occasion he seized on the note, hurriedly screwed it up, and singed it. Eduard, noticing the mistake, snatched it from his hand. Soon afterwards he sat down to write it again but he found it less easy to write the second time. He felt a certain misgiving and apprehension but he managed to overcome them. He pressed the note into Ottilie's hand the first moment he was able to get near her.

Ottilie did not delay replying. He stuck her note unread into his waistcoat which, being fashionably short, did not retain it very well. It slipped out and fell to the floor without his noticing. Charlotte saw it and picked it up and handed it to him with a hasty glance. 'Here is something in your hand-writing which you may not want to lose,' she said.

He was taken aback. 'Is she pretending?' he asked himself. 'Does she know what is in the note or has she really been misled by the similarity in the handwriting?' He hoped and believed it was the latter case. He had been warned, he had been warned twice, but his passion could not read these strange fortuitous signs through which a higher being seems to be speaking to us, they led him rather on and on, so that the constraint in which he felt he was being kept became more and more irksome. His friendly sociability disappeared. His heart was hardened and when he had to be together with his wife and his friend he found it impossible to discover or rekindle in his heart his former affection for them. He silently reproached himself for this and that was an additional discomfort. He tried to surmount it by resorting to a kind of humorousness but because his humour was now without love it also lacked the charm it used to have.

Charlotte was helped over all these trials by the state of mind she was in. She was conscious always of how earnestly she had resolved to forswear her affection, fair and noble though it was.

She wishes very much to come to the aid of the other couple too. She feels that distance alone will not be enough to cure the disease, it is too grave for that. She makes up her mind to speak to the good child about it but she cannot: the memory of her own inconstancy stands in her way. She tries to talk about it in general terms: generalities apply to her own case too and she shrinks from talking about that. Every word of advice she wants to give Ottilie strikes back into her own heart. She wants to warn her and feels that she herself may be in need of warning.

She continues to keep the lovers apart and to say nothing and this does not improve matters. Gentle hints which escape her from time to time have no effect on Ottilie: Eduard has convinced Ottilie of Charlotte's affection for the Captain and convinced her that Charlotte herself wants a divorce and that he is now thinking of a decent way of bringing one about.

Ottilie, borne by the feeling of her innocence along the path to the happiness she desires, lives only for Eduard. Fortified in all that is good by her love for him, because of him happier in all that she does, more open towards other people, she lives in a heaven on earth.

So they carry on with their daily lives, each in his own way, reflecting and not reflecting. Everything seems to be going on as it always does. Because even in momentous times, when everything is at stake, you do go on with your daily life as if nothing is happening.

CHAPTER FOURTEEN

MEANWHILE a letter from the Count had arrived for the Captain. Two letters in fact. One, for letting the others read, described vaguely the prospects opening up for the Captain, which were said to be very fair; the other, which contained a definite present offer of an important court and administrative post, the rank of major, a considerable salary and other benefits, was on account of various attendant circumstances to be kept secret for the time being. The Captain kept it secret, he told his friends only about the hopes being held out to him and concealed what was imminent.

He went on vigorously meanwhile with the work in hand and quietly arranged that everything would go forward unhindered when he had left. It is now in his own interest that a definite finishing date should be fixed for many things, that Ottilie's birthday should hasten many things. The two friends, although they have come to no express understanding, now work well together. Eduard is now very content for them to have augmented their funds by drawing money in advance. The whole operation is moving forward as fast as it can.

The Captain would now have liked to advise altogether against converting the three lakes into one great lake. The lower dam had to be strengthened, the middle dams removed, and the whole thing was in more than one sense momentous and dubious. But both works, in so far as they could be fitted in together, had already been started on, and here a young architect, a former pupil of the Captain, arrived at very much the right moment. Partly by appointing craftsmen who knew how to do the work, partly by contracting the work out wherever possible, he furthered the operation and promised it a secure and lasting foundation; on seeing which the Captain was secretly pleased, because it meant he would not be missed when he left. He made it a rule not to leave an uncompleted task once he had taken it up until he knew his place had been adequately filled. He despised people who deliberately leave confusion behind them so that their departure shall be noticed and who, ignorant egoists that they are, want to destroy anything they can no longer be involved with.

So they worked on and put all their effort into the work, and the object of the work was the glorification of Ottilie's birthday, although nobody said so or even honestly admitted it to himself. Charlotte thought, and it was not out of envy, that it could not be made into a definite celebration. Ottilie's youth, her circumstances, her relationship to the family did not justify her appearing as queen of the day. And Eduard did not want to mention it because according to his idea everything was supposed to happen as if of its own accord and come as a pleasant surprise.

They all therefore came to an unspoken agreement to pretend the pavilion was to be finished on this particular day without any reference to what other significance this day might have, and that this would offer an occasion for announcing a celebration and for inviting the local populace as well as their friends.

But Eduard's affection was boundless. As his desire to possess Ottilie was without measure so in sacrificing, giving, promising he likewise knew no measure. For the presents he wanted to give Ottilie on this day Charlotte had made a number of suggestions but they were far too niggardly. He consulted his valet, one of whose tasks was to take care of his wardrobe and who was consequently always in touch with the dealers in the latest fashions; and the valet, who was not unfamiliar with the most acceptable sort of gifts nor with the most agreeable way of presenting them, at once ordered in the town the most elegant chest covered in red morocco, secured by steel pins, and filled with presents worthy of such a container.

He also suggested something else to Eduard. They had a small collection of fireworks which they had always intended to let off but had never done so. It would be easy to add to these, to buy more of the sort they had got and other sorts they had not got. Eduard seized on the idea and the valet undertook to take care of it. The matter was to remain a secret.

Meanwhile as the day drew closer the Captain had been instituting the policing arrangements he considered so necessary whenever a crowd had been summoned or induced to assemble. He had even taken thorough precautions against begging and other inconveniences which spoil the pleasure of a celebration.

Eduard and his confidant were occupied above all with the fireworks. They were to be set off beside the middle lake in front of the great oak-trees; the audience was to stand under the plane-trees on the opposite side of the lake where, in safety and comfort, they could observe the effect from the proper distance, see the reflections in the water and watch the fireworks which were intended to burn while floating on the water.

Under another pretext Eduard had the space beneath the plane-trees cleared of undergrowth, grass and moss, and only now on the cleared ground did it appear how magnificently high and broad the trees had grown. The sight gave Eduard the greatest pleasure. 'It was about this season of the year I planted them. How long ago could that have been?' he asked himself. As soon as he was back in the house he consulted the diaries his father had kept very regularly especially when he was in the country. It was true the planting of the plane-trees would not be mentioned, but another event of domestic importance which happened on the same day and which Eduard could still remember well must inevitably have been recorded. He skims through several volumes. He finds the event he has in mind. But he is astonished, he is delighted, when he notices the most miraculous coincidence. The day, the year when he planted the trees is also the day, the year when Ottilie was born.

CHAPTER FIFTEEN

At last the morning Eduard ardently longed for dawned. Gradually the guests arrived, many guests, for invitations had been sent out far and wide and many who had missed the laying of the foundation-stone and had heard so much about it were the more determined not to miss this second celebration.

Before the meal the carpenters appeared in the courtyard of the mansion playing instruments and carrying a swaying ornate garland composed of foliage and flowers laid in alternate stepwise layers. They spoke their greeting and prevailed upon the women to hand over silk kerchiefs and ribbons with which, in accordance with tradition, the carpenters adorned themselves. They continued with their triumphal procession while the ladies and gentlemen were dining, and after stopping for a time in the village, where they also deprived the women and girls of many ribbons, they at last came to the hill where the completed pavilion stood, accompanied by a great crowd and with a great crowd awaiting them.

After the meal Charlotte delayed the company for a little. She wanted no solemn formal procession and they found their way to the spot gradually in separate groups without regard to rank or formality. Charlotte hung back with Ottilie and this did not improve matters, because since Ottilie was in fact the last to arrive it seemed as if the trumpets and drums had been waiting only for her, as if proceedings had to start at once now she had arrived.

To take the newness off the pavilion they had decorated it with an ornament of branches and flowers according to the Captain's directions, only without his knowledge Eduard had

had the architect inscribe the date in flowers across the cornice. That might be let pass, but the Captain arrived in time to prevent Ottilie's name too from blazing forth from the pediment. He was able tactfully to stop this undertaking and to have the flower-letters already in place taken down.

The garland was hoisted up and could be seen from far and wide. Ribbons and kerchiefs fluttered many-coloured in the air and a short speech was for the most part lost in the wind. The solemnities had ended, the dance on the levelled and foliage-enclosed space in front of the building could now begin. A smartly-dressed apprentice led a lively peasant girl up to Eduard and invited Ottilie, who was standing close by, to dance. The two couples were at once joined by others and Eduard very soon changed partners, taking Ottilie and circulating with her. The younger guests joined happily in the dance, while the older guests were content to look on.

Then, before the dance broke up and the people dispersed among the walks and paths, it was agreed to assemble again at sunset under the plane-trees. Eduard arrived there first, saw that everything was in order and held a consultation with the valet who, in company with the fireworks expert, had to look after the spectacle on the other side of the lake.

The Captain regarded the arrangements made for this entertainment with misgiving and he was going to speak to Eduard about the pressure of spectators that was to be expected when Eduard asked him somewhat brusquely to leave this part of the celebrations to him.

The tops of the dams had been staked out and cleared of grass and the soil was uneven and insecure. The people had already crowded on to them. The sun went down, twilight came on, and while waiting for it to grow darker the company under the plane-trees was served with refreshments. They found the spot incomparable and looked forward to the future view they would have of a great and so variously bounded lake.

A calm evening, not a breath of wind, all seemed right for the nocturnal festival, when suddenly a terrible shrieking and shouting started up. Big lumps of earth had come away from the dam, several people could be seen falling into the water. The earth had given way under the pressure and trampling of the ever-increasing crowd. Everyone wanted the best position and now no one could go forward or back.

Everyone not on the dam leaped up and ran towards it, but more to see what had happened than to do anything about it, for what could anyone do, since no one could reach the place where it had broken? The Captain with a few others who had their wits about them raced to the dam and drove the crowd down from it on to the bank so as to leave room for people on the dam to try to pull out those who had fallen into the lake and were going under. Partly through these efforts, partly through their own they were all soon back on dry land, except a boy whose panicky strugglings had taken him away from the dam instead of bringing him back to it. His strength seemed to leave him, only fitfully did he bring up a hand or foot. The boat was unfortunately on the other side of the lake filled with fireworks, it was a slow job unloading it, and it looked as if any assistance from that quarter would come too late. The Captain had made up his mind what he should do, he threw off his outer clothing, all eyes were on him, and his splendid strong figure was a sight to inspire confidence; but a cry of surprise nonetheless broke from the crowd when he dived into the water. Every eye followed him as, swimming skilfully, he soon reached the boy and brought him back to the dam. The boy appeared to be dead.

The boat then came up, the Captain boarded it and inquired of everyone around whether they were sure there was no one else missing. The doctor comes and takes charge of the boy who appears to be dead. Charlotte also appears and begs the Captain to look after himself, to get back to the house and get changed. He hesitates to leave and does not do so until certain responsible, sensible people who have been close to the scene and have themselves helped with the work of rescue assure him solemnly that everyone has been saved.

Charlotte watches him go back to the house, she remembers that wine, tea or whatever else he might need are locked away, and that on occasions like this people often lose their bearings, and she hurries through the confused company still standing about under the plane-trees. Eduard is telling everyone to stay where they are, he is soon going to give the signal for the fireworks to start. Charlotte goes up to him and asks him to postpone an entertainment which is now out of place, which cannot properly be enjoyed at that present time. She asks him to show some consideration for the boy and his rescuer. 'The doctor is already doing what he can,' Eduard replied: 'he has everything he needs and our interference would only hinder him.'

Charlotte stuck to her point and gestured to Ottilie, who at once made to leave. Eduard seized her hand and cried: 'Don't let us end this day in the hospital! She is too good to be a sister of charity. The apparently dead will reawaken and the living will dry themselves even without our assistance.'

Charlotte said nothing and walked away. Some of them followed her, some stayed with Eduard and Ottilie. Finally no one wanted to be the last to stay and they all followed. Eduard and Ottilie found themselves alone under the plane-trees. She begged, she implored him to go back with her to the mansion but he insisted on staying where they were. 'No, Ottilie!' he cried. 'Extraordinary things don't come about smoothly, don't happen in an everyday way. The unexpected accident this evening has brought us together more quickly. You are mine! I have told you so and vowed it so often: let us leave saying and vowing, now it shall be so in fact!'

The boat from the other side floated across. The valet was

in it. He was at a loss to know what to do and asked what was now going to be done about the fireworks. 'Set them off!' Eduard shouted across to him. 'It was for you alone I got them Ottilie, and now you alone shall see them! Permit me to sit beside you and enjoy them with you.' He sat down beside her gently and modestly, he did not touch her.

Rockets roared, maroons exploded, fireballs floated up, squibs coiled around and burst, catherine-wheels foamed sparks, at first singly, then in pairs, then all together, more and more violently one after the other and all at once. Eduard, whose heart was aflame, followed this fiery spectacle with shining eyes and a feeling of satisfaction. To Ottilie's tender agitated heart the roaring and flashing, the sudden bursting forth and vanishing, was rather distressing than pleasurable. She leaned herself shyly against Eduard and when he felt her draw near him so trustfully he felt she now belonged to him entirely.

Night had hardly resumed her reign before the moon arose and illumined the course of Eduard and Ottilie as they returned to the mansion. A figure stepped before them hat in hand and begged alms, saying he had received none that festive day. The moonlight revealed his face and Eduard recognized the importunate beggar of a former occasion. But he was too happy, too happy to be angry, too happy to remember that begging had been strictly prohibited and on that day especially. He searched in his pocket and found a gold piece and gave it to the beggar. Since his own happiness seemed to be without limit he wanted to make everybody happy.

At home everything had meanwhile been going well. The doctor had worked, everything needed had been to hand, Charlotte had assisted, all had collaborated together and the boy had been restored to life. The guests dispersed, partly to see something of the fireworks from a distance, partly to get back to their own quiet homes after such scenes of confusion.

The Captain had quickly changed and he too had taken an active part in the first-aid operation. Now it was all quiet, and he found himself alone with Charlotte. He gently confided to her that he would very soon be leaving. She had gone through so much that evening that this revelation made little impression on her. She had seen how her friend had been ready to sacrifice himself, how he had rescued others and had himself been rescued. These strange events seemed to her to presage a significant but not an unhappy future.

Eduard came in with Ottilie and he was likewise told of the Captain's coming departure. He suspected that Charlotte had known all about it earlier but he was far too involved with himself and his plans to trouble his head about that.

On the contrary, he heard attentively and with satisfaction of the good and honourable position the Captain was to take up. His secret desires raced impetuously ahead of events. Already he saw the Captain united with Charlotte, himself with Ottilie. No finer present could have been given him to mark this festive day.

But how astonished Ottilie was when she went to her room and found the exquisite little chest on her table. She opened it at once. Inside everything was packed and arranged so beautifully she could not bring herself to disturb it, she hardly liked to keep the lid open. Muslin, cambric, silk scarves and lace vied with one another in delicacy, elegance and costliness. There was jewellery there too. She could see she had been given enough to clothe her from head to foot several times over, but it was all so costly and unfamiliar she did not dare to think it hers.

CHAPTER SIXTEEN

THE following morning the Captain had gone. He had left behind a note for his friends telling them of his gratitude. He and Charlotte had said a brief halting farewell the previous evening. She felt they were parting for ever and she acquiesced in it : the Captain had at last shown her the Count's other letter and in that letter the Count also spoke of the prospect of an advantageous marriage; and although the Captain did not make any mention of that point, she took it for a certainty and wholly and entirely renounced him.

On the other hand, she now thought she could demand of others the same self-control she was exercising over herself. It had not been impossible for her, it ought to be possible for others. It was with this idea in mind that she took her husband aside and spoke with him. She spoke frankly and confidently because she felt the matter had now to be cleared up once and for all.

'Our friend has left us,' she said. 'We are now back together as we were before, and it is now up to us whether we want to go back completely to our former life.'

Eduard, who heard nothing but what flattered his passion, believed that by these words Charlotte meant her former state of widowhood and that she was, if in an indirect way, holding out to him the hope of a divorce. He therefore replied with a smile : 'Why not? It would only be a question of coming to an arrangement.'

He was therefore very painfully disabused when Charlotte replied : 'We have to come to a decision now so that Ottilie too can be found another situation. There is at the moment a double opportunity to offer her a life she would find very desirable. Since my daughter has now gone to live with her great-aunt, Ottilie can return to the boarding-school, or she can be received into a house of repute and there enjoy with an only daughter all the advantages of an education appropriate to that station.'

'In the meantime,' Eduard replied, keeping himself tolerably in check, 'Ottilie has been so spoiled by our friendly companionship any other would hardly be welcome to her.'

'We have all been spoiled,' said Charlotte, 'and you not the least. Nevertheless, this is an epoch which challenges us to reflect and seriously admonishes us to think of what is best for all the members of our little circle and not to refuse any sacrifice that may be demanded of us.'

'At any rate, I think it unfair that Ottilie should be sacrificed,' Eduard replied, 'and that is what it would mean if we took her now and planted her down among strangers. Good fortune found the Captain while he was here, we can see him go without any trepidation, with satisfaction even. Who knows what is waiting for Ottilie? Why should we be over hasty?'

'It is pretty clear what is waiting for us,' Charlotte replied with some agitation, and since she intended to speak her mind once and for all she went on: 'You are in love with Ottilie, you are getting accustomed to having her about. And on her side too affection and passion are springing up and growing. Why should we not put into words what every hour proclaims and confesses? Ought we not to have enough foresight even to ask ourselves what this is going to lead to?'

Eduard controlled his feelings. 'If we cannot answer that question straight away,' he said, 'this much can be said, that when we cannot say for certain how something is going to turn out we must resolve to wait and see what the future will teach us.'

'To prophesy here,' said Charlotte, 'requires no great wisdom, and this much can at any rate be said straight away, that neither of us is any longer young enough to go blindly ahead on a course that will take us where we do not want to go or ought not to go. There is no longer anybody to look after us, we have to be our own friends and our own instructors. No one expects us to wander into an extremity of folly, no one expects us to make ourselves blameworthy, not to speak of ludicrous.'

'Can you blame me,' answered Eduard, who was incapable of responding to his wife's frankness, 'can you reproach me if I have Ottilie's happiness at heart? And not some future happiness that can never be counted upon, but her happiness now? Imagine, honestly and without self-deception, imagine Ottilie torn from us and handed over to strangers – I at least do not think I could be cruel enough to demand she should endure such a change.'

Charlotte was well aware of the resolution that lay behind her husband's dissimulation. Only now did she feel how far he had removed himself from her. With some agitation she exclaimed: 'Can Ottilie be happy if she comes between us! If she deprives me of a husband and your children of a father!'

'I would have thought our children were taken care of,' said Eduard with a cold smile, but added more amiably: 'We are surely not thinking yet of going to such extremes.'

'Extremes and passion go hand in hand,' Charlotte said. 'While there is still time do not insist on refusing the good advice, the help I offer us both. When troubles come the one who sees most clearly must be the one to act. This time I am that one. Dear, dearest Eduard, leave things to me! Can you ask me to give up my well-earned happiness, my most treasured rights, without more ado, can you expect me to give you up?'

'Who is asking you to do that?' Eduard replied with some embarrassment.

'You yourself are,' Charlotte replied. 'When you want to keep Ottilie beside you are you not conceding everything that must follow from that? I am not trying to talk you round, but if you are not able to master yourself at least you will no longer be able to deceive yourself.'

Eduard felt how much she was in the right. A spoken word is terrible when it says in a moment what the heart has for long allowed itself in secret; and it was only to put off the issue that Eduard answered: 'I am not clear even yet what it is you have in mind.'

'It was my intention,' Charlotte replied, 'to discuss with you these two suggestions about Ottilie's future. Both have much to recommend them. The boarding-school would be the most suitable when I consider how the child is now. But the wider sphere promises more when I consider what she ought to become.' She thereupon described the two possibilities in detail and concluded with the words: 'If it were left to me I would prefer the house of that lady, for several reasons but especially because I do not want to encourage the affection, I may say passion, Ottilie has aroused in a young man at the school.'

Eduard gave the impression he approved of what she said. In reality he was only seeking a respite. Charlotte, who wanted to get something definite done, at once seized on the fact that Eduard had not directly objected, to make firm arrangements for Ottilie's departure in a few days' time, an event for which she had quietly made all the necessary preparations.

Eduard went cold. He considered himself betrayed and that his wife's honeyed words had been calculated deliberately to sever him from his happiness for ever. He made as if to leave the matter entirely to her. But secretly he had come to his decision. Merely so as to get his breath, so as to avert the imminent incalculable disaster of Ottilie's going away, he resolved to leave home himself. He was not able to conceal his intention entirely from Charlotte, but he explained it by saying he did not want to be there when Ottilie left, indeed from that moment on he wanted never to see her again. Charlotte, who believed she had won, gave him every assistance. He ordered his horses, gave his valet the necessary instructions about what to pack and how to follow afterwards, and then, as if on the spur of the moment, he sat down and wrote.

Eduard to Charlotte

The evil that has befallen us, my dear, may be curable or it may not – but this I know: if I am not to give way to immediate despair I must find a respite for myself and for us all. Since I am making a sacrifice I can make a demand. I am leaving my house and I shall not return to it until prospects are more favourable and more peaceful. You may occupy it in the meantime, but with Ottilie. I want to know she is with you and not among strangers. Take care of her, treat her as you always have, or with even more love and tenderness. I promise not to seek any clandestine relationship with Ottilie. Let me rather live for a time in ignorance of how you are: I will think the best. Think likewise of me. The only thing I ask, and I ask it with all the warmth at my command, is that you will make no attempt to send Ottilie elsewhere and set her up in a new situation. Outside the confines of your house, of your park, entrusted to strangers, she belongs to me and I shall have her. But if you respect my affection, my desires, my grief, if you flatter my hopes and illusions, then I for my part will not resist recovery should the power to recover be given me.

This last phrase came from his pen not his heart, and when he saw it on the page he began to weep bitterly. He had promised to renounce the happiness of loving Ottilie, the unhappiness of loving her, he had promised in some way or other to do that! It was only now he realized what he was doing. He was going away without knowing what his going away would produce. He was not going to see her again, at least not for the present, and how could he be sure he would ever see her again? But the letter was written, the horses were standing at the door. At any moment he might catch sight of Ottilie somewhere in the house and have his resolution brought to nothing. He pulled himself together. He remembered he could come back any time he wanted to, that it was by going away that he was getting closer to the goal of his desires. On the other hand, he imagined Ottilie thrust out of the house if he stayed. He sealed the letter, hurried down the steps and swung himself on to his horse.

As he rode past the inn he saw sitting under the trees the beggar he had given to so generously the previous night. The beggar was comfortably enjoying his midday meal. He stood up and bowed respectfully and more than respectfully to Eduard. The sight of the very figure which had appeared before him when he had had Ottilie on his arm the previous day reminded him painfully of the happiest hour of his life. His grief grew more intense, the thought of what he was leaving behind was unbearable. He looked at the beggar again: 'You are to be envied!' he cried: 'you still enjoy your alms of yesterday, but my happiness of yesterday is gone!'

CHAPTER SEVENTEEN

OTTILIE went to the window when she heard somebody riding away and she saw Eduard's departing back. She thought it strange he should have left the house without seeing her, without having spoken to her. She became disquieted and more and more pensive when Charlotte took her for a long walk and talked about all kinds of things but refrained, deliberately as it seemed, from mentioning her husband. She was thus doubly perplexed to find when they got back that the table was laid only for two.

We never like having to go without what we are used to but we find this deprivation really painful only when what we have to go without is of some consequence. Eduard and the Captain were missing, for the first time Charlotte had herself set the table, and it seemed to Ottilie as if she had been discharged. The two women sat opposite one another. Charlotte talked quite dispassionately about the Captain's appointment and of the unlikelihood that they would be seeing him again for some time. Ottilie's only consolation was that she could imagine the reason Eduard had ridden away was to accompany the Captain on part of his journey.

Only when they rose from the table they saw Eduard's carriage outside the window, and when Charlotte asked somewhat indignantly who had ordered it she was told it was Eduard's valet, who had a few more things to pack up and take away in it. It took all the self-command Ottilie possessed to conceal her anguish and amazement.

The valet came in and asked to be allowed to take away a number of things, a cup, a couple of silver spoons, and other things which all seemed to Ottilie to point to a long journey and a long absence. Charlotte refused him quite brusquely:

she could not see what he was talking about, did he himself not have command of everything that concerned his master? The cunning fellow, whose real objective was merely to talk with Ottilie and for that purpose to get her out of the room under some pretext, apologized for his intrusion but repeated his request. Ottilie wanted to let him have his way but Charlotte continued to refuse, the valet was obliged to depart, and the carriage rumbled away.

It was a terrible moment for Ottilie. She could not understand, she could not conceive what had happened, but she sensed that Eduard had been torn from her for a considerable time. Charlotte felt with her and left her alone. We cannot attempt to describe her anguish and her tears. She suffered immeasurably. She only prayed to God that he would help her get through this day. She got through the day and the night that followed and when she came to herself again it seemed to her she was a different being.

But she had not overcome her feelings, she had not acquiesced in her situation; although she had suffered so great a loss she was still there and had more still to fear. The first thing to worry her after she was conscious of herself again was that now the men had gone away she too would have to go away. She suspected nothing of Eduard's threats through which her residence with Charlotte was secured but the way Charlotte behaved did serve to calm her to some extent. Charlotte tried to keep the good child occupied and seldom left her side if she could help it; and although she well knew how ineffectual words are against resolute passion, she also knew the power of self-possession and self-knowledge and she therefore spoke openly to Ottilie about many things that concerned them.

Hence it was a great comfort to Ottilie when Charlotte on one occasion deliberately let fall the wise observation: 'People are terribly grateful when we quietly help them out of the difficulties and embarrassments their passions have led them into. Let us cheer up and take in hand what the men have left unfinished. Let our temperance preserve and advance what their impetuousness and impatience would have destroyed. That is the best way we can spend our time until they return.'

'Since you speak of temperance, dear aunt,' Ottilie replied, 'I cannot help saying I am reminded of the intemperance of the men especially when it comes to wine. I have often been awfully worried to see how they lose all reason, prudence and consideration for others and become utterly uncharming and unlikeable even for hours on end, and how often evil and confusion threaten to break in and displace all the good a fine man is capable of doing. How often may this not be the cause of sudden violent decisions!'

Charlotte agreed with her but did not pursue the conversation because she felt only too certain that even now Ottilie was thinking only of Eduard, who had been known to increase his pleasure, volubility and vigour with the aid of wine, not as a habit, to be sure, but still more often than he should have.

If this remark of Charlotte's had given Ottilie occasion for thinking about the men again and particularly about Eduard, another remark did so all the more strikingly: Charlotte said the Captain would be getting married soon, and spoke of this eventuality as of something altogether certain and well-known, and this gave everything a very different complexion from what Ottilie had been led to imagine by Eduard's earlier assurances. As a result of all this Ottilie began to scrutinize every remark Charlotte made and to observe her every gesture, her every action, her every step much more closely than before. Without realizing it Ottilie had become shrewd, sharp-witted, suspicious.

In the meantime Charlotte made a detailed appraisal of the estate and everything concerning it and set to work on it with her customary efficiency. She always insisted that

Ottilie participate too. She resolutely reduced the household expenses, and when she looked into them properly she came to consider the emotional events which had taken place a blessing in disguise, because if they had gone on as they had been going on they could easily have got themselves involved in limitless expense and before they knew it their impetuous way of living and working would have, if not destroyed, at any rate seriously undermined their fortune and the comfortable circumstances that went with it.

She did not interrupt the work already in progress in the new park; on the contrary, she was glad to let it go on, since it would have to provide the basis for future development, but when that much was done it would have to stop, because when her husband came back she wanted him to find enough pleasurable activity left to do to keep him busy.

In all this work and preparation she found the architect's endeavours beyond praise. Within a short time the great lake spread out before her and the newly created banks were attractively grassed and decorated with plants of many kinds. All the rough work on the pavilion was done and all that was necessary to conserve it taken care of, and then she called a halt at a point where it would be pleasurable to take it up again. While this was going on she was relaxed and cheerful. Ottilie only seemed to be. All she looked for in anything was whether it was a sign Eduard was expected back soon or not. This was the only thing that interested her.

That being so, she welcomed a new arrangement under which the peasant lads were collected together with the object of keeping the now very extensive park clean and tidy. Eduard had entertained the idea before. A kind of cheerful uniform was made for them which they put on in the evening after they had scrubbed themselves thoroughly. The uniforms were kept in the mansion, the most intelligent and careful of the boys were entrusted with looking after them, the architect supervised the whole thing, and before you knew it all the boys had acquired a certain aptitude. It was not hard to train them and when they went to work it was with a kind of military precision. In fact, when they marched along with their scrapers, garden knives, rakes, trowels and hoes and brooms, and others came along behind them with baskets for carrying off weeds and stones, and others came pulling the huge iron garden-roller, it made a very pretty procession. To the architect it suggested a succession of poses for the frieze of a garden-house; Ottilie, on the other hand, saw it only as a kind of parade which was soon to greet the returning master of the house.

This encouraged her to want to receive him with something similar on her own account. They had been trying for some time to encourage the village girls in sewing, knitting, spinning and other womanly accomplishments, and these virtuous activities too had been more in evidence since they had begun the cleaning and beautification of the village. Ottilie had taken part, but only occasionally and when she felt inclined. Now she thought of going to work more thoroughly and consistently. But girls cannot be formed into a troop in the way boys can. She followed her own good sense and without being too specific she attempted no more than to imbue each girl with a sense of devotion to her home, her parents and her brothers and sisters.

With many she succeeded. But there was one lively little girl about whom she heard nothing but complaints that she was without any aptitude and would never do anything about the house. Ottilie could not dislike the girl because the girl was always very friendly towards her, seemed drawn towards her and came and went with her whenever she was allowed to. When she was with Ottilie she was active, cheerful and untiring. Her need seemed to be to attach herself to an admired mistress. At first Ottilie tolerated the child's company, then she was taken with an affection for her, finally they became inseparable and Nanni accompanied her mistress everywhere.

Ottilie often went to the garden and took pleasure in the way everything was growing. The season for cherries and berries was coming to an end, although there was still enough left for Nanni to enjoy the last of them. The rest of the fruit, which promised such a rich harvest in the autumn, always made the gardener think of the master and he never thought of him without wishing him back. Ottilie very much enjoyed listening to the good old man. He knew his job inside out and he never tired of talking about Eduard.

When Ottilie said how glad she was the new shoots grafted that spring were all coming on so well, the gardener answered doubtfully: 'I only hope the good master may be able to enjoy them. If he was here this autumn he could see what good kinds are still standing in the walled garden from the time of his father. Nowadays your orchard gardeners are not so reliable as the monks used to be. The names in the catalogue are fine enough, but when you have grafted them and brought them on, the fruit you get doesn't make it worth while having such trees in the garden.'

But almost every time the faithful servant saw Ottilie what he most repeatedly asked about was the master's return and when that was going to happen. And when Ottilie could not tell him the good man did not hide from her that he was sorry to think she did not trust him. This brought home to her how ignorant she was of what was happening and she found that feeling very painful. But she could not stay away from these flower-beds and borders. They had sown some of the flowers together and planted all the plants, and now everything was in full bloom, it needed hardly any further attention, except that Nanni was always ready to water it. The late flowers were only now appearing, and Ottilie watched them appear with deep emotion; she had often promised herself she was going to celebrate Eduard's birthday and these flowers were, in all their splendour and abundance, supposed to deck out that celebration, an expression of her affection and gratitude. But her hopes of ever seeing that day celebrated were not always equally lively. Doubt and uneasiness were whispering constantly at the good child's soul.

It was not likely either that she would ever get on to a frank friendly footing with Charlotte again, because the two women were in very different situations. If everything stayed as it was before, if they went back to their old regular life, Charlotte would be happier than she was now and a happy prospect would open up for her for the future, but Ottilie would on the contrary lose everything. Yes, everything is the right word: in Eduard she had discovered for the first time what life and joy were, with things as they were now she was conscious of an infinite emptiness of which she had hitherto hardly had any conception. A heart that is seeking something feels there is something it lacks, a heart that has lost something feels its loss. Desire changes into ill-humour and impatience and a woman accustomed to wait passively now wants to step out of her usual confines, wants to become active, wants to do something to promote her own happiness.

Ottilie had not renounced Eduard. She could not do so, notwithstanding Charlotte was, despite her conviction to the contrary, shrewd enough to pretend she had, and that the fact was known, and to take it as settled that a calm friendly relationship was possible between her husband and Ottilie. Very often, when she had shut herself in her room for the night, Ottilie would kneel in front of the open chest and look at the birthday presents. She had touched none of them. Very often she would hurry out of the house at daybreak, out of the place where she had formerly found all her happiness, into the open, into the country which had formerly had no attraction for her. She would even want to get off the land itself, she would leap into the boat and row to the middle of the great lake, and there she would take out a travel-book and let herself be rocked by the waves and read and dream herself into a far country; and there she would always discover her friend, he would tell her she had always been close to his heart, she would tell him he had always been close to hers.

CHAPTER EIGHTEEN

WE have already got to know Mittler and something of the curious way in which that gentleman occupied his time, so it will come as no surprise to learn that, as soon as he heard of the misfortune which had struck these friends of his, he felt a strong inclination to prove his friendship and demonstrate his dexterity in this instance too, notwithstanding none of the parties involved had as yet called upon him for assistance. Yet he also felt it would be advisable to delay a while first; he knew only too well that when cultured people get themselves into a moral muddle they are more difficult to assist out of it than are uncultured people in a like predicament. For that reason he left them for a time to their own resources. But at last he could endure it no longer and, since he had already got on to Eduard's track during his period of inactivity, he now hurried to seek him out.

His path led him to a pleasant valley. The green meadow which lay at the bottom of the valley was well wooded and the full-flowing sparkling stream which flowed through it sometimes meandered and sometimes rushed along. Fertile fields and well-stocked orchards stretched away over the gently rising slopes. The villages lay not too close together, the place as a whole had a peaceful character and, if its individual parts were not exactly suitable for painting, they seemed eminently suitable for living in.

A well-preserved farmstead with a neat little house surrounded by gardens at last caught his eye. He conjectured that this must be Eduard's present residence, and he was not mistaken.

Of our solitary friend we can say this much: in the silence of his solitude he had given himself over completely to contemplating his passion. He had evolved plans of all kinds, nourished hopes of all kinds. He found it impossible to deny that he wanted to have Ottilie there, that he wanted to bring her, entice her there, and he could not deny there were other thoughts too, of things permissible and impermissible, which would not be stilled. And then, working on these thoughts, his imagination would evoke one possibility after another. If he was not to possess her there, if he could not legitimately possess her, then he would make over to her the possession of his estate. There she should live as an independent person, there she should be happy, even – when his self-tormenting imagination took him that far – happy with somebody else.

Thus did his days pass in a never-ending vacillation between hope and torment, between tears and serenity, between plans, preparations and despair. He was not surprised by the sight of Mittler. He had long expected him and so he half welcomed his arrival. If he had been sent by Charlotte, Eduard had already armed himself with excuses and procrastinations of all kinds and then with certain more definite suggestions; if he brought some news of or from Ottilie, Mittler was as welcome as a messenger from heaven.

Eduard was therefore depressed and annoyed to learn that Mittler had not come from the mansion but was there on his own initiative. His heart was hardened and conversation would not at first get under way. But Mittler knew well that a heart preoccupied with love has an urgent need to express itself, to pour out to a friend what is going on within it, so after a certain amount of desultory chatter he was content to step out of his usual role and, deserting the role of mediator, to play the old comrade.

In this character he took it upon himself to rebuke Eduard gently for the solitary life he was leading, but Eduard replied: 'Oh I cannot imagine a more pleasant way of spending my time! I think about her constantly, I am always with her. I possess the inestimable privilege of being free to imagine where Ottilie is, where she goes, where she stops, where she rests. I see her before me acting as she always does, doing things and planning other things – admittedly always things which are most flattering to me. But it does not stop at that, because how can I be happy away from her! I set my imagination to work to decide what Ottilie has to do in order to come to me. I write myself sweet intimate letters and sign them with her name, I reply to them, and then I preserve the letters together. I have promised not to approach her in any way and that promise I shall keep. But what is stopping her from turning to me? Has Charlotte perhaps been so cruel as to demand from her a promise and vow not to write to me or let me have news of herself? It would be natural enough, I even think it probable, and yet the idea seems to me monstrous and unendurable. If she loves me, as I believe she does, as I know she does, why does she not resolve, why does she not dare to flee the house and come and throw herself in my arms? I often think that is what she ought to do, that is what she could do if she wanted to. Whenever I hear a noise in the hallway I look up at the door: "It's her!" I think, I hope. And since what is perfectly possible is apparently impossible, I imagine the impossible must be possible. When I awake at night and the lamp throws an uncertain light over the bedroom her figure, her spirit, an intuition of her ought to be wafted across to me, approach me, seize me, for no more than a moment, so that I could have some kind of assurance she is thinking of me, that she is mine.

'One joy alone remains to me. When I was near her I never dreamt of her, now we are apart we are together in dreams, and strange to say it is only since I have got to know other charming people here in this neighbourhood that her image appears to me in dreams, as if she were trying to say: "Look about you as you will, you will find nothing more lovely than me!" And so her image comes into all my dreams. All that befalls me with her in dreams is mixed and mingled together. Sometimes we are putting our names to a contract: there is her hand and there is mine, there is her name and my name, they efface one another, they blend together. But these rapturous illusions of fantasy can be painful too. Sometimes she does something that offends the pure idea I have of her, and it is only then I know how much I love her, because I am then distressed beyond all power of description. Sometimes she teases and torments me in a way quite unlike her, and then straightway her image alters, her heavenly little round face grows longer, and she is somebody else; but still that does not appease me, my torment continues, and I am thrown into confusion.

'You can smile at me, my dear Mittler, or not smile, just as you like! Oh I am not ashamed of this attachment, of this foolish mad infatuation if you want to call it that. No, I have never loved before, it is only now I know what love is. Everything in my life was until now merely prologue, merely delay, merely pastime, merely waste of time, until I came to know her, until I came to love her, until I wholly and truly loved her. People have reproached me, not exactly to my face but certainly behind my back, with being only a bungler, with being only a dabbler and an incompetent in most things. It may be so, but I had not yet found that in which I can now show myself a master. I should like to see the man who has a greater talent for love than I have.

'It is a lamentable talent, I know, it is one full of tears and suffering, but it comes so naturally to me, I find it so congenial, that I should be hard put to it ever to give it up again.'

While Eduard had certainly relieved his feelings by this energetic outpouring, it had also all at once brought every detail of his singular situation clearly into focus and, overwhelmed by the painful conflict, he burst into tears and his tears flowed the more freely in that his heart had been softened through disclosing what was in it.

Mittler, when he saw himself being deflected far from the

object of his journey by Eduard's painful and passionate outburst, found his natural impetuosity and inexorability of mind even less tractable than usual and he expressed his disapproval bluntly and with candour. Eduard ought to pull himself together (so he informed him); ought to consider what he owed to his dignity as a man; ought not to forget that what redounded most to a person's honour was to be composed in face of misfortune; ought to remember that to endure suffering with equanimity and decorum was the way to be respected, esteemed and held up as an example to all.

Agitated and miserably distressed as he was, Eduard could not help thinking these expressions vain and hollow. 'It is very well for the happy man to talk,' he cried, flying into a passion, 'but he would feel ashamed if he could see how intolerable he is to one who is not happy. You are supposed to have infinite endurance and patience, but infinite suffering is a thing your smug contented man refuses to recognize. There are occasions – yes there are such occasions! – when all consolation is base and it is a duty to despair. Isn't there a noble Greek who knows how to paint heroes who nonetheless does not disdain, when his heroes are overwhelmed with grief, to let them weep? He even has a proverb which says: Men who give way easily to tears are good. I have nothing to do with those whose hearts are dry and whose eyes are dry! My curse on the happy who see in the unhappy no more than a spectacle to be watched. Let a man be tortured, physically and mentally tortured, in the cruellest way imaginable, still he is supposed to bear himself bravely so as to win their applause and so that when he dies they will go on applauding him, as if he were a gladiator perishing with decorum in the arena. My dear Mittler, I am grateful for your visit, but you would be doing me a great favour if you would disappear for a while and take a walk round the garden or the valley. Come back again later. I will try to be more composed and more like yourself.'

But Mittler preferred continuing the conversation to breaking it off, because he felt he would not find it very easy to resume. Eduard too was not really averse to continuing and the conversation was in any event moving, if painfully, towards its objective.

'Thinking round and round and talking back and forth is of no help, that I know,' said Eduard. 'But it was only as we were talking that I came to know my own mind, that I felt quite definitely what I ought to do, what I had in fact already decided to do. I see my life before me as it is now and as it will be. My only choice is between misery and happiness. My dear chap, I want you to help me get a divorce. That is what I need and that is what has already in effect taken place. Get Charlotte to agree to it. I won't go into why I think she will be amenable. Go to her, my dear fellow, set all our minds at rest, make us happy again!'

Mittler faltered. Eduard went on: 'My fate and Ottilie's are inseparable, and we shall not perish. Look at this cup! Our initials are cut into it. At a moment of rejoicing a man threw it into the air, nobody was to drink out of it again, it was to shatter on the stony ground, but it was caught before it could fall. For a high price I bought it back and now I drink out of it every day, so that every day it tells me that when fate has decreed something that thing is indestructible.'

'Heaven help us,' cried Mittler, 'but what forbearance my friends demand of me! Superstition is it now? Is that the latest? I abominate it, it is the worst thing that ever plagued the human race. We play with prophecies, intuitions and dreams, and use them to try to give some significance to everyday life. But when life has for once got some real significance of its own, when everything buffets and blows about us, these ghosts and spirits only serve to make the storm blow harder.'

'Leave the needy heart,' cried Eduard, 'tossed as it is between hope and dread in the uncertainty of this life, some guiding star it may look up to even if it cannot steer by it.'

'That would be all very well,' Mittler replied, 'if only people who believe in such things would show some consistency. But I have always noticed that no one pays any attention to warning or admonitory signs, the only signs that are believed in or paid attention to are fair and flattering ones.'

Since Mittler could see he was being led into mystic regions in which he felt the more uncomfortable the longer he stayed, he was now somewhat more disposed to accede to Eduard's urgent desire he should go to Charlotte. Why should he oppose it? His own objective must now be to gain time so as to find out what the women were thinking and doing.

He hurried to Charlotte and found her, as usual, cheerful and composed. She was glad to tell him of all that had happened: from Eduard he had been able to gather only the effect of what had happened. He cautiously advanced his own view of the matter, but could not bring himself to utter the word divorce even in passing. He was therefore very surprised and astonished and in his own fashion exhilarated when, after so much disagreeableness, Charlotte concluded by saying: 'I must believe and hope that all will be well again and that Eduard will come back again. How can it be otherwise, since you find me in a certain condition.'

'Do I understand you aright?' Mittler interjected. 'Perfectly,' Charlotte replied. 'A thousand blessings on this news!' he cried, clapping his hands. 'I know how strongly this argument works on the heart of a man. How many marriages have I not seen hastened, strengthened, revived by it! One such expectancy has more effect than a thousand words. Indeed, of all we can expect from life, this expectancy is surely the best, is it not! – But,' he went on, 'so far as I am concerned I might have every cause for annoyance. I can see that in this case my vanity is not going to be flattered. I shall get no thanks from you, that I can see. I remind myself of a friend of mine, a doctor, who was always able to cure the poor, which he did for the love of God, but could seldom cure a rich man who was willing to pay. Fortunately, in this case the matter is going to settle itself, for my efforts and admonitions would certainly have got nowhere.'

Charlotte now asked him to take the news to Eduard, to take him a letter from her, and see what was to be done. He declined. 'Everything has already been done,' he cried. 'Write to him! Any courier will do as well as I. I have to make off to where I am more needed. I shall only come back to congratulate you. I shall come to the christening.'

Charlotte had often before been displeased with Mittler and she was so this time. In his impetuous way he had done much good, but this same precipitancy had led to many a disaster. No one was more subject to sudden prejudices.

Charlotte's courier was sent to Eduard, who received him half in dread. She could equally well have said Yes or No. For a long time he did not dare open the letter. When he did open it and read it he was taken very much aback, and he stood as if petrified when he read the paragraph with which it ended:

'Recall to mind those nocturnal hours when you visited your wife romantically as a lover, drew her irresistibly to you, enclosed her in your arms as if she were a mistress or a bride. Let us reverence this strange chance as a dispensation of heaven which joined us together anew at the very moment when our life's happiness seemed as if it was going to fall apart and vanish away.'

It would be hard to describe what went on in Eduard's soul after he had read that. But in such a dilemma as he then found himself what finally happens is that old habits and old inclinations reassert themselves as a way of killing empty time and filling empty life. For the nobleman war and hunting are an ever-ready aid of this description. Eduard longed for danger from without to counterbalance the danger from within. He longed for destruction because existence was threatening to become unendurable: he even found consolation in the thought he was going to cease to exist and that by doing this he could make happy his friends and those he loved. There was no one to oppose his will in this because he kept his intentions secret. He drew up a formal last will and testament: he made over the estate to Ottilie and to be able to do that gave him a delicious sensation. He made provision for Charlotte, for the unborn child, for the Captain, for his servants. That war had broken out again was a fortunate chance. In his youth he had found the superficialities of military life a burden, it was because of them he had left the service, but now it was a glorious feeling to set out under a general of whom he could say: Under his command death is probable, victory certain.

When she too learned of Charlotte's secret, Ottilie was as confounded as Eduard, and more so, and she withdrew into herself. She had nothing more to say. She could not hope and she should not desire. But a glimpse of her soul is provided by a journal which she kept, from which we propose to offer a number of extracts.

PART TWO

CHAPTER ONE

WE often encounter in everyday life something which, when we encounter it in art, we are accustomed to attribute to the poet's artistry: when the chief characters are absent or concealed, or lapse into inactivity, their place is at once taken by a second or third character who has hardly been noticed before, and when this character then comes fully into his own he seems just as worthy of our attention and sympathy and even of our praise.

This is what happened as soon as Eduard and the Captain had gone: the architect came more and more to the fore with every day that passed. The preparation and carrying out of so many tasks depended solely on him and he proved himself precise, informed and energetic in that work and also able to give support to the ladies in all sorts of ways and to keep them amused in hours of idleness. His appearance was in itself one to inspire confidence and awaken affection. He was a young man in every sense, well-built, slim, tall, perhaps a little too tall, modest but not timid, familiar but not importunate. He was happy to take on any responsibility and to take care of any task, and because he had no difficulty in doing the accounts he soon knew all about the household and its running, and his beneficent influence was felt everywhere. He was usually the one to receive callers and he knew how to turn away an unexpected visitor, or if he could not do that, at any rate to prepare the women so that they suffered no inconvenience.

One caller who gave him a certain amount of trouble was a young solicitor who was sent along one day by a neighbouring aristocrat to discuss a subject which, although not very important in itself, was disturbing to Charlotte. We have to give our attention to this incident because it supplied an impetus to various things which might perhaps otherwise have lain dormant for a long time.

Let us recall those alterations Charlotte had made in the churchyard. All the gravestones had been moved from their places and set up against the wall and against the base of the church. The ground had been levelled and, except for the broad walk which led to the church and then past it to the little gate beyond, sown with various kinds of clover, which provided a fine green and flowery expanse. New graves could be added from the end of this expanse, but each time the ground was to be levelled again and sown with clover. No one could deny that this arrangement provided a dignified and cheerful prospect when you went to church on Sunday or feast-days. Even the parson who, stricken in years and riveted to the old ways, had at first not been very happy about the new dispensation, now found pleasure in sitting, a Philemon with his Baucis, under the ancient lime-trees before his backdoor and having before him a gaily coloured carpet instead of a field of rough and rugged gravestones. This patch of ground was, moreover, to be for the permanent benefit of his household, since Charlotte had provided that its use would be guaranteed to the parsonage.

But for all that, there were some parishioners who had already expressed disapproval that the place where their ancestors reposed was no longer marked, and that their memory had thus been so to speak obliterated. There were many who said that, although the gravestones which were preserved showed who was buried there, they did not show where they were buried, and it was where they were buried that really mattered.

This opinion was shared by a neighbouring family which had many years before reserved a plot in this burial ground and in exchange made a small bequest to the church. Now the young solicitor had been sent to revoke the bequest and to give notice that no further payments would be made, because the condition under which payments had hitherto been made had been unilaterally abrogated and all protests and representations ignored. Charlotte, the originator of this change, wanted to talk to the young man herself. He stated his and his client's case firmly but politely and gave them all much to think about.

'You will understand,' he said, after a brief preamble justifying his presumption in coming, 'you will understand that all persons, the highest and the humblest, are concerned to mark the place in which their loved ones lie. To the poorest peasant burying one of his children it is a kind of comfort and consolation to set upon its grave a feeble wooden cross, and to decorate it with a wreath, so that he may preserve the memory of that child for at any rate as long as his sorrow for it endures, even though such a memorial must, like that grief itself, at last be wiped away by time. The prosperous employ, instead of wood, iron, make their cross fast and firm and in various ways protect it, and already one may speak of a memorial which will endure through the years. But because even these at length must fall and lose their brightness, the rich feel no stronger call than the call to erect a stone which will endure for many generations and which their posterity can refurbish and renew. But it is not the stone itself which draws us to the spot, but that which is preserved beneath it, that which is entrusted to the earth beside it. The question here is not so much of the memorial as of the person himself, not of the memory but of the present fact. I can embrace the departed far more readily in a grave than in a monument, for a monument has in itself little real meaning: it should rather be a landmark around which wives, husbands, relatives, friends continue to assemble even after their departure hence, and the survivor should retain the right to turn strangers and ill-wishers away from his dear ones at rest.

'I therefore consider my client entirely justified in revoking his bequest, and that in so doing he is being more than fair and reasonable, for the members of this family have been injured in a way that precludes all possibility of recompense. They have been deprived of the bitter-sweet sensation of sacrificing to their dear departed and of the consoling hope of one day reposing beside them.'

'The matter is not so important,' Charlotte replied, 'that one should trouble oneself with a law-suit over it. I so little regret my action that I shall be glad to make up to the church whatever it will be losing. I must confess to you quite frankly that your arguments have not convinced me. The pure feeling that, at least after death, we are all one and all equal, seems to me more comforting than this obstinate obdurate continuing on with the personalities, attachments and circumstances of our life. What do you think?' she asked the architect.

'In such a matter as this,' the architect replied, 'I have no wish either to contend or to pronounce judgement. Let me say, with respect, what my art and my way of thinking suggest to me. We are no longer so fortunate as to be able to press to our heart the remains of a beloved one in an urn; we are neither rich nor happy enough to be able to preserve them entire in great ornate sarcophagi; we cannot even find room for them inside the church, but are directed out into the open-air; all this being so, we have every reason to approve the style which you, madam, have introduced. If the members of a parish lie side by side they are still reposing beside their loved ones and with them, and if the earth is to receive us one day I can think of nothing more natural or more cleanly than that the mounds which have arisen fortuitously and are gradually subsiding should be levelled without delay, so that the earth, since it is now borne by all together, shall lie more lightly on each.'

'And are all these people to pass on without any kind of memorial, without anything to be remembered by?' said Ottilie.

'By no means!' said the architect. 'It is only a particular place we ought to renounce, not a memorial. The architect and the sculptor are vitally interested that mankind should expect from them, from their art, from their hand, a perpetuation of its existence, and that is why I should like to have well-conceived, well-executed monuments, not scattered about all over the place but erected on a spot where they can expect to remain. Since even saints and kings forgo the privilege of being laid to rest in the church in person, let us at least set up memorials and inscriptions there, or in galleries around our burial grounds. They might assume a thousand forms, and be ornamented in a thousand ways.'

'If artists are as rich in ideas as that,' said Charlotte, 'tell me why we can never get away from the form of a petty obelisk, a truncated column or a funeral urn. Instead of the thousand designs of which you boast I have never seen anything but a thousand repetitions.'

'That may well be so with us,' the architect replied, 'but it is not so everywhere. And in general I would say that designs and their proper application are a ticklish business. In the present case especially there are many difficulties to overcome: it is hard to make a grave subject attractive, or when dealing with a joyless one not to produce something joyless. I have a large collection of sketches for monuments of all kinds and I occasionally display it: but a man's fairest memorial is still his own portrait. It gives a better idea of what he was than anything else can do. It is the best text to the music of his life, whether there was much music or little. Only it has to be painted during his best years, and this is usually neglected. No one gives thought to preserving living forms, and when they do, they do so very inadequately. A mask is taken of a dead man, and this death-mask mounted on a block, and they call it a bust. How rarely can an artist impart life to such a thing!'

'Perhaps without knowing or intending it,' said Charlotte, 'you have turned this conversation entirely in my favour. A portrait is an independent thing; wherever it stands, it stands in its own right, and we shall not require that it should mark the actual grave. But shall I confess a strange feeling I have? I feel a kind of aversion even towards portraits. They always seem to be uttering a silent reproach. They point to something distant and departed and remind me how hard it is to do justice to the present. Think how many people we have seen and known and how little we meant to them and how little they meant to us! We meet the witty man and we do not talk with him, we meet the learned man and we do not learn from him, we meet the much-travelled man and we discover nothing through him, we meet the amiable man and we show him no love in return.

'And, unhappily, this is not the case only with passing acquaintances. Societies and families behave so towards their finest members, towns towards their worthiest citizens, peoples towards their most admirable princes, nations towards their greatest men.

'I once heard it asked why one always speaks well of the dead, but of the living more circumspectly. The answer was: because we have nothing to fear from the former, while the latter could still cross our path. So impure is our concern for the memory of others: it is mostly no more than a selfish joke; while it is, on the other hand, a deadly serious matter to keep our relations with the living constantly alert and alive.'

CHAPTER TWO

UNDER the inspiration of this incident and the discussions attending it, they went along to the burial-ground next day and the architect put forward several happy suggestions for brightening and embellishing it. And it was agreed that his efforts should also be extended to include the church, a building which had attracted his attention from the very first.

This church, strongly constructed in the Gothic style and pleasingly ornamented, had stood there for several centuries. It was apparent that the architect of a nearby monastery had exercised his skill on this smaller building too, and it still made a solemn impression, although the redecoration of the interior for the Protestant service had robbed it of something of its repose and majesty.

The architect did not find it difficult to extract from Charlotte a moderate sum which he intended using to restore both exterior and interior to their original condition and to harmonize them with the churchyard. He was himself very dextrous and it was agreed to keep on some of the workmen still engaged in building the pavilion until this pious work too should have been completed.

They were now in a position to examine the building itself with all its surrounds and adjuncts, and to the great delight and astonishment of the architect they found a little side-chapel which had previously been hardly noticed and which was even more ingeniously and delicately constructed and assiduously and pleasingly ornamented. And it also contained many carved and painted remains of the older form of worship, in which feast-days were denoted by different images and vessels and each was celebrated in its own particular way.

The architect could not resist at once including this chapel in his plans: his particular intention was to restore it as a monument to the taste of a bygone age. In his mind's eye he had already decorated the blank walls according to his own inclination, and he looked forward to being able in this connection to exercise his talents as a painter. Only for the moment he kept all this a secret from the others.

But first of all he kept his promise to show the ladies his collection of drawings and sketches of ancient tombs, monuments, urns and other such objects and, when conversation turned to the simple grave-mounds of the Norse peoples, he brought out his collection of weapons and utensils found in such graves. They had been cleaned and set out in portable drawers and compartments fixed to carved cloth-covered boards, so that these ancient solemn objects had taken on a certain modishness, as if they were in the showcase of a shop. And now that he had begun displaying his collections, and since the solitude in which they were living demanded the production of some entertainment, he began to appear every evening with some portion of his treasures. They were mostly of German origin: old coins and seals and other objects of that kind. All these things took the imagination back to more ancient times, and when he finally started to illustrate his talks with woodcuts, the earliest copperplates, and with other examples from the beginning of printing, and since the church was at the same time also growing back into the past day by day, they at length had to ask themselves whether they were really living in modern times, or whether it was not a dream, and they were now dwelling among quite different customs, habits and ways of life.

Prepared for in such a fashion, a large portfolio which he brought out last of all produced its maximum effect. It contained, to be sure, only figures drawn in outline, but, because they had been traced directly from the pictures they represented, they had entirely preserved their antique character. And how fascinating they found this antique character to be! Purity radiated from all the figures: if they were not all noble, it was clear they were all good. Cheerful composure, happy acknowledgement of one above us, silent submission in love and expectation, was inscribed on every countenance and expressed in every gesture. The old man with the bald head, the boy with abundant locks, the cheerful youth, the earnest man, the transfigured saint, the hovering angel, all seemed blessed in an innocent contentment, a pious expectation. The commonest action had in it a touch of ethereal life, and the character of each of the figures seemed to be fitted for an act of worship.

Into such a sphere most people gaze as into a vanished golden age, a lost paradise. Perhaps Ottilie alone was situated to feel she was among her own kind.

After this, it was impossible to resist the architect's offer to paint the space between the pointed arches of the chapel after the model of these ancient pictures, and so preserve his memory in a place where things had gone so well for him. He spoke of this with a certain sorrow: he could see that, the way things were going, his stay among such splendid society could not last for ever, but might perhaps even have to end quite soon.

For the rest, these days were not very eventful, but there were many occasions for talking seriously together, and we are therefore taking the opportunity here to offer a number of extracts from what Ottilie noted of these conversations in her journal; and we can think of no better way of introducing them than recording an image that leaps to our mind as we leaf through the beloved pages.

We understand that the English navy has a certain arrangement by which every rope in the royal fleet, from the stoutest to the finest, is spun in such a fashion that a red thread runs through it which cannot be extracted without unravelling the whole rope, so that even the smallest piece of this rope can be recognized as belonging to the Crown.

Similarly, there runs through Ottilie's journal a thread of affection and inclination that binds everything together and characterizes the whole. It is this thread which turns into the peculiar property of the writer these observations, thoughts, aphorisms copied down, and whatever else is there, and makes them significant for her. Every single passage we have selected bears indisputable testimony to the truth of this.

From Ottilie's Journal

To repose one day beside those you love is the pleasantest idea you can have when you come to think about the Beyond. 'To be gathered to your fathers' is such a heartfelt expression.

There are many kinds of memorial and memento which bring us closer to those who are far away and those who have departed, but none is more meaningful than the portrait. There is something exciting about being with a much-loved portrait, even if it is not a good likeness, just as there is sometimes something exciting about arguing with a friend. You have the pleasant feeling that you are divided, and yet can never be separated.

Sometimes you are with a real person in the same way as you are with a portrait. He does not have to speak, or look at you, or concern himself with you at all: you see him and feel what he means to you, indeed he can even come to mean more to you, without his doing anything about it, without his realizing in any way that his relationship with you is merely that of a portrait.

You are never satisfied with a portrait of people you know; which is why I have always felt sorry for portrait painters. You rarely ask the impossible, but that is what you ask of them. They are supposed to incorporate into their portrait everyone's feelings towards the subject, everyone's likes and dislikes; they are supposed to show, not merely how they see a particular person, but how everyone would see him. I am not surprised when such artists gradually grow insensitive, indifferent and self-willed. This would itself be a matter of indifference if it did not mean one would have to go without the likenesses of so many dearly-loved people.

It is indeed true: the architect's collection of weapons and ancient utensils, which were, together with the body, covered with great mounds of earth and rock, testifies to us how vain is man's provision for the preservation of his personality after death. And how inconsistent we are! The architect admits he has himself opened these graves of our ancestors, and yet he continues to occupy himself with monuments for our posterity.

But why take it all so seriously? Is everything we do done for eternity? Do we not dress in the morning so as to undress again at night? Do we not travel in order to return? And why should we not wish to repose beside our own people, even if it is only for a hundred years?

When you see all the gravestones which have sunk down and been worn away by the feet of churchgoers, and even that the churches themselves have collapsed over their own tombs, you can still think of life after death as a second life, which you enter into as a portrait or an inscription, and in which you remain longer than you do in your actual living life. But sooner or later this portrait, this second existence, is also extinguished. As over men, so over memorials time will not let itself be deprived of its rights.

CHAPTER THREE

It is so pleasant a sensation to occupy yourself with something you can only half do that you should never reproach the dilettante if he engages in an art he will never learn or blame the artist if he feels inclined to go beyond the boundaries of his art into a neighbouring field.

It is with such accommodating thoughts as these that we observe the architect's arrangements for painting the chapel. The colours were ready, the measurements taken, the sketches drawn. He had renounced all claim to originality, he kept close to his outlines, all he was concerned with was to distribute the sitting and hovering figures over the blank space so that they would tastefully decorate it.

The scaffolding was up, the work was progressing and, since he had already completed something worth looking at, he could not object to Charlotte's coming with Ottilie to see it. The living angel faces and the flowing garments against the blue background of heaven were a delight to the eye, and the quiet piety of their demeanour engendered composure and a feeling of great tenderness in the heart.

The women had climbed up to him on the scaffolding, and Ottilie took paint and brush and, following his directions, painted a pleated robe. She painted skilfully and with neat clean lines. She seemed all at once to have command of everything she had learned in her school lessons. She hardly noticed how easy it was.

Charlotte, who was always happy to see Ottilie in any way occupied and distracted, left the couple to themselves and went away to ponder her own thoughts and to work out for herself the cares and worries she could share with no other.

When ordinary people get passionately worked up over the

common difficulties of everyday we can only give them a pitying smile, but we regard with reverence a soul in which the seed of a great destiny has been sown, which must await the unfolding of this conception, and which cannot and must not seek to accelerate either the good or the evil, the happiness or the unhappiness, which is to arise from it.

Eduard had sent Charlotte a reply by the courier she had sent to him in his solitude. His reply had been friendly and sympathetic, but composed and serious rather than confiding and affectionate. Shortly afterwards he had disappeared and Charlotte could get no news of him, until eventually she chanced to see his name in the gazette, where he was cited with honours among those who had distinguished themselves in a major incident of the war. She now knew what path he had chosen. She learned that he had come through great dangers, but she was at the same time convinced he would seek out greater. She could see all too clearly that he was hardly going to be kept from going to extremes in any sense of that word. She kept these cares, which were always with her, to herself, and they went round and round in her mind, but however she considered them she could not lay them to rest.

Ottilie, suspecting nothing of all this, had meanwhile been seized by the greatest enthusiasm for the work in the chapel and she had no difficulty at all in getting Charlotte's permission to continue with it regularly. Now it went rapidly forward and the azure heaven was soon populated with inhabitants worthy of it. Practice on the earlier pictures had given Ottilie and the architect greater facility, and the later pictures were obviously better. And the faces, which were left for the architect alone to paint, gradually took on a very singular quality: they all began to look like Ottilie. The young man had had no preconceived faces in his mind, whether drawn from nature or from art, and what must have happened is that the proximity of the beautiful child must have made so lively an impression on his soul that what his eye had seen his hand was gradually able to depict with nothing lost in the process, until finally both eye and hand were acting in unison. Be that as it may, one of the last of the little faces was a complete success, so that it seemed as if Ottilie herself were looking down from the vault of heaven.

The ceiling was now finished. It had been decided to leave the walls and simply to paint them over a lighter brown than they were already. The delicate columns and sculptured ornamentation were to be picked out in a darker brown. But as in matters of this sort one thing always leads to another, it was decided to add hanging clusters of fruit and flowers, which were supposed, so to speak, to link heaven and earth. Here Ottilie was altogether in her element. The gardens provided the finest examples they could desire and, although the garlands were very liberally fitted out, the work was completed sooner than they had expected.

But everything still looked disordered and unfinished. The scaffolding was still in position, the planks were thrown one on top of the other, the uneven floor was even more disfigured by the spilt paint. The architect now asked the ladies to give him a week and during that time not to enter the chapel. At length, one fine evening he invited them both to betake themselves there; and he begged to be excused accompanying them, and bowed himself out.

'Whatever surprise he may have prepared for us,' Charlotte said when he had gone, 'I do not at the moment feel like going down there. You go on your own and tell me all about it. He is certain to have arranged something very nice. I shall enjoy it first in your description, and then I shall be glad to go and see it in reality.'

Ottilie, who well knew that Charlotte had to be careful about what she did, avoided all emotional excitement, and guarded especially against being taken by surprise, at once set off alone. She instinctively looked around for the architect, but he was nowhere to be seen and must have hidden himself. She found the church door open and went in. The church had been completed, cleaned and consecrated earlier on. She went to the door of the chapel, its ponderous brass-studded weight swung back easily before her, and she halted in surprise at the unexpected appearance of the familiar room.

A grave many-coloured light was coming through the single high window, which had been set with stained glass, giving the whole interior a strange glow and evoking a peculiar atmosphere. The beauty of the vault and the walls was enhanced by the decoration of the floor, which now consisted of tiles specially shaped and laid after a handsome pattern and joined together with plasterwork. The architect had had these tiles, together with the stained-glass panes, prepared in secret and had been able to have them installed very quickly. There were also seats in the chapel now: a number of finely carved choir stalls had been discovered among the antiquities of the church and these were now disposed very becomingly around the chapel walls.

Ottilie was delighted to see things familiar to her thus brought together into an unfamiliar whole. She stood, walked back and forth, looked and examined. At length she sat in one of the stalls, and as she gazed up and around it seemed to her that she was and was not, she felt her existence and did not feel it, she felt that all this before her might vanish away and that she too might vanish away, and only when the sun ceased to illumine the window did Ottilie come to herself and hurry back to the mansion.

She did not hide from herself at what special epoch this unexpected event had befallen her. It was the eve of Eduard's birthday. She had indeed hoped to celebrate it very differently from this: how brightly everything was to have been adorned for this celebration! But still the whole wealth of autumn flowers stood ungathered. The sunflowers still turned their faces to the sky, the asters still gazed ahead in modest stillness, and those flowers that had been bound in garlands had been used to decorate a place which, if it was not to remain a mere artist's whim, if it was to be put to any sort of use, seemed to be fit only to be a communal tomb.

She could not help recalling the bustling which had attended Eduard's celebration of her own birthday, she could not help thinking of the newly erected pavilion under whose roof they had promised themselves so much pleasure. The fireworks exploded again before her eyes and in her ears; the lonelier she was, the more she lived in imagination; yet the more she lived in imagination, the more alone she felt. She leaned upon his arm no more, and had no hope of ever being able to lean on it again.

From Ottilie's Journal

I must make a note of a remark made by the young artist: The case of the craftsman and the sculptor supplies the clearest evidence that man is least able to make his own that which most completely belongs to him. His works desert him as the bird deserts the nest in which it was hatched.

The architect above all has in this the strangest of destinies. How often he employs his whole mind and his whole love in the production of rooms from which he himself must be excluded. Kingly halls owe to him their splendour, but he cannot enjoy them at their most effective. In temples, he fixes a boundary between himself and the holy of holies, he may no longer mount the steps he himself has erected, just as the goldsmith may worship only from afar the monstrance he has made. The architect hands over to the rich man with the keys of his palace all the ease and comfort to be found in it without being able to enjoy any of it himself. Must the artist not in this way gradually become alienated from his art, since his work, like a child that has been provided for and left home, can no longer have any effect upon its father? And how beneficial it must have been for art when it was intended to be concerned almost exclusively with what was public property, and belonged to everybody and therefore also to the artist!

Ancient peoples had a solemn conception which can seem dreadful to us. They imagined their ancestors as sitting in great caverns on a circle of thrones in silent converse with one another. When a newcomer came in they stood up, if he was worthy of it, and bowed a welcome to him. When I was sitting in the chapel yesterday, and saw the other stalls ranged around the one I was sitting on, this idea seemed to me a very pleasing one. 'Why can't you go on sitting here,' I thought to myself, 'go on sitting here quietly and turned in upon yourself, for a long long time, until at last your friends come and you rise for them and show them to their places with a friendly bow?' The stained glass turns the day to solemn twilight, and somebody ought to install an ever-burning lamp, so that the night too should not be wholly dark.

However you imagine yourself, you always think of yourself as seeing. I believe people have dreams only so as not to stop seeing. It may well be that one day the inner light will come forth out of us, so that we shall then no longer need any other light.

The year is dying. The wind blows across the stubble and finds there is nothing left for it to shake. Only the red berries on their slender trees still seem to want to remind us of something merrier, and the beat of the thresher awakens in us the thought of how much life and nourishment lies hidden in the cut-down ear of corn.

CHAPTER FOUR

How strangely then, after such events as these, after the rise of this sensation of transcience and passing away, was Ottilie affected by the news, which could no longer be kept concealed from her, that Eduard had delivered himself over to the varying fortunes of war. She was, alas, spared none of the reflections to which such news could be expected to give rise. But happily a human being can comprehend misfortune only up to a certain degree; what goes beyond this degree destroys him or leaves him indifferent. There are situations in which fear and hope become one, annul one another, and are lost in a black numbness and apathy. How otherwise could we know that those we love best stand in hourly danger of death and yet go on living our ordinary lives?

So it was as if a benevolent spirit had taken Ottilie into its care when it suddenly brought into this silence, into which she seemed in her lonely idleness to be sinking, a wild throng of young people, a crowd which, by keeping her thoroughly occupied and rousing her out of herself, excited in her the feeling of her own powers.

Charlotte's daughter Luciane had hardly left the boarding-school and gone out into the great world, had hardly taken her place among the numerous company which frequented her aunt's house, before her desire to attract really did attract someone and a young man, a very rich one, was taken with a violent desire to possess her. His great wealth gave him the right to take the best of everything for his own, and it seemed to him that all he lacked was a perfect wife on whose account he would be the envy of the world as he already was in every other respect.

It was this family affair which had been keeping Charlotte so busy. She had been devoting all her thoughts and all her correspondence to it, in so far as these were not engaged in trying to get more detailed news of what Eduard was doing; and it was the reason Ottilie had lately been left more to herself. She knew Luciane would be coming, she had been making necessary preparations in the house, but she did not realize she would be coming so soon. She still had a lot left to arrange and discuss when the storm suddenly broke over the mansion and over Ottilie.

Maidservants and manservants, baggage-carts with trunks and chests, came driving up; you would have thought you already had a houseful of guests, but the actual guests were only now arriving: the great-aunt with Luciane and her lady friends, the young man likewise not alone. The entrance hall was now full of cases, valises and other leather containers, it was a problem to sort out whose box was whose, there was no end to the dragging about of baggage. In the meantime there was a violent downpour, which did nothing to reduce the discomfort. Ottilie faced this tumult with equanimity; she went calmly to work, and her cheerful competence in fact showed itself at its finest, for it was not very long before she had reduced everything to order. They were all installed in their rooms, they were all comfortable in their own fashion, and they all thought they were being well looked after because they were not hindered from looking after themselves.

After a very hard journey they would all now have liked to relax, the future son-in-law would have liked time to ingratiate himself with his future mother-in-law – but Luciane could not rest. She had at last attained the happiness of being allowed to ride a horse. The future bridegroom possessed some beautiful horses and they had to be mounted straight away. Wind and weather, rain and storm, were of no account: it was as if you lived only to get wet and dry yourself again. If she fancied going out on foot she did not bother what clothes she had on or what shoes she was wearing: she simply had to go and see the park of which she had heard so much. What could not be reached on horseback had to be scoured on foot. Soon she had seen everything and passed judgement on it. With the vivacity of her temperament she was not easy to contradict. The company had a lot to put up with from her, especially the maidservants, who were never finished with washing and ironing, mending and stitching.

She had hardly exhausted the mansion and its environs before she felt obliged to start paying visits in the neighbourhood, and since they rode and drove very fast, the 'neighbourhood' meant quite a large tract of country round about. The mansion was inundated with return calls, and so that they should not be out when the return callers came definite appointments were soon being made.

While Charlotte was involved in settling affairs with the aunt and the future bridegroom's secretary, and Ottilie and her staff of servants were seeing to it that, with such a crowd in the house, nothing should be lacking for their entertainment (trappers and gardeners, fishermen and shopkeepers were all kept busy), Luciane still continued to appear like a flaming comet drawing a long tail behind it. She soon began to find insipid the entertainment and conversation which commonly attended neighbourly visiting. She hardly let even the most elderly guest sit quietly at the card-table, and anyone she was in the least able to move – and whom was she not able to move with the charm of her importunity? – had to get up and join, if not in the dancing, at any rate in the games of forfeits and other lively party pursuits. And although all this, including the redemption of forfeits, centred upon Luciane herself, on the other hand no one, and especially no man, whatever sort of man he might be, went away quite empty; indeed, she succeeded in altogether winning over a number of older people of consequence by discovering when their birthday or nameday fell and arranging a celebration of it. A skill quite her own in this sort of thing was very useful, so that, while everyone was favoured, each thought he was the most favoured of all, a weakness which the oldest man in the company was in fact most obviously guilty of.

If she seemed to have the fixed intention of winning over to herself every man of rank, reputation, fame or any prospect of these, of trampling wisdom and discretion under foot, and of gaining the toleration of even the quiet and thoughtful for her wild and whirling ways, she was still willing to pay plenty of attention to the young: every young person had his share, his day, his hour when she went out of her way to charm and captivate him. So she had soon had her eye on the architect; but he had so unaffected an air beneath his long black locks, he stood at a distance so erect and composed, he replied to everything so concisely and judiciously but without showing any inclination to be drawn further, that at last, half of set purpose, half because she could not help it, she resolved to make him the hero of the day and so win him too for her court.

It was not for nothing she had brought so much luggage with her (indeed a large quantity had also come after her arrival): she had provided herself with endless changes of clothes. If she took pleasure in changing three or four times a day into a succession of ordinary dresses such as would be seen anywhere in society, she also appeared sometimes in actual fancy-dress, as a peasant or a fishergirl, a fairy or a flowergirl. She did not shrink from dressing up as an old woman, so that her youthful face would look out all the more freshly from under her cowl, and she so confounded the actual with the imaginary that you really thought you were dealing with the *Saalnixe*.*

*The 'nymph of the hall', a character in Ferdinand Kauer's Viennese operetta *Das Donauweibchen*, which was produced at Weimar.

But what she chiefly used these fancy-dresses for was mimed tableaux and dances, in which she was a skilled performer. A young gentleman of her court had acquired sufficient dexterity at the keyboard to accompany her gestures with what little music was required: a brief discussion and they were in instant rapport over what he had to play.

During a pause in a lively party one evening somebody invited her, apparently on the spur of the moment though in fact at her secret instigation, to give them one of her performances. She affected surprise and embarrassment and had to be asked several times. She appeared undecided, left the choice to others, asked someone to give her a theme as if she were an improvisator, until at last the piano-playing gentleman, with whom she no doubt also had a prior arrangement, sat himself down at the keyboard, began to play a funeral march, and invited her to give them her Artemisia, a role she had so admirably perfected. She allowed herself to be persuaded and, after a brief absence, she reappeared to the sad caressing tones of the death-march in the figure of the royal widow, with measured tread and bearing before her a funeral urn. Behind her there was borne a large blackboard and a sharp piece of chalk fixed into a drawing-pen.

She whispered something to one of her admirers and adjutants, and he at once went up to the architect and invited and pressed him to take part in the performance, indeed to some extent physically pushed him into it: he was to draw on the blackboard the tomb of Mausolus and thus play a central role in the proceedings. However embarrassed he might outwardly appear – in his plain black modern suit he presented a strange contrast to all the gauze, crepe, valances, spangles, tassels and coronets – he was keeping himself tightly under control inwardly, which unfortunately only made him seem even odder. With the greatest gravity he stationed himself before the blackboard, which was being held up by a couple of pageboys, and drew with much care and deliberation a tomb which, while it would have been more appropriate to a Lombard king than to the King of Caria, was so well-proportioned, seriously conceived, and ingeniously ornamented that its execution excited general delight and the finished work general admiration.

During all this time he had paid hardly any attention to the queen, devoting it all to the task in hand. When he eventually turned and bowed to her, and indicated he believed he had now carried out her commands, she held out to him the urn and intimated her desire to see it represented at the top of the tomb. He did as he was bid, though he did it reluctantly, since it could not be made to harmonize with the rest of his drawing. Luciane watched him impatiently until he had finished, for it had by no means been her intention that he should give her a conscientious performance : her desires and objective would have been better served if he had merely sketched in a few strokes something that might pass for a monument and then devoted the rest of the time to her. The way he had in fact acted had, however, brought her into the most embarrassing straits : for although she had tried to vary her postures and gestures to express her approval of the gradually evolving tomb, and had once or twice almost taken hold of him and pulled him round so as to establish some sort of communication with him, he had been so unresponsive and had borne himself so stiffly that she was again and again driven to resorting to the urn, pressing it to her heart and gazing up to heaven, until, because such performances necessarily grow more and more exaggerated, she finally came to look more like the Widow of Ephesus than the Queen of Caria. The representation consequently became somewhat protracted. The piano-player, who was normally patient enough, no longer knew what key he was supposed to be playing in, and he breathed a thankful prayer when he saw the urn at last standing on top of the tomb and, as the queen was about to express her gratitude, he instinctively struck up a merry tune, so that, if the representation was thereby deprived of its solemn character, the audience was restored to perfect good humour and at once proceeded to applaud the lady for the wonderful expressiveness of her performance and the architect for the elegance and artistry of his drawing.

The husband-to-be especially was intent on engaging the architect in conversation. 'I am sorry your drawing is so transient,' he said. 'But you will at least allow me to have it taken up to my room and discuss it with you.'

'If you like I can show you some carefully done drawings of structures and monuments of this sort,' said the architect. 'This is no more than a fleeting sketch.'

Ottilie was standing not far off and she went up to the two men. 'Do not neglect to let the Baron see your collection,' she said to the architect. 'He is a connoisseur of art and antiquities. I should like you to get to know one another better.'

Luciane came up and asked : 'What are you discussing?'

'A collection of works of art,' the Baron replied, 'which this gentleman owns and which he would like to show us some time.'

'Let him bring it right away,' Luciane cried. 'You will bring it right away, won't you?' she added coaxingly and taking hold of him by both hands. 'This may not be the right moment for it,' the architect replied.

'What !' Luciane cried imperiously, 'are you refusing to obey a command of your queen?' and fell to raillery and cajoling.

'Don't be obstinate,' Ottilie said in a whisper.

The architect took himself off with a bow that was neither a bow of agreement nor one of refusal.

He was hardly gone before Luciane set off again round the room like a tornado. She chanced to run into her mother. 'Oh how miserable I am!' she cried. 'I have left my monkey behind. They advised me not to bring him, but it's only because my servants are too lazy to look after him that I am deprived of the pleasure of his company. But I'm going to have him brought here, somebody shall go and fetch him. If only I had a picture of him I'd be happy. I am going to have his portrait done and it shall never leave my side.'

'Perhaps I can console you,' Charlotte replied. 'I have in the library a whole volume of the most marvellous pictures of monkeys. Would you like me to send for it?' Luciane cried aloud for joy and the volume was fetched. The sight of these repulsive manlike creatures, made even more manlike by the artist's brush, gave Luciane the greatest pleasure, but she was transported when she discovered a resemblance between each of these animals and people she knew. 'Doesn't that one look exactly like uncle?' she exclaimed cruelly. 'And that one like M—, the dealer in fancy goods? And that one like Pastor S—? And this one is what's-his-name to the life! Monkeys are your real *Incroyables** and I cannot understand why people want to keep them out of the best society.'

It was in the best society that she said this, but no one took it amiss. They had got so used to making so many allowances for the sake of her charm that at last her ill-breeding could get away with anything.

Meanwhile Ottilie was talking with the Baron. She was hoping the architect would come back: his collection, a more serious and tasteful one, would free the company from all this nonsense with the monkeys. It was in anticipation of this that she had entered into the conversation. But the architect was still absent, and when at last he did return he at once disappeared among the company without having brought anything with him and as if no one had expected

*Derogatory nickname applied to themselves by Parisian dandies of the Directory period.

him to. For a moment Ottilie was – how shall we put it? – annoyed, indignant, taken aback; she had put in a good word for him and she would have liked the Baron to have passed an hour with him in a way he would have found pleasant, for, his boundless love for Luciane notwithstanding, he seemed to be suffering from her behaviour.

The monkeys had to give place to supper. Party games, more dancing even, finally a joyless sitting around punctuated with efforts to whip up again a mirth that was already extinct went on, this time as on previous occasions, until well after midnight. For Luciane was already accustomed to not being able to get out of bed in the morning or into it at night.

During this period there are fewer events noted in Ottilie's journal, but she records more frequently maxims and aphorisms drawn from and applicable to life. But because most of them cannot have sprung from her own reflections, it seems probable that someone had passed on to her a book from which she copied what appealed to her. That much in them possesses a deeper and more personal meaning for her will be apparent from the red thread of which we spoke.

From Ottilie's Journal

The reason we so much like to look into the future is that we would so much like to deflect to our own advantage the as yet undetermined events which hover there.

When we find ourselves in a great gathering it is hard not to think that chance, which brings so many together, ought also to lead our friends to us.

In however much seclusion you live, before you know it you are either a debtor or a creditor.

If we meet someone who owes us a debt of gratitude we remember the fact at once. How often we can meet someone to whom we owe a debt of gratitude without thinking about it at all !

It is natural to communicate yourself to others, but to receive the communication of others without falsifying it requires culture.

We would not say very much in company if we realized how often we misunderstand what others say.

When we repeat what others have said, the reason we falsify it so much is probably that we have not understood it.

He who addresses others for very long without flattering them provokes antipathy.

Every assertion provokes its contrary.

Contradiction and flattery both make bad conversation.

The pleasantest company is that in which a cheerful mutual deference and respect prevails.

Human beings reveal their character most clearly by what they find ridiculous.

The ridiculous originates in the perception of an act which conflicts with custom or morality but does so harmlessly.

The sensual man often laughs when there is nothing to laugh at. His reaction to whatever stimulus he may receive never fails to reveal his inner complacency.

The clever man finds almost everything ridiculous, the wise man almost nothing.

A man of advancing years was criticized for continuing to concern himself with young women. 'It is the only way of staying young oneself,' he replied, 'and that, after all, is what everyone wants.'

We are willing to acknowledge our shortcomings, we are willing to be punished for them, we will patiently suffer much on their account, but we become impatient if we are required to overcome them.

Certain shortcomings are essential for the individual's existence. We would not like it if our old friends were to abandon certain of their peculiarities.

People say 'He will die soon' when someone does something contrary to his usual habits.

What kind of shortcomings ought we to retain, even cultivate in ourselves? Those which rather flatter than injure other people.

Passions are shortcomings or virtues intensified.

Our passions are phoenixes: as the old one burns away a new one immediately rises from its ashes.

Great passions are illnesses without hope of cure. That which would cure them is that which first makes them really dangerous.

Passion is both enhanced and alleviated by confession. Perhaps the middle course is nowhere more desirable than in confiding in and keeping quiet before those we love.

CHAPTER FIVE

THUS did Luciane continue to drive herself on in an unceasing round of pleasure. Her court expanded with every day that passed, in part because her riotous behaviour excited and attracted others, in part because she knew how to grapple others to her by acts of kindness. She was generous in the highest degree : for, since her aunt's and her fiancé's affection had brought her in a short space of time so many beautiful and costly gifts, she seemed to possess nothing of her own and not to realize the value of the things she had heaped up around her. She did not hesitate for a moment to take off a costly shawl and drape it around a woman who seemed to her to be too poorly clad compared with the others, and she did it so lightheartedly no one could have refused such a present. One of her court always had a purse and a standing instruction to ask after the oldest and the sickest in the places they visited and to ease their condition at any rate for the time being. As a result she acquired throughout the entire region a name for benevolence which could sometimes be inconvenient, since it attracted to her all too many burdensome sufferers.

But nothing served to enhance her reputation more than did the constant attention she paid to a certain unfortunate young man who avoided society because, although otherwise handsome and presentable, he had lost his right hand in battle. This mutilation so upset him, he was so weary of having to explain it to every new acquaintance, that he preferred to hide himself away, devote himself to reading and other studies, and once and for all have nothing further to do with society.

She came to learn of this young man's existence. He had

to come and join her, at first in an intimate group, then in a bigger, then in the biggest. She was more charming towards him than towards anyone else. She especially managed to make him conscious of the value of what he had lost, in as much as by her importunate readiness to be of service to him she sought to replace it. At table he had to sit beside her and she cut up his food so that he needed to use only a fork. If older people or those of more exalted rank interposed themselves, she kept an eye on him from the other end of the table and the hurrying servants had to render him the assistance of which her removal from his side threatened to deprive him. Finally she encouraged him to write with his left hand. He had to address all his attempts at writing to her, and so whether she was near or far she was always in touch with him. The young man did not know what had happened to him, and indeed that moment saw for him the start of a new life.

It might perhaps be thought that this kind of behaviour would have been displeasing to the Baron, but the opposite was the case. He thought very highly of her for these efforts, and his equanimity was the more complete in that he knew of her almost exaggerated caution where anything the least little bit risky to herself was concerned. She wanted to amuse herself with everyone just as it took her fancy, everyone was in danger of being badgered, pulled, pushed or otherwise teased by her at some time or other, but no one was permitted to do the same to her, no one could play fast and loose with her, no one could even think of taking with her the liberties she herself took; and thus she kept the rest strictly within those bounds of propriety which she seemed at any moment to be on the point of overstepping herself.

In general you might have thought she had made it her principle to expose herself to an equal measure of praise and blame, affection and disaffection. If she tried in a dozen ways to win people over, she usually managed to alienate them again through the sharpness of her tongue, which spared nobody. They never paid a visit in the neighbourhood, she and her companions were never hospitably received in some house or mansion, without she made it clear on the way home in the most uninhibited way how inclined she was to find all human affairs merely ridiculous. Here there were three brothers who had politely waited for one to be the first to get married while old age overtook them; here there was a little young wife with a big old husband; there, contrariwise, a cheerful little husband and a clumsy giantess. In one house you could not move a step without treading on children, another she thought empty-looking even when crowded because there were no children in it. Certain elderly husbands ought to get themselves buried as soon as possible so that, since there were no legal heirs, someone could for once have a good laugh in the house again. Certain married couples ought to travel because they were in no way fitted to keep house. And as she criticized the people, so did she criticize their goods, their homes, their furniture, their crockery. Wall decorations of any kind especially excited her mockery. From the most ancient wall-carpets to the latest wallpaper, from the most venerable family portraits to the most frivolous current copperplates, all had to go through it, she pulled them all to pieces, so that you had to marvel that anything for five miles around continued to exist.

There may not perhaps have been any actual malice in this destructiveness; usually it was no doubt merely selfish mischievousness; but in her relations with Ottilie real bitterness had developed. She looked down with contempt on the dear child's constant quiet industriousness which everyone else approved and applauded, and when it was mentioned how great an interest Ottilie took in the gardens and greenhouses, she made fun of that fact, not only by affecting surprise that there seemed to be no flowers or fruit about (unmindful that they were now in the depth of winter), but by thenceforth having so much greenery, branches and whatever else was beginning to show life brought into the house and squandered on daily decoration of the rooms and the table that Ottilie and the gardener saw with dismay their hopes destroyed for the coming year and perhaps for many years after that.

She was equally reluctant to let Ottilie stay quietly in the house, where she was happy. Ottilie had to come with her on their sleigh rides and outings, she had to come to the parties held in the neighbourhood, and, since the others were not worried by snow and cold and raging night storms, she had to brave them too. The delicate child suffered not a little under this treatment, but Luciane gained nothing by it: although Ottilie always went dressed very simply she was still, or at least she always seemed to the men, the loveliest girl there. A gentle attraction drew all the men around her, no matter where she might be in the great halls where the parties were held; indeed, Luciane's young man himself often spent his time with her, and he was the more anxious to do so in that he wanted her advice and assistance in a matter he was engaged on.

He had now become better acquainted with the architect, had talked with him a great deal over his art collection about the history of the past, and from other converse with him, especially when inspecting the chapel, had come to appreciate his talent. The Baron was young and rich, he collected and he wanted to build, his enthusiasm was great but his knowledge small, and he believed he had found in the architect a man with whose help he could achieve several of his ambitions simultaneously. He had told Luciane of his intentions and she had signified her approval, and was in fact highly delighted at the idea, although perhaps the reason was rather that she would have liked to take this young man away from Ottilie – for she thought she had noticed signs of something like affection for her on his part – than any intention of employing his talents. For although he had been very active at her extemporary festivities and had offered his services in preparing this or that performance, she always thought she knew better how to go about these things and, since her ideas were usually commonplace, they could be executed as well by a skilled valet as by the finest artist in the world. When she wanted to celebrate somebody's birthday or some other special occasion, her imagination was incapable of rising above sacrifices on an altar and a crowning with wreaths, whether it was a plaster or a real head that was crowned being a matter of indifference.

The Baron wanted to know what the architect's position in the house was, and Ottilie was able to tell him precisely. She knew Charlotte had already been looking around for a post for him, for if the present company had not arrived he would have left as soon as the chapel was finished, because all building had to stop during the winter, and it was therefore very desirable he should be found a new patron to employ and advance him.

Ottilie's relations with the architect were altogether pure and unaffected. She had enjoyed his pleasant and lively presence as if it were that of an elder brother. Her feelings towards him remained on the quiet passionless level of blood relationship, for there was no room left in her heart for anything else, it was filled entirely with her love for Eduard and only the Divinity which permeates all things could occupy this heart with him.

Meanwhile, the deeper the winter, the wilder the weather, the more impassable the roads, the more attractive did it seem to pass the waning days in such good company. Its numbers altered, but after every ebb the house was soon flooded again. Officers from more distant garrisons began to attend, the cultivated ones to their own great advantage, the coarser ones to the embarrassment of the company; there was also no lack of the non-military; and quite unexpectedly the Count and the Baroness one day came driving up together.

Their presence seemed to create for the first time a real court. The men of quality surrounded the Count and the ladies paid homage to the Baroness. They did not have to wonder for long how they came to be together and in so happy a mood: it was revealed that the Count's wife had died and that a new marriage would be celebrated as soon as propriety allowed. Ottilie recalled their previous visit, she recalled every word they had said about marriage and divorce, uniting and separating, about hope and expectation and privation and renunciation. Then they had both been quite without prospects, now they stood before her so near to their hoped-for happiness, and an involuntary sigh welled up from her heart.

As soon as Luciane heard that the Count was a lover of music, she set about organizing a concert. She wanted them to hear her singing to a guitar. And this is what happened. She was not without skill on the instrument, she had a pleasant voice, but as far as the words were concerned they were as incomprehensible as they usually are when a German young lady sings to a guitar. But everyone agreed she had sung with great expression and the loud applause she received was enough to satisfy her. Only she had a singular piece of misfortune on this occasion. Among the company there was a poet whom she especially hoped to charm over because she wanted him to write one or two songs for and about her, and for that reason the songs she had sung that evening had mostly been his. He was polite about her performance, like everyone else, but from him she had hoped for something more than politeness. She tried several times to get that something more out of him but without any success, until at last in exasperation she sent one of her courtiers to him to sound him as to whether he had not been delighted to hear his wonderful poems sung so wonderfully. 'My poems?' the poet replied in astonishment. 'Excuse me, sir,' he added, 'but I heard nothing but vowel sounds, and I did not hear all of those. However, I can see I do owe it to her to show myself grateful for her kind intentions.' The courtier said no more and refrained from passing on what the poet had said. The latter sought to escape with a few well-turned compliments. Luciane dropped him an obvious hint that she would very much like to possess something he had composed especially for her. He felt like offering her the whole alphabet, so that she could herself construct any panegyric she fancied to fit any available tune, but he refrained because that really would have been too impolite. But she was not to escape from this incident without some injury to her feelings. Shortly afterwards she learned that that very evening the poet had written a beautiful poem to one of Ottilie's favourite tunes, and that the words were more than merely complimentary.

And now Luciane, who like everyone of her type was for ever incapable of distinguishing the profitable from the unprofitable, wanted to try her luck at recitation. She had a good memory but her performance was, not to mince words, unintelligent, and vehement without being passionate. She recited ballads, tales and whatever else is customarily produced at such declamatoria, and she had acquired the unfortunate habit of accompanying whatever she was reciting with gestures, so that what ought to be simply epic and lyrical was unpleasantly confused rather than united with what is dramatic.

The Count, who was a man of discernment, very quickly took the measure of the company, its inclinations, passions and favoured entertainments, and he suggested to Luciane, fortunately or otherwise, a new kind of performance well suited to her personality. 'There are so many well-proportioned people here,' he said, 'who are certainly capable of impersonating the movements and postures of paintings. Have you not yet tried representing real well-known pictures? Such tableaux demand a great deal of troublesome arrangement, I know, but they produce an unbelievable effect.'

Luciane grasped at once that here she would be altogether in her element. Her fine proportions, her full figure, her regular yet individual face, her braided light brown hair, her slim neck, were all as if made for portraiture, and had she known that she looked more beautiful when she stood still than when she walked, since a certain lack of grace became perceptible when she walked, she would have thrown herself into the preparation of these *tableaux vivants* with even greater enthusiasm.

There was now a search for copperplates of famous paintings. The first to be chosen was the Belisarius of Van Dyck. A tall well-built gentleman of mature years was to represent the seated blind general and the architect the sorrowing warrior standing before him (whom he did in fact somewhat resemble). Luciane had, with a sort of modesty, selected for herself the role of the young woman in the background counting out a generous alms from a bag on to the flat of her hand, while an older woman seems to be dissuading her and telling her she is giving too much. Another female character actually giving alms had not been forgotten.

They occupied themselves very seriously with this and other pictures. The Count gave the architect a few hints about how the tableaux ought to be mounted and the architect at once erected a stage for them and looked after the lighting that would be needed. They were already deeply involved in the arrangements before they realized that such an undertaking would demand considerable expenditure and that very many of their requirements were not to be had in the country in the middle of winter. But, so that things should not be delayed, Luciane allowed virtually her entire wardrobe to be cut up to provide material for the costumes which the artists had, arbitrarily enough, assigned to their characters.

The evening arrived and the performance was given before a large audience and to universal approbation. Solemn music heightened the sense of expectancy. The Belisarius inaugurated the proceedings. The figures corresponded so well to their originals, the colours were so happily chosen, the lighting so artistic, you thought you had been transported to another world, the only disturbing factor being a sort of anxiety produced by the presence of real figures instead of painted ones.

The curtain fell but the audience insisted it be raised again several times. They were then entertained by a musical interlude while a picture of a more elevated description was prepared. It was Poussin's famous representation of Esther before Ahasuerus. This time Luciane had given herself a better role. In the figure of the unconscious swooning queen she was able to display all her attractions, and she had prudently selected for the maidens surrounding and supporting her only girls who, while pretty and shapely enough, could not for a moment endure comparison with her. To represent the king, a very Zeus on his golden throne, she had chosen the handsomest and most robust-looking man in the company, so that this tableau really did attain an incomparable perfection.

As the third they had selected the so-called *Instruction paternelle* of Gerald Terborch, and who does not know Wille's wonderful copperplate of this painting? A noble knightly father sits with one leg over the other and seems to be admonishing the daughter standing before him. His daughter, a magnificent figure in a white satin dress which hangs in abundant folds, is seen only from behind, but her whole attitude seems to indicate that she is restraining herself. That the admonition is not violent or shaming can be seen from the father's expression and bearing, and as for the mother, she seems to be concealing a slight embarrassment by looking down into a glass of wine which she is in the act of drinking.

This picture was to be the occasion for Luciane to exhibit herself at her very best. Her braids and the shape of her head and neck were lovely beyond conception, and her figure, of which little was discernible under the mock classical dress worn by modern women, was wonderfully slim and dainty and light, and was shown to the greatest advantage in the older costume; and the architect had taken care to lay the many folds of white satin in the most artistic way, so that this living copy was beyond question inordinately superior to the original picture and provoked universal rapture. The encores were unending, and the wholly natural desire also to see the face of so lovely a creature when you had seen enough of her back view gained the upper hand of the audience to such an extent that, when one impatient wag shouted out the words you sometimes write at the end of a page – 'Tournez s'il vous plaît' – he excited universal applause and approval. But the performers knew too well where their advantage lay, and had grasped the sense of these artistic representations too thoroughly, to yield to this general demand. The shamed-seeming daughter remained motionless without granting the audience a sight of her facial expression, the father remained seated in his admonitory posture, and the mother kept her eyes and nose riveted to the transparent glass, in which, although she appeared to be drinking, the wine never grew less. – A number of little pieces followed, depicting Dutch inn scenes and market scenes, but they need not detain us.

The Count and the Baroness departed, promising to return in the first happy weeks of their approaching marriage, and now, after two weary months, Charlotte hoped to be likewise rid of the remaining company. She was assured of her daughter's happiness once she had put behind her the giddiness of adolescence, for her husband-to-be considered himself the happiest man in the world. Despite his great wealth and the moderation of his temperament, he seemed to be in a strange way flattered by the prospect of possessing the additional advantage of a wife everyone was bound to like. He was so much inclined to relate everything to her, and to himself only through her, that it disturbed him if a newcomer did not at once devote all his attention to her but neglected her and concerned himself with him, which older people especially often did. The architect's future was soon settled: in the New Year he was to follow the Baron and spend the carnival season with him in the city, where Luciane promised herself the greatest delight from a repetition of the beautiful tableaux and from a hundred other things, a delight which seemed all the more certain in that her aunt and her future husband appeared to begrudge none of the expenditure her pleasures demanded.

Now it was time to separate, but it stood to reason that this could not be done in a normal manner. There was on one occasion some rather loud joking to the effect that Charlotte's supplies for the winter would soon be exhausted, whereat the gentleman who had played the role of Belisarius but was himself not exactly poor, carried away by Luciane's attractions, to which he had been paying homage for so long, cried out impulsively: 'Let us all go Dutch! Come to my place and eat me out of house and home too, then let's go on to someone else's place and then to someone else's!' No sooner said than done. Luciane agreed, and the next day they collected their goods together and the whole pack pounced on another estate. There was sufficient room there but fewer comforts and amenities, which gave rise to many improprieties that Luciane found wholly delightful. Their existence grew ever more turbulent and disorderly. *Battue* expeditions in the deep snow and whatever other uncomfortable excursions they could think of were organized, the women were no more permitted to exclude themselves than the men were, and so they went, hunting and riding, sleighing and rioting, from one house to another, until at last they came to the Residenz, where the reports and stories they heard of the entertainments to be found at court and in the city turned their fantasy in that direction and, the aunt having already gone on ahead, drew Luciane and her whole entourage irresistibly out of their old way of life into a new.

From Ottilie's Journal

In the world everyone is accepted as he is, but he has to be something. The troublesome are endured more willingly than the insignificant are suffered.

You can do anything in society except anything that has consequences.

We do not get to know people when they come to us; we have to go to them to learn what they are like.

I find it almost an instinct with us to find fault with visitors and judge them unkindly as soon as they have gone : for we have as it were a right to assess them according to our own standards. Even fair and sensible people can hardly abstain from sharp comment on such occasions.

On the other hand, when we visit other people and see them in their habitual surroundings, in the circumstances of life which are necessary and unavoidable to them, and how they influence or accommodate themselves to their environment, then it requires ill-will and want of understanding to find that ridiculous which ought to seem to us in more than one sense worthy of respect.

The object of what we call deportment and good manners is to attain that which can otherwise be attained only by force or not even by force.

Association with women is the element of good manners.

How can character, the individuality of a human being, be reconciled with good breeding?

It is good breeding which ought first to bring out and emphasize what is individual. Everyone desires significant qualities but no one wants them to be uncomfortable and troublesome.

The greatest advantages, in society as in life in general, are possessed by a cultivated soldier.

Uncultivated warriors are at least faithful to their character and, since good naturedness usually lies concealed behind their violence, you can also get along with them if you have to.

No one is more burdensome than an uncultivated civilian. Since he does not have to do with anything coarse, you have a right to expect refinement of him.

If we live with someone who is sensitive about propriety we are anxious for his sake when anything improper occurs. Thus I always feel for and with Charlotte if anyone rocks back and forth in his chair, because she finds that unendurable.

No one would come into a private room wearing spectacles if he realized that we women at once lose all desire to look at or talk with him.

Familiarity where there should be respect is always ridiculous. No one would throw down his hat when he has hardly taken it off in greeting if he realized how funny that looks.

There is no outward mark of politeness that does not have a profound moral reason. The right education would be that which taught the outward mark and the moral reason together.

Behaviour is a mirror in which everyone exhibits his image.

There is a politeness of the heart; it is related to love. It gives rise to the most comfortable politeness of outward behaviour.

Voluntary dependence is the best position to be in, and how would that be possible without love?

We are never further from our desires than when we imagine we possess what we desire.

No one is more a slave than he who thinks he is free without being so.

You have only to declare yourself free to feel at that moment dependent. If you venture to declare yourself dependent, you feel free.

When another person is vastly superior to you there is no remedy but to love him.

There is something terrible about a superior man of whom fools are proud.

No man, they say, is a hero to his valet. But that is merely because it takes a hero to appreciate a hero. A valet would presumably know how to appreciate a valet.

There is no greater consolation for mediocrity than that genius is not immortal.

The greatest human beings are always linked to their century by some weakness.

People are usually considered more dangerous than they really are.

Fools and clever people are both harmless. It is the half-crazy and the half-wise who are dangerous.

You cannot escape from the world more certainly than through art, and you cannot bind yourself to it more certainly than through art.

Even in the moment of our greatest happiness and that of our greatest misery we need the artist.

Art is concerned with the difficult and the good.

To see the difficult dealt with easily gives us an intuition of the impossible.

The difficulties increase the closer we approach the goal.

Sowing is not so hard as reaping.

CHAPTER SIX

THE great upheaval Charlotte had endured during this visit was compensated for by the fact that she had now come fully to understand her daughter. Her knowledge of the world had been of great assistance to her in encompassing this understanding. It was not the first time she had encountered so unusual a personality, although she had never encountered one at this level of intensity. Yet experience had taught her that such people, disciplined by life, by manifold experience, by family tradition, are capable of attaining a very pleasant and amiable maturity once their egoism has been softened and their erratic energies have been harnessed to some definite purpose. As a mother Charlotte was all the more ready to put up with exhibitions that others might perhaps find unpleasant, since it is right and proper for parents to look for signs of hope where strangers will look only for enjoyment or have no reason to look at all.

Yet even after her daughter's departure another blow, characteristic but unexpected, had still to fall on her. It originated in the bad reputation Luciane had left behind her, arising this time not from what was blameworthy in her behaviour but from what might have been thought praiseworthy. She seemed to have made it a rule to be, not only cheerful with the cheerful, but also sad with the sad and, faithful to the spirit of contradiction, sometimes to annoy the cheerful and cheer the sad. Whenever she visited a family she asked about the sick and infirm who were unable to join the company. She visited them in their room, played the doctor and pressed upon them the powerful physic she kept in the travelling medicine-chest which accompanied her everywhere; whether such a cure failed or succeeded was, as might be imagined, a matter of chance.

In this sort of philanthropy she was altogether inhuman and it was quite impossible to dissuade her from it, since she was firmly convinced she was acting splendidly. But one experiment she made in moral regeneration went seriously wrong and it was this which later gave Charlotte a great deal of trouble, because it had consequences and everybody talked about it. She heard of it only after Luciane had gone; Ottilie, who had been present, was obliged to give her a circumstantial account.

One of the daughters of a respected house had had the misfortune to be responsible for the death of one of her younger brothers and was unable to get over it. She lived in her room quietly and busily occupied and she could bear the sight even of her own family only if they came one by one, for whenever several were there together she at once suspected they were discussing her and her condition. But she would act rationally to each individually and would talk with him for hours.

Luciane had heard of this and she at once secretly resolved that when she came to visit that house she would, as it were, perform a miracle and restore the girl to society. She bore herself more circumspectly than usual, managed to gain access to the mentally sick patient and, as far as one could tell, win her confidence by talking about and playing music. But finally she made a mistake, for, because she wanted as always to produce a sensation, she one evening brought the pale beautiful child, whom she thought she had sufficiently prepared, unexpectedly out into a noisy glittering assemblage; and perhaps this too would have been a success had the company itself not behaved ineptly out of curiosity and apprehension, crowding around the invalid and then avoiding her and making her confused and agitated by whispering and putting their heads together. The highly-strung girl could not endure it. She fled, emitting fearful shrieks that sounded like cries of terror at some approaching demon. The company scattered in alarm and Ottilie was one of those who attended the utterly prostrate girl back to her room.

Luciane had then given the company a stern talking-to, without realizing for a moment that all the guilt in this matter was hers and without letting this failure or other failures deter her from her activities.

The invalid's condition had grown worse from that time on; indeed, she had become so bad that the poor child's parents could no longer keep her in the house but had to put her into a public institution. All Charlotte could do was to try to mitigate the pain her daughter had caused that family by treating them with especially tender consideration. On Ottilie the affair had made a profound impression; she was all the more sorry for the poor girl since she was convinced, as she did not deny to Charlotte too, that she could certainly have been cured had she received more consistent treatment.

And because people do discuss past unpleasantness more than they do pleasant events, there was also talk about a little misunderstanding which had arisen between Ottilie and the architect, and had perplexed her about him, on that evening when he had been unwilling to exhibit his collection although she had requested him so politely. This refusal of his had remained fixed in her soul and she herself could not say why. Her feelings were altogether justified, for what a girl like Ottilie is capable of asking for, a young man like the architect ought not to refuse. But the latter, when she now and then gently reproached him, made fairly acceptable excuses for his behaviour.

'If you knew,' he said, 'how roughly even cultivated people treat works of art you would forgive me if I am disinclined to bring mine out in a crowd. No one seems to know he should take a medallion by the edges. They all finger the most beautiful impressions and the cleanest backgrounds, and pass the most valuable pieces around between forefinger and thumb, as if this were the way to examine artistic objects. Without thinking that a large sheet of paper has to be held with two hands, they reach out with one hand for some invaluable copperplate, some irreplaceable drawing, like some pothouse politician taking hold of a newspaper and by the way he crumples it publishing in advance his judgement on the events of the day. It seems not to occur to anyone that if twenty people handle a work of art like that one after another there will not be very much left for the twenty-first to see.'

'Haven't I too sometimes embarrassed you in that way?' Ottilie asked. 'Haven't I occasionally harmed your treasures without realizing it?'

'Never,' the architect replied, 'never! You could not do it, it would be impossible for you to do it: good-breeding and propriety are inborn in you.'

'Be that as it may,' Ottilie replied, 'it would not be a bad idea in future to insert in books of etiquette, after the chapters on how to eat and drink in company, a detailed chapter on how to treat art collections and behave in museums.'

'Custodians and art lovers would then certainly be happier to show their rareties,' said the architect.

Ottilie had long since forgiven him, but as he seemed to have taken the reproach very much to heart and continued to assure her he really did like showing his collection and was glad to put himself out for his friends, she realized she had hurt his tender susceptibilities and felt a sense of guilt towards him; so that she could not very well directly refuse a request he made her as a consequence of this conversation, although, when she consulted her feelings on the matter, she could not see how she could grant it.

It was like this. He had been extremely hurt that Luciane's jealousy had excluded Ottilie from the picture tableaux; he had also noticed with regret that Charlotte had been able to attend this most splendid part of the social entertainment only now and then, because she had not been feeling well: now he did not want to leave them without expressing his gratitude by organizing to the honour of the one and for the entertainment of the other a far finer representation than the previous ones had been. Perhaps there was another secret motive too, of which he was unconscious: he found it very hard to leave this house and this family, indeed it seemed to him impossible he could ever tear himself away from Ottilie's eyes, for during recent weeks he had virtually lived on their quiet friendly glance.

Christmas was approaching and he suddenly realized that the art of representing pictures by three-dimensional figures had actually originated in the so-called Crib, in the pious representation devoted, during this holy season, to the divine mother and child, and showing how, in their apparent lowliness, they are worshipped firstly by shepherds and then by kings.

He had perfectly visualized how such a picture might be made. He had found a fine healthy boy baby, there would be no shortage of shepherds and shepherdesses, but the thing could not be brought to fruition without Ottilie. The young man had elevated her in his mind to the role of the Mother of God, and if she were to refuse there was, so far as he was concerned, no question but that the undertaking would have to be dropped. Ottilie, half embarrassed by his proposal, referred him to Charlotte. The latter gladly gave him permission and also managed to persuade Ottilie out of her reluctance to assume that sacred figure. The architect laboured day and night so that on Christmas Eve nothing should be lacking.

And day and night it literally was. He had in any case few needs, and Ottilie's presence seemed to serve him in place of all other refreshment: working for her sake, it was as if he needed neither sleep nor food. So that when the solemn evening came all was finished and ready. It had proved possible to assemble a group of wind instruments to play an overture and evoke the desired atmosphere. When the curtain went up Charlotte was genuinely surprised. The picture represented before her had been repeated so often that no new impression was to be expected from it. But in this case there were particular advantages in presenting actuality in the form of a picture. The whole room was closer to night than twilight and yet individual details were not obscure. The incomparable idea of having all the light proceed from the child had been realized by the artist through an ingenious lighting device concealed by the shadowed figures in the foreground, which were illumined only by sidelights. Happy girls and boys were disposed around the scene, their youthful faces sharply illumined from below. And there were angels too, and the light that proceeded from them seemed to be darkened by the divine light and their ethereal bodies seemed heavy and opaque compared with the human-divine body.

Happily the child had fallen asleep in the most charming posture, so that there was no distraction when your glance dwelt on the mother, who had with boundless charm raised part of the child's bands to reveal the treasure hidden within them. It was at this moment that the picture appeared to have been caught and fixed. Dazzled and surprised, the people standing round seemed just to have turned away their eyes and to be in the act of looking back again in happy curiosity, their expressions showing more of amazement and pleasure than admiration and reverence, although these had not been forgotten and their expression had been assigned to a number of older figures.

But Ottilie's figure, gestures, expression and eyes surpassed anything ever depicted by a painter. The sensitive connoisseur, seeing this vision, would have trembled lest anything move, and he would have doubted whether anything could ever again please him so well. Unhappily there was no one present capable of appreciating this effect to the full. Only the architect, who as a tall slim shepherd looked from the side over the heads of those who were kneeling, derived full pleasure from it, although he was not in the best position to see it. And who could describe the expression worn by the new-made Queen of Heaven? The purest humility, the loveliest sense of humbleness before a great undeserved honour, an incomprehensible immeasurable happiness, suffused her features, expressing what she herself felt as well as her conception of the role she was playing.

Charlotte was delighted with the lovely picture, but what affected her most was the child. Tears streamed from her eyes and there came vividly into her mind how she hoped soon to be holding a similar dear creature in her arms.

The curtain had been lowered, in part to give the performers some relief, in part to allow a change of scene. The artist had intended to transform the first picture of night and lowliness into one of daylight and glory, and to that end had set up on all sides a vast increase in lighting, which was being lit during this interval.

Ottilie had until then been greatly relieved that, apart from Charlotte and one or two other members of the household, no one had witnessed this pious mummery. She was therefore somewhat taken aback to hear, during the interval, that a stranger had arrived and that Charlotte had welcomed him into the hall. No one could tell her who he was. She wanted to cause no disturbance, so she raised no objection. Lights and lamps were burning and a boundless brightness surrounded her. The curtain went up and presented the audience with a surprising view: the scene was all light, and in place of the now abolished shadows there remained only colours which, by being skilfully selected, produced a moderating influence on the light. From beneath her long eyelashes Ottilie saw a man sitting next to Charlotte. She could not make out who it was, but she thought she recognized the voice of the young schoolmaster from the boarding-school. A strange feeling took possession of her. How much had happened since she had last heard that voice! The succession of joys and sorrows she had experienced passed like lightning through her soul and awoke in her the question whether she dared admit and confess it all to him. 'And how little worthy you are to appear before him in this sacred form,' she thought. 'And how strange it must be for him to see you thus disguised.' With a celerity with which nothing else can be compared, feeling and thought reacted one against the other within her. Her heart beat fast and her eyes filled with tears, while she strove to stay as still as a statue; and how glad she was when the boy began to stir and the artist found himself under the necessity of signalling for the curtain to be lowered.

If the painful feeling of not being able to hurry to greet a worthy friend had been added during these last moments to Ottilie's other sensations, she now found herself in an even more embarrassing predicament. Should she go to meet him in this strange costume and attire? Ought she to change? She did not hesitate, she did the latter, and in the meantime tried to collect and calm herself, and she succeeded in regaining her composure only when she was at last able to greet the new arrival in her ordinary clothes.

CHAPTER SEVEN

SINCE the architect had the best interests of his patronesses at heart, it was pleasant for him, now he at last had to leave, to know they were in the good company of the estimable schoolmaster; yet, since he was also interested in retaining their favour himself, he found it a little painful to see himself so soon and, as his modesty would have it seem, so well, indeed so completely replaced. Hitherto he had procrastinated, now he was eager to be gone : for what he would have to put up with after he had left he at least did not want to have to endure while he was still there.

In order to cheer him a little, the ladies made him a farewell gift of a waistcoat; he had long seen them both at work knitting it and had felt a silent envy of the unknown fortunate man for whom it was intended. Such a present is the pleasantest an affectionate man can receive : for when he thinks of the tireless play of the lovely fingers that made it he cannot help flattering himself that in so long drawn out a labour the heart too cannot have been altogether indifferent.

The women now had a new man to look after towards whom they felt well-disposed and who they wanted to feel comfortable while he was with them. The female sex inwardly cherishes its own unalterable interest from which nothing in the world can sunder it; in external social affairs, on the other hand, it is happy to let itself be easily swayed by the man of the moment, and thus, by what it accepts and what it rejects, by obstinacy and complaisance, it is really the female sex which directs the regime from which no man in the polite world dares to withdraw.

If the architect had exercised his talents for the entertainment and profit of the ladies more or less as he pleased, and the business and entertainment of the household had been conducted from this point of view, the presence of the schoolmaster very soon brought about a change in their mode of life. His great gift was to speak well and to discourse on human affairs, particularly the education of the young. And thus there developed a new way of living perceptibly different from the old, and it was the more different in that the schoolmaster did not altogether approve of what they had previously been exclusively engaged in.

Of the *tableau vivant* which had greeted him on his arrival he said nothing. But when he was complacently shown the church and the chapel and the things pertaining to them, he was unable to refrain from voicing his opinion. 'So far as I am concerned,' he said, 'I do not in the least like this assimilation of the sacred and the sensual, this compounding of them together. Nor do I like it that certain particular rooms have to be set aside, consecrated and adorned for the preservation and enjoyment of pious feelings. The sense of the divine ought to be accessible to us everywhere, even in the most commonplace surroundings; it can accompany us wherever we are and hallow every place into a temple. I like to see family prayers conducted in the room where the family usually eats and assembles for social occasions and dancing. The highest excellence in man is without form and one should beware of giving it any form other than that of the noble deed.'

Charlotte, who already had a general knowledge of his outlook and quickly discovered more of it in detail, at once gave him an opportunity to be active in his own sphere by having the garden brigade, which the architect had assembled just before his departure, marched into the great hall. They looked very fine as they came in with arms swinging and dressed in their bright clean uniforms. The schoolmaster inspected them after his own fashion and by questioning and talking with them had very soon brought out the particular temperament and abilities of each boy; moreover, without appearing to do so he had in the course of less than an hour given them some real instruction.

'However do you do it?' Charlotte asked as the boys filed out. 'I listened very closely, there was nothing exceptional about what you discussed, yet I really do not know how I would go about getting them to talk so sensibly in such a short time.'

'Perhaps one should make a secret of the tricks of one's trade,' replied the schoolmaster, 'but I cannot hide from you the quite simple rule which will enable you to achieve this and much more. Take some subject, some matter, some idea – call it what you will. Take a really firm grip on it. Be clear about it in your own mind in all its parts. It will then be easy, by talking to a group of children, to discover what they already know of it and what they still have to learn. No matter how inappropriate their answers are or however far from the point they wander, so long as your next question draws their minds and thoughts back to the subject in hand, so long as you do not let them draw you away from it, the children are bound in the end to think and understand only what and in the way the teacher wants them to. The greatest mistake a teacher can make is to let his pupils draw him away from the point, is to be incapable of keeping them fixed to the subject he is at that moment treating. Try doing it yourself, and you will find it very interesting.'

'How neat,' said Charlotte: 'good teaching is, it seems, exactly the reverse of good breeding. In society one ought not to dwell too long on anything, and in school the first commandment is to resist all distraction.'

'Variety without distraction would be the best motto for life and learning, if only this laudable balance were not so hard to achieve,' said the schoolmaster, and would have gone on had Charlotte not called him to watch the boys again, as their gay procession was just then passing across the courtyard. He said he was glad to see they had put the boys into uniform. 'Men,' he said, 'ought to wear uniform from their youth up, because they have to get used to acting together, to mixing with their own kind, to obeying *en masse* and to working within the whole. Any kind of uniform, moreover, encourages a military attitude of mind, as it does a smarter and more straightforward bearing, and in any case every boy is a born soldier: you have only to look at the games they play, their fighting and mock battles.'

'So on the other hand you will not disapprove,' said Ottilie, 'when you see I do not dress my girls all alike. I hope that when I present them to you, what you will find delightful is the mixture of colours.'

'I approve very heartily,' the schoolmaster replied. 'Women ought all to be dressed differently, each according to her own style and nature, so that each may learn to perceive what looks well on her. A more important reason is this: because women are destined to stand alone and act alone their whole life long.'

'That seems to me very paradoxical,' Charlotte replied. 'Surely we women hardly ever live for ourselves.'

'Oh yes you do!' replied the schoolmaster. 'With respect to other women you certainly do. Think of a woman as a lover, as a bride, as wife, housewife and mother: always she stands isolate, always she is alone and wants to be alone. Yes, even the vain woman is in the same case. Every woman by her nature excludes every other woman: for every woman is required to do everything the whole sex is required to do. With men it is otherwise. A man desires another man: if there were no other man he would create him: a woman could live an eternity without its occurring to her to bring forth her own kind.'

'If you put the truth in a strange way,' said Charlotte, 'what is strange finally appears true. Let us extract what is best from your remarks and still, as women, hold together

208

with women, and cooperate together too, so as not to allow the men too great advantages over us. Indeed, you must not take it amiss if we feel a little malicious pleasure, as we must do all the more after this, when the gentlemen too fail to get on especially well together.'

The wise schoolmaster now examined with great application the way in which Ottilie handled her little pupils and indicated his decided approval. 'You are quite right,' he said, 'to teach your charges only what is of immediate applicability. Cleanliness makes children glad to take some pride in themselves, and the whole battle is won if they can be inspired to do what they have to do with cheerfulness and self-confidence.'

He found, moreover, to his great satisfaction that nothing had been done for the sake of appearance, but everything was directed towards the most essential necessities. 'In how few words,' he exclaimed, 'might the whole business of education be summed up if anyone had ears to hear.'

'Would you not like to try if I have ears to hear?' Ottilie asked amiably.

'Very gladly,' said the schoolmaster, 'only you mustn't give me away. Boys should be educated to be servants and girls to be mothers, and all will be well.'

'The ladies could well be willing to be educated as mothers,' said Ottilie, 'since, even if they are not mothers, they always have to prepare themselves for being attendants of some kind; but our young men would certainly consider themselves too good to be servants, since it is easy to see each of them regards himself as more capable of commanding than serving.'

'And therefore let us keep silent,' said the schoolmaster. 'We flatter ourselves when we embark on life, but life does not flatter us. For how many people would allow of their own free will what they are finally compelled to allow? But let us leave these reflections, which here do not concern us.

'You are fortunate in being able to apply to your pupils a

correct method of instruction. If your youngest girls occupy themselves with dolls and patch together a few rags for them, if older sisters look after the younger and all the members of the household take care of one another, then the further step into adult life is not a great one, and a girl so brought up will find with her husband what she left behind with her parents.

'But in the cultivated classes the task is very involved. We have to take account of more elevated, more delicate, more refined circumstances, and we have especially to take account of social relationships. We others, therefore, have to cultivate our pupils in an outward-looking direction; that is unavoidable and necessary, and it can turn out very well provided one does not go too far in the process: for in seeking to educate children for a wider circle of life one can easily push them out into boundless spheres without keeping in view the real requirements of their inner nature. Here lies the task of education which educators are, to a greater or less degree, succeeding or failing in.

'I am concerned at many of the things we provide our girls with at the school, because experience tells me of how little future use it will be to them. How much is not at once discarded, how much not consigned to oblivion, as soon as a woman finds herself a housewife and mother!

'Nonetheless, since I have dedicated myself to this work, I cannot renounce the devout desire one day to succeed, in company with a faithful companion, in cultivating in my pupils all that which they will need when they go off to lead their own lives, and to be able to say of them that in this sense their education is complete. A fresh education then begins, of course, an education which is renewed every year of our lives, if not by us ourselves then by the circumstances in which we live.'

How true Ottilie thought this observation! What had an unanticipated passion not taught her in the year just gone!

What tests and trials did she not see ahead of her even if she looked only to the most immediate future !

It was not without premeditation that the young man had mentioned a companion, a wife : for, all his modesty notwithstanding, he could not forbear to indicate in an indirect way what his intentions were; indeed, circumstances and events had inspired him to employ this visit to advance a few steps nearer to his goal.

The headmistress of the boarding-school was no longer young and she had been casting about among her colleagues for someone to enter into a partnership with her; and she had finally settled on her young assistant, whom she had every reason to trust : she had proposed to him that he should continue to direct the establishment with her, should act in it as if it were his own, and after her death become her heir and sole inheritor. The main consideration seemed to be for him to find a wife willing to share this existence. He secretly had Ottilie in mind and in his heart, and his doubts on this head had to some extent been stilled by a number of fortunate events. Luciane had left the school and it would now be easier for Ottilie to return; it was true that something of her affair with Eduard had become known but, like other similar episodes, this too was not taken very seriously, and it might even contribute to bringing Ottilie back. But no decision would have been made, no steps taken, had an unexpected visit not, in this case too, supplied a definite stimulus. Because the appearance of strong individuals in any circle can never fail to produce consequences.

The Count and the Baroness, who, because almost everyone is perplexed about the education of their children, often found themselves asked about the merits of this or that school, had decided to find out all about this one, of which they had heard so many good reports, and in their new circumstances they were able to conduct such an investigation together. But the Baroness had something else in view too. During her last stay with Charlotte she had had a thorough and circumstantial discussion with her about everything concerning Eduard and Ottilie. She insisted again and again that Ottilie must be sent away. She tried to inspire in her the courage to take this step, for Charlotte was still fearful of Eduard's threats. They talked over the various solutions to their problem, and when the boarding-school was mentioned they also spoke of the young schoolmaster's affection for Ottilie, and the Baroness became all the firmer in her resolve to undertake the proposed visit.

She arrived and met the schoolmaster, and they inspected the establishment and talked of Ottilie. The Count, too, was glad to talk of her since he had come to know her better during his latest visit. She had drawn closer to him, indeed he had attracted her, because she thought to learn through his informed conversation what had hitherto been quite unknown to her. And, as in Eduard's company she had forgotten the world, so in that of the Count the world had for the first time come to seem to her desirable. All attraction is mutual. Ottilie inspired in the Count such an affection that he was glad to regard her as a daughter. Here too, for a second time and more dangerously than the first time, she was in the Baroness's way. Who knows what this lady might not have plotted against her in the days when her passions were more vehement! Now it was sufficient to reduce the threat to wives which she constituted by getting her married.

She therefore gently but effectively instigated the schoolmaster to arrange a little visit to the mansion, so that he could without delay hasten the accomplishment of the plans and the achievement of the desires of which he made no secret to the lady.

It was thus with the full approval of the headmistress that he undertook his journey and cherished within him the liveliest hopes. He knows Ottilie is not unfavourably inclined towards him; and if there existed some inequality of rank between them, the disposition of the age would make light of that. The Baroness had, moreover, given him to understand that Ottilie would always be poor. To be related to a wealthy house, she had said, was of no help to anyone: for, even in the case of the largest fortune, one would have a conscience about depriving of any considerable sum those who, by virtue of closer relationship, seemed to possess greater right to the property.

And, indeed, it is a strange fact that men very seldom exercise the great privilege of disposing of their goods even after they are dead to the benefit of their favourites but, seemingly out of respect for tradition, favour only those who would get their property even if they had no will in the matter.

On the journey he felt that he and Ottilie were altogether equal. A friendly reception raised his hopes. It is true he found Ottilie less frank and open with him than formerly, but she was at the same time more grown-up, more cultivated and, if you will, more communicative than he had previously known her. She confided to him much that had a bearing on his profession of schoolmaster, but when he thought to advance his own objective in being there a certain inner reserve always held him back.

But one day Charlotte gave him an opportunity by saying in Ottilie's presence: 'Well, now you have examined pretty well everything going on in my circle, what do you think of Ottilie? You need not be afraid to speak before her.'

The schoolmaster thereupon told, with a great deal of discernment and in a quiet tone, how he had found Ottilie changed very much to her advantage in respect of a more relaxed manner, an easier conversation and a greater insight into worldly affairs, which manifested themselves more in her actions than her words, but that he believed it would be very advantageous to her to return to the school for a time, so as to acquire permanently and thoroughly, in proper regular sequence, that which the world taught only partially, to the confusion rather than the satisfaction of the pupil, and indeed sometimes taught only when it was too late. He had no wish to expatiate on the subject: Ottilie herself best knew out of how coherent a programme of lessons she had been torn.

Ottilie could not deny the truth of what he said, but neither could she confess her feelings on hearing it, because she hardly knew how to interpret them. All the world seemed to her coherent when she thought of the man she loved, and she could not see how anything could be coherent without him.

Charlotte responded to this proposition with prudent affability. She said both she and Ottilie had long desired a return to the boarding-school, only at the present time she found so dear a friend and helper indispensable to her; later on, however, she would raise no objection if it was still Ottilie's desire to go back for as long as was needed to complete what she had begun and follow through to the end what had been interrupted.

The schoolmaster joyfully accepted this offer; Ottilie could say nothing against it, although she shuddered at the mere thought. Charlotte, on the other hand, was thinking to gain time; she hoped that Eduard would meanwhile have returned as a happy father and then, she was convinced, all would be well and Ottilie too would somehow be taken care of.

After a weighty conversation which has given all the participants something to think over, there usually supervenes a pause or standstill which looks very much like general embarrassment. They wandered up and down the room, the schoolmaster browsed among the books, and eventually came upon the folio which had been left lying about since Luciane's visit. When he saw it contained nothing but monkeys he at once slammed it again. This incident may nonetheless have given rise to a conversation, the traces of which we find in Ottilie's journal.

From Ottilie's Journal

How can anyone bring himself to expend such care on depicting horrid monkeys! It is debasing simply to regard them as animals, but it is really more malicious to succumb to the temptation of seeking in them the likeness of people you know.

It positively requires a certain perverseness to want to devote one's time to caricatures and grotesques. I have our good schoolmaster to thank that I have never been plagued with natural history; I could never take kindly to worms and beetles.

He has now admitted that he feels the same way. 'We should know nothing of nature,' he said, 'except that of it with which we are in immediate living contact. With every tree around us which blossoms, bears leaves and brings forth fruit, with every shrub we pass by, with every blade of grass upon which we tread, we have a true relationship, they are our genuine compatriots. The birds which hop upon our branches and sing amid our foliage belong to us, they speak to us from our youth up and we learn to understand their language. Consider whether every strange creature torn from its natural surroundings does not produce in us an uneasy feeling, dulled only by familiarity. A variegated noisy life is needed to make monkeys, parrots and Moors endurable around you.'

Sometimes when I have been seized by curiosity to see such exotic things I have envied the traveller who can behold these wonders in an everyday living relationship with other wonders. But then he too suffers a change. You cannot walk among palmtrees with impunity, and your sentiments must surely alter in a land where elephants and tigers are at home.

Only that naturalist is worthy of respect who is capable of describing and depicting the strange and exotic together with its own locality, with all its environs, in its own proper element. How I should like to hear Humboldt* on this subject.

* Alexander von Humboldt (1769–1859), naturalist, greatly admired by Goethe, of whom he became a close friend.

A museum of natural history can seem like an Egyptian tomb where various animal and vegetable idols stand around embalmed. It may be very well for a priestly caste to tend such things in a mysterious twilight, but they ought not to be introduced into general education, the less so in that they can easily push aside more immediate and worthier things.

The teacher who can rouse our feelings by a single good deed, a single good work of art, achieves more than one who passes on to us in form and name whole rows of inferior natural creatures, for the only result of that is what we know anyway, namely that the human form bears uniquely the image of the divine.

The individual is free to occupy himself with whatever attracts him, with whatever gives him pleasure, with whatever seems to him useful: but the proper study of mankind is man.

CHAPTER EIGHT

Few are capable of concerning themselves with the immediate past. Either the present holds us forcibly or we lose ourselves in the distant past and try to call back and restore the totally vanished, whatever it may have been. Even in great and wealthy families which owe a great deal to their ancestors it is usual to think more of the grandfather than the father.

Such were the reflections which thrust themselves upon our young schoolmaster as, on one of those beautiful days when departing winter deceives us that spring has already come, he had been walking through the ancient great walled garden and admiring the avenues of tall lime-trees and the formal plots which were the work of Eduard's father. They had flourished wonderfully in the fashion desired by him who had planted them and, now they were ready to be appreciated and enjoyed, no one mentioned them any longer; they were hardly ever visited and all the enthusiasm and expenditure was directed another way, out into the unenclosed open country.

He remarked as much to Charlotte on his return, and she was inclined to agree with him. 'As life draws us along,' she replied, 'we think we are acting of our own volition, ourselves choosing what we shall do and what we shall enjoy; but when we look more closely we see they are only the intentions and inclinations of the age which we are being compelled to comply with.'

'To be sure,' said the schoolmaster; 'and who can withstand the current of his environment? Time moves on, and sentiments, opinions, prejudices and fancies move on with it. If a son's youth happens to coincide with an age of transition, you may be sure he will have nothing in common with his father.

If the father lived in a period in which there was a desire to acquire property and to secure, limit and enclose it and to fortify one's pleasure in it through seclusion from the world, then the son will try to expand, open out, spread abroad and unlock the gates.'

'Whole ages are like this father and son you have described,' said Charlotte. 'We can scarcely imagine the days in which every little town had to have its walls and moats, every manor-house was built in the middle of a marsh, and the meanest castle was accessible only by a drawbridge. Even the bigger cities are now taking down their walls, the moats even of the castles of princes are being filled in, the towns are now only market-towns without defences, and when you travel around and see all this you might think universal peace had been established and the Golden Age to be at hand. If we are to enjoy our gardens they have to look like open country; there should be no evidence of art or constraint, we want to breathe the air in absolute freedom. Do you think, my friend, that we could go back from this state of things to another, earlier state?'

'Why not?' the schoolmaster replied. 'Every state of things has its difficulties, the restricted as much as the free. The latter presupposes superfluity and leads to prodigality and waste. Let us stick to your example, which is a sufficiently striking one. As soon as shortages occur, self-restriction at once returns. Men who are compelled to make use of their land again erect walls around their gardens to secure to themselves its produce. Out of this there gradually arises a new outlook on things. Utility again gets the upper hand, and even he who possesses much finally comes to feel obliged to put everything he owns to use. Believe me, it is quite possible that your son will turn his back on all your parklands and retire again behind the grave walls and among the tall lime-trees of his grandfather.'

Charlotte was delighted to hear a son foretold her and

for the sake of that she pardoned the schoolmaster his somewhat unamiable prophecy of what might one day happen to
her beloved park. She therefore replied: 'Neither of us is
old enough to have experienced such a conflict more than
once; but if we think back to our early youth and remember
what older people were then complaining about, and remember too the history of cities and nations, then what you say
can hardly be gainsaid. But ought we not to do something to
halt this natural process? Ought we not to be able to bring
about some accord between father and son, parents and
children? You have been kind enough to prophesy a son for
me: does he have to stand opposed to his father, destroy
what his parents have built up, instead of completing and
enhancing it by continuing with it in their spirit?'

'There is indeed a rational remedy for this,' the schoolmaster replied, 'although it is seldom applied. The father must
raise his son to the status of partner, he must let him work
and plant as an equal, and he must allow him the same freedom in harmless caprice as he allows himself. The activities
of the one can be interwoven with those of the other instead
of being patched on to them. A young shoot is easily grafted
on to an old stem, a grown branch cannot be grafted at all.'

The schoolmaster was glad to have chanced to say something that pleased Charlotte and thus fortified her goodwill
towards him at the moment when he saw he would have to
be saying farewell. He had already been too long away from
the school, but he could not bring himself to return there
until he had become thoroughly convinced that Charlotte's
approaching confinement would first have to come and go
before he could hope for any decision about Ottilie. He then
accommodated himself to this state of things, and with these
hopes and prospects in view took himself back to his headmistress.

Charlotte's confinement drew near. She kept more to her
own rooms, and her own private circle of women which had

collected about her kept her company. Ottilie looked after the household and scarcely dared think what she was doing. It is true she had resigned herself utterly; she desired to go on being as useful as she could to Charlotte, to the child, to Eduard; only she could not see how that was going to be possible. Only by doing her duty every day could she save herself from utter confusion.

A son was successfully brought into the world and the women all affirmed he was the image of his father. Ottilie alone could secretly see no resemblance when she went to congratulate the mother and to welcome the child with all her heart. Charlotte had already sorely missed the presence of her husband during the arrangements for her daughter's wedding; now the father was not to be present at the birth of his son either, he was not to decide on the name by which the boy would be known.

The first of all their friends to put in an appearance to offer congratulations was Mittler, who had made special arrangements to be informed of the event as soon as it had happened. He entered upon the scene looking extremely pleased and complaisant. Far from concealing his triumph that Ottilie was still there, he proclaimed it to Charlotte, and assured her she need have no further worries about immediate problems and necessities, since he was the man to take care of them all. The baptism, he said, ought not to be long delayed. The ancient parson, who already had one foot in the grave, would with his blessing cement together past and future; the child ought to be called Otto: he could bear no other name than the name of his father and his father's friend.

It required the determined importunity of this gentleman to set aside the hundred-and-one misgivings, objections, hesitations, falterings, knowings-better and knowings-otherwise, vacillatings, opinionizings and changings and re-changings of opinion that eventuated; since, on such occasions as this, when one misgiving arises, new misgivings keep arising out of it, and by trying to satisfy everybody and settle everything you always annoy somebody and unsettle something.

Mittler took upon himself all the birth announcements and invitations to stand godparent; they were to be prepared immediately, for he was highly concerned to acquaint the rest of the world – including that part of it given to malicious gossip – with a happy occurrence he considered so significant for the family. And indeed the passionate events which had taken place had not eluded the notice of the public, which in any case lives in the conviction that everything that happens happens only so that it shall have something to talk about.

The baptismal solemnities were to be, although worthy of the occasion, brief and unostentatious. They assembled and Ottilie and Mittler were, as witnesses, to hold the child. The ancient clergyman, sustained by the sexton, advanced with slow tread. The prayers were spoken, the child was laid in Ottilie's arms, and when she looked affectionately down at him she was not a little startled to see in his open eyes the very image of her own. Such a resemblance must have struck and surprised anyone who looked at them. Mittler, who next received the child, was likewise taken aback, but what he saw was an incredible similarity between its features and those of the Captain; he could not remember ever having seen anything of the kind before in the whole course of his experience.

The infirmity of the good old parson had prevented him from accompanying the baptism with anything more than the bare liturgy. But while this was going forward, Mittler, full of the occasion, had called to mind his own former sacerdotal functions, and he was in any event inclined on any occasion to start composing speeches in his head and to imagine himself delivering them. In the present circumstances he found it the harder to contain himself in that he was surrounded by a small congregation composed exclusively of friends. Consequently, towards the conclusion of the proceedings he commenced complaisantly to substitute himself for the officiating clergyman and to expatiate in a hearty address on his duties as godfather and on the hopes he entertained for the child, upon which hopes and duties he dwelt all the longer in that he thought he saw in Charlotte's contented expression a sign of her approval.

That the good old man would have very much liked to sit down escaped the tireless speaker, but what escaped him even more completely was that he was about to produce an even worse evil: for after he had impressively described the relationship of everyone present to the child, and had thereby put Ottilie's self-control through something of a test, he finally turned to the ancient parson with the words: 'And you, reverend elder, can now say with Simeon: Lord, now lettest thou thy servant depart in peace, for mine eyes have seen the salvation of this house.'

He was launched on a resounding peroration when, holding the child out to the old man, he saw him apparently bend forward to receive him but then suddenly sink back. He was only just caught as he fell and taken to a stall, where, all that could be done for him notwithstanding, he had to be pronounced dead.

To see birth and death, coffin and cradle, juxtaposed so closely, and to see this terrible antithesis not in imagination but with their own eyes, was a hard lesson for those who were standing by, and it was the harder in that it was so sudden. Ottilie alone regarded the dead man, whose features still retained the amiable expression which characterized them, with a kind of envy. The life of her soul had been killed, why should her body remain alive?

If the disagreeable events of the day had led her often and often to meditate on transcience, on parting and loss, she was granted, as consolation, strange nocturnal visions which assured her of her beloved's existence and cheered and fortified her own. When at evening she had lain down to rest, and was hovering still in that sweet sensation between sleep and wake, it seemed to her as if she were gazing into a bright yet softly illumined room. There she saw Eduard, quite clearly, dressed, not as she had seen him in life, but in the garb of a soldier, and each time his figure held a different posture, always a natural one, with nothing fanciful or grotesque in it: standing, walking, lying, riding. The figure, delineated to the smallest detail, moved before her of its own volition without her having to do anything, without her having to want it or to make an effort of imagination. Sometimes she saw him surrounded by shadowy forms, and especially by something that moved that was darker than the bright background, but she could hardly distinguish what they were, they might be people or horses or trees or mountains. Usually she fell asleep while watching these visions, and when she awoke on the morrow after a peaceful night she was refreshed and comforted: she felt convinced Eduard was still alive and that she was still his and he was still hers.

CHAPTER NINE

SPRING had come, later but also more suddenly and joyfully than usual. Ottilie now found in the garden the fruit of her foresight: all was budding and blossoming and putting out leaf in its proper season; much that lay ready under the glass of greenhouses now reached out towards the world of nature outside, which had at last grown active, and everything that had to be done was now no longer mere hopeful labour but a joy and a delight.

But she had to console the gardener for many a gap in the rows of potted plants and the spoiled symmetry of the tree-tops caused by Luciane's ungoverned behaviour. She encouraged him by saying that all would soon be restored, but he had too deep a feeling for his craft and too pure an idea of it for these consolations to be of much effect. Just as the gardener must not let himself be distracted by other interests and inclinations, so the peaceful progress of the plant towards lasting or transient perfection must not be interrupted. Plants are like self-willed people with whom you can do anything provided you handle them properly. A tranquil eye, an un-ruffled consistency in doing, each season of the year, each hour of the day, precisely what needs to be done, are perhaps required of nobody more than they are of the gardener.

The good man possessed these qualities to a high degree, which was another reason Ottilie so enjoyed working with him; but for some time he had found it impossible to practise his real vocation with any sense of pleasure. For although he knew perfectly well how to undertake everything demanded by an orchard or a kitchen garden, and was equal to the older type of ornamental garden – as indeed a man will succeed better with this task or that – and although in the management of an orangery, of flower-bulbs, of carnation and auricula plants, he could have challenged nature herself, yet the new ornamental trees and fashionable flowers were still to some extent strange to him, and of the endless field of botany that time was bringing to light and of the strange names buzzing about in it he had a kind of awe that put him out of humour. What the Lord and Lady had started to bring in the previous year he regarded all the more as useless expenditure and wasteful squandering in that he had to see many a costly plant thrown away and was on no good terms with the market-gardeners, who, as he thought, treated him with something less than perfect honesty.

After experimenting in various ways he had evolved for himself a sort of programme in respect of all this, a programme in which Ottilie encouraged him all the more in that it really depended on Eduard's returning – in this matter, as in many others, his absence was felt more and more with every day that passed.

As the plants now put down ever more roots and put out ever more branches, Ottilie too felt more rooted to this ground. Just a year ago she had come there as a stranger, as a creature of no importance; how much had she not acquired since that time! But how much, alas, had she not since that time lost again! She had never been so rich and never been so poor. Her feelings of wealth and poverty alternated one with the other with every passing minute, they met and crossed one another in the depths of her soul, and she knew no way out but to attack whatever task lay immediately to hand with sympathetic, with passionate involvement.

That anything particularly dear to Eduard also exercised the strongest claim on her attention may well be imagined; indeed, why should she not hope that he himself, soon returned, would remark with gratitude the loving care she had devoted to him in his absence?

But she was also called upon to work on his behalf in quite

another direction. The principal task she had undertaken was to look after the child, whom she could care for the more completely in that it had been decided to bottle-feed him and not put him out to nurse. In that fair season he was to enjoy the open air, and so she liked best to take him out herself and to carry the sleeping child among the flowers and blossoms that were one day to smile upon his childhood, among the young shrubs and plants that seemed by their own infancy to be destined to grow up with him. When she looked about her she was conscious of how grand and rich a heritage the child was born to, for almost everything the eye could see was one day to belong to him. How desirable it was then that he should grow up before the eyes of his father and mother and be the confirmation of a union renewed and happy.

Ottilie felt all this so genuinely, she thought of it as actually coming to pass, and without considering her own situation in the slightest. Under that clear heaven, in that bright sunshine, it suddenly became clear to her that, in order to become perfect, her love would have to become utterly unselfish; indeed, there were moments when she believed she had already attained this height. She desired only Eduard's welfare; she believed she was capable of renouncing him, even of never seeing him again, if only she knew he was happy. But for herself she was quite decided never to belong to another.

That autumn would be as glorious as spring was already assured. Every kind of so-called summer flower, all those which cannot cease blooming in autumn and go on bravely growing in face of the cold, asters especially, had been sown in the greatest abundance and, planted out everywhere, were to make a firmament of stars over the earth.

We are in the habit of copying into our journals good ideas we have read or striking remarks we have heard, but if we would also take the trouble to transfer there specific observations, original views, fleeting witty phrases from the letters we receive from our friends, we should acquire a very ample collection. We preserve letters, never to read them again; we finally destroy them one day for reasons of discretion, and so the fairest and most immediate breath of life vanishes for us and for others. I am going to resolve to make good this omission.

So once more the year's tale is starting again from the beginning. Now we are once more, thanks be to God, at its prettiest chapter. Violets and lilies-of-the-valley are like the chapter headings or vignettes. It always gives us pleasure when we come upon them again in the book of life.

We reproach the poor, especially the youthful poor, if they stand about the streets begging. Do we not notice that they immediately become active as soon as there is something to do? Nature has hardly disclosed its treasures before the children have started making a business of them; there is no longer any begging, each of them offers you a bouquet; he has gathered it before you were awake, and he looks at you with as smiling a face as does the gift he offers. No one puts on the appeal of wretchedness when he feels he has some right to make a request.

Why is the year sometimes so long, sometimes so short, why does it seem so short and yet in retrospect so long? That is how the past year appeared to me, and nowhere more strikingly than in the garden: what is transient and what endures are involved one with another. And yet nothing is so fleeting but it leaves some trace of itself behind.

We can take pleasure even in winter. We feel we can stretch ourselves more freely when the trees stand before us so spectral and transparent. They are nothing, but they likewise conceal nothing. But when buds and blossom come we grow impatient for the full leaf, for the landscape to take on bodily form, and the tree to lean towards us like a living being.

Everything perfect of its kind must transcend its kind: it must become something other, something incomparable. In many of its notes the nightingale is still a bird; then it rises above its type and seems to want to show all the feathered tribe what singing really is.

A life without love, without the presence of the beloved, is only a *comédie à tiroir*. You pull out one drawer and shut it again and hurry on to the next. Everything, even the good and significant, hangs together very poorly. You must everywhere be starting again from the beginning and would be glad to end anywhere.

CHAPTER TEN

CHARLOTTE, for her part, was feeling happy and fit. She found great joy in the hearty boy, whose form and features, which promised so much for the future, were the occupation of her eyes and heart every hour of the day. Through him she found a new and different contact with the world and with her home; her old energetic industry revived; wherever she looked she saw how much had been done over the past year and rejoiced over it. Inspired by a curious desire, she went up to the moss-hut with Ottilie and the child, and when she laid him on the little table as upon a domestic altar and re-garded the two empty places, she thought of the times that had been and there arose in her new hope for herself and for Ottilie.

Young women perhaps look modestly around, quietly sizing up this young man or that to see whether they would like him for a husband; but whoever has to make provision for a daughter or a young female ward casts about in a wider sphere. And that was what Charlotte had in mind at that moment, for it seemed to her not impossible that Ottilie might marry the Captain, for had they not sat together side by side in this very hut? It was not unknown to her that that pros-pect of an advantageous marriage had failed to materialize.

Charlotte climbed further up and Ottilie carried the child. Charlotte was sunk deep in thought. Even on dry land it was possible to be shipwrecked; to recover from it as quickly as possible was a fine and praiseworthy thing. Life was, after all, only a matter of profit and loss. How many plans went awry ! How often one was diverted from one's chosen course ! How often we were turned aside from a clearly envisaged goal so as to achieve a higher ! The traveller on his way breaks a wheel and is greatly annoyed by it, yet through this unpleasant accident he makes the most agreeable connections and acquaintances, which then go on to influence his entire life. Fate grants us our desires but it does so in its own fashion, so that it can give us something over and above what we desire.

It was with these and similar reflections that Charlotte was occupied as she climbed to the top of the hill, where their truth was fully confirmed. For the view of the surrounding country was far finer than could ever have been imagined. Every distracting petty feature had been removed, every good feature of the landscape produced by nature and the passing of time stepped unobstructedly forth, and already the young vegetation intended to fill out certain gaps and bind pleasingly together the separate parts of the terrain was putting on green.

The pavilion itself was practically habitable; the view, especially from the upper rooms, was as varied as could be desired. The longer you looked, the more beautiful things you discovered. What changing effects must the different times of the day, the sun and the moon, here produce! How delightful it would be to stay here, and how quickly the desire to construct and create reawoke in Charlotte now she found all the rough work completed! A joiner, an upholsterer, a painter who knew how to handle stencils and gilding: that was all that was needed, and soon the building was ready for use. Cellar and kitchen were quickly fitted out: for at this distance from the mansion you had to have everything you needed installed about you. And so from then on the women lived with the child up in the pavilion and, with this lodging as a new centre, unexpected paths and walks opened up for them in the country round about. The weather was beautiful and now they breathed the free fresh air of a higher region.

Ottilie's favourite walk, sometimes alone, sometimes with the child, led down to the plane-trees by a comfortable footpath and then to the place where one of the boats used for crossing the lake was moored. She sometimes liked to take a trip on the water, only, because Charlotte evidenced some anxiety about taking the child, she always left him behind. But she did not fail to visit the gardener in the walled garden every day and take a friendly interest in the many young plants he was rearing, which had now all been brought out into the open air.

In this fair season, Charlotte found very opportune the visit of an Englishman who had come to know Eduard while on his travels, had met him several times, and was now curious to see the beautiful grounds of which he had heard so much. He brought with him a letter of recommendation from the Count and at the same time introduced a quiet but very pleasant man as his companion. As he now went around the domain, sometimes with Ottilie and Charlotte, sometimes with the gardeners and local huntsmen, sometimes with his companion and sometimes alone, the observations he made showed him to be an amateur and connoisseur of such landscape parks, of which he must himself have laid out many. Although advanced in years, he took a cheerful interest in anything that would enhance the charm of life or augment its significance.

It was in his presence that the women first really learned to appreciate their surroundings. His experienced eye took in every effect as if it were brand new and he took all the greater pleasure in what had been effected in that he had not known the place before and hardly knew how to tell what had been done artificially from what nature had provided.

It could well be said that his observations enlarged and enriched the park. He knew in advance what the new struggling plantations promised. No spot escaped his notice where some kind of beauty might be introduced or brought into prominence. Here he drew attention to a spring which, made clear and bright, promised to ornament a whole group of bushes, there to a cavern which, cleared and enlarged, could provide a much desired resting place, while they had only to fell a few trees to gain a view from it of magnificent cliffs towering up. He congratulated the occupiers that they had so much work left to do and begged them not to hurry it but to reserve for the coming years the pleasure of this creating and contriving.

Outside these companionable hours he was, moreover, in no way a burden, for he occupied himself the greater part of the day in capturing the picturesque views of the park in a portable *camera obscura* and then drawing them, thus preserving for himself and others the fruit of his travels. He had been doing this for many years in every significant region he visited and had thus provided himself with the most pleasant and interesting collection. He showed the ladies a big portfolio he carried with him and entertained them with the pictures and his commentary on them. They were delighted to range through the world thus comfortably in their solitude and to watch coasts and harbours, mountains, lakes and rivers, cities, castles and many another spot with a name in history moving before their eyes.

Each of the two women had a special interest: Charlotte's was more general, she was interested in those places where something historically noteworthy had taken place, while Ottilie preferred to dwell on those regions of which Eduard had used to speak, where he liked to stay, whither he often returned; for every man has certain places, near and distant, which attract him, which, in accordance with his nature, especially appeal to or excite him, whether because of the first impression they made on him, or because of certain circumstances connected with them, or because he is used to them.

She would therefore ask the English nobleman what places he liked best and where he would now make his home if he had to choose. He could then point to more than one lovely spot and in his singular French expound to them what had happened to him there to render the place dear to him.

But to the question where he usually stayed now, where he most liked to return to, he replied without hesitation, yet to the surprise of the ladies: 'I have got myself used to being at home everywhere, and by now nothing contents me more than that others should build and plant and make domestic arrangements on my behalf. I have no desire to return to my own estate, partly on political grounds but chiefly because my son, for whose sake I really built it up, to whom I hoped to bequeath it, and with whom I hoped to enjoy it during my lifetime, has no interest in any of it, but has taken himself off to India, where, like many another, he proposes to devote his life to higher ends, or even to throw it away altogether.

'We expend far too much on paving our way through life, and that is a fact. Instead of settling down right away to enjoy ourselves in moderate circumstances, we expand more and more and make things more and more uncomfortable for ourselves. Who now has the benefit of my buildings, my park, my gardens? Not I, not even my family: unfamiliar visitors, inquisitive strangers, travellers passing through.

'Even when we are well off we are never more than half at home, especially when we are in the country, where we lack so much we are used to in town. The book we particularly want is not to hand, and precisely what we need most has been forgotten. We never set up house but we go dashing off out of it again, and if it is not our own will and fancy that drives us out, chance, necessity, passion, circumstances and I don't know what else drives us out instead.'

The nobleman had no suspicion how nearly he had touched his lady friends by these observations. And how often may any of us not run into like danger if we venture some general observation, even in company whose circumstances are, except on this one point, known to us? A chance hurt of this sort, even from people who meant no harm, was nothing new

233

to Charlotte, and in any event she saw the world so clearly that she felt no special pain if anyone inconsiderately compelled her to turn her eyes upon this or that unpleasantness. Ottilie, on the other hand – who in her half-aware youthfulness was given more to intuition than observation, and might, indeed must turn her eyes away from what she did not want and ought not to see – Ottilie was thrown into a terrible state by these confidences: they tore the veil from her eyes and it seemed to her now that all that had been done for the home and the household, for the garden and the park, and for all the domain around, had been done utterly in vain, because he to whom it all belonged could not enjoy it, because he too, like this present guest, had been driven by his nearest and dearest out to roam the world and, yes, out to face the greatest of the world's dangers. She was used to listening and keeping silent, but this time she found her situation an agony which was rather exacerbated than eased by the stranger's further discourse, which he cheerfully proceeded with in his cautious and idiosyncratic French.

'I believe,' he said, 'that I am now on the right path. I regard myself at all times simply as a traveller who gives up much so as to enjoy much. I have grown accustomed to change, indeed it has become a necessity to me, just as at the opera you always expect to find a new scene and set because there have been so many different scenes and sets before. I know what I can expect from the best inn and from the worst: let it be never so good or never so bad, it will not be what I have had before, and in the long run it comes to the same thing whether you are dependent on a habit grown to a necessity or on the most capricious fortuitousness. In any event, I no longer experience the annoyance of finding that something has been lost or mislaid, of being unable to use my living room because I have had to have it redecorated, that a favourite cup has been broken and that for a whole week I cannot enjoy drinking out of any other. I am raised above things of this kind, and if the house starts to burn down about my ears, my servants quietly pack up and off, and we get out into the courtyard and away to town. And with all these advantages, when I work it out, by the end of the year I haven't spent any more than it would have cost me to stay at home.'

During the course of this description Ottilie had before her only Eduard: she saw him too struggling in want and hardship along trackless paths, lying down in the field with danger and distress for companions and, surrounded by so much hazard and uncertainty, accustoming himself to being without home or friend and to throwing all away merely so as not to run the risk of losing it. Happily the company now broke up for a time, and Ottilie found somewhere to weep her heart out in solitude. None of the dull vague pain she had felt had seized on her more violently than did this clarity of vision, which she strove to make even clearer to herself – for when we are tormented from without we usually react by also tormenting ourselves.

Eduard's condition appeared to her so miserable and so wretched she resolved that, whatever it might cost her, she would do all she could to reunite him with Charlotte; she would hide her love and grief in some quiet spot and, by keeping occupied with any sort of activity whatever, escape and elude them.

In the meantime, the nobleman's companion, a quiet, sensible and observant man, had noticed the *faux pas* his friend had committed, and had revealed to him how similar his situation was to that at the house they were visiting. The latter knew nothing of the family's circumstances; but his companion, whose interest while on his travels was aroused by nothing more than it was by singular situations produced by natural or social circumstances and by the conflict between law and violence, commonsense and reason, passion and prejudice, had acquainted himself in advance, and further after his arrival, with all that had happened and was still happening.

The nobleman regretted what he had done without growing confused or embarrassed over it. You would have to keep utterly silent in society if you wanted to be certain of never committing a blunder of this sort, for not only weighty observations but the most trivial remarks are capable of giving offence. 'We will make up for it this evening,' he said. 'We shall avoid all general conversation. Let the company hear something of the many amusing and instructive tales with which you have enriched your memory and filled your portfolio in the course of our travels.'

But even with the best of intentions, the visitors did not succeed this time either in providing their friends with harmless entertainment. For after the nobleman's companion had engaged their attention and aroused their interest to the highest pitch with a succession of singular, instructive, amusing, touching and terrible tales, he thought to close with the narration of an event which, though singular indeed, was of a more tender description than those preceding: he little suspected how familiar the story would be to his audience.

The Wayward Young Neighbours

A Novella

The children of two neighbouring families of rank and position, a boy and a girl, were of an age that would allow them one day to become man and wife. They were brought up together with that pleasant prospect in view, and their parents looked forward to a future union. Very soon, however, it began to appear that their intention was going to miscarry, since a strange antipathy sprang up between these two admirable young people. Perhaps they were too much alike. Both were self-engrossed, both clear as to what they wanted and firm in their intentions, loved and respected by their companions, always enemies when they met, constructive when alone, mutually destructive when together, never competing but always fighting with one another, altogether kind and well-behaved, and vicious, indeed malignant, only towards one another.

This wayward relationship was already apparent in their childhood games, and it was apparent as they grew older. And as boys are accustomed to play war-games, dividing up into sides and doing battle against one another, the bold defiant girl on one occasion placed herself at the head of one of the armies and fought the other with such violence and animosity it would have been beaten shamefully from the field if the only boy who ventured to oppose her had not borne himself very manfully and at length disarmed and captured his fair opponent. But even then she struggled so fiercely that, to preserve his eyes without injuring his foe, he was compelled to tear off his silk neckerchief and tie her arms behind her back.

This act she never forgave him; indeed, she engaged in so much secret plotting against him with the object of harming him that the parents, who had long been aware of these strange passions, came to a mutual agreement to separate the two inimical creatures and abandon their romantic hopes for them.

The boy soon distinguished himself in his new sphere, and profited from every sort of instruction. Well-wishers and his own inclination marked him for a military career. He was admired and respected wherever he went. He seemed to have nothing but a beneficial and pleasing effect on others and, without formulating the fact clearly in his mind, he was happy to have parted company from the only enemy nature had provided him.

The girl, on the other hand, suddenly changed. Her years, an increasing culture, and even more a certain inner change of feelings, drew her away from the rough games she had hitherto played in the company of boys. On the whole she seemed to be lacking something: there was nothing in her vicinity worth her hatred and she had not yet found anyone she was able to love.

A young man, older than her former neighbour and foe, of rank, wealth and standing, admired in society and sought after by women, turned all his attentions in her direction. It was the first time a man had offered himself to her as friend, lover and servant. That he should prefer her to many who were older, more cultivated, more brilliant and had more claim to attention, pleased her very well. His constant concern for her, which never became importunate, his loyal support on certain unpleasant occasions, his wooing of her parents – which was, though open, quiet and no more than hopeful, since she was, to be sure, still very young – all this charmed and captivated her, and custom, the relations between them which the world now took for granted, also played its part. She had been referred to so often as betrothed, she finally came to consider herself betrothed, and neither she nor anyone else thought any further time of trial necessary when she exchanged rings with him who had for so long passed as her fiancé.

The quiet course the whole affair had taken was not at all accelerated by the engagement. Both sides agreed to let everything go on as before; they enjoyed one another's company and wanted to continue to bask in this pleasant season as in the springtime of the more earnest life to come.

In the meantime, her now distant neighbour had made himself into the finest type of young man, had risen to a well-deserved eminence in his profession, and came home on leave to visit his family. It was quite natural, and yet it seemed strange to them, that he should once again meet his beautiful companion of former years. She had of late known only the feelings of a girl in the midst of her family and about to be married; she was in harmony with all around her; she believed she was happy, and she was in fact happy after a fashion. But now, for the first time for a long time, she encountered something from outside: it was not something to be hated; she had become incapable of hatred; indeed, her childish hatred, which had in reality been only an obscure recognition of an inner worth, now expressed itself in a joyful astonishment, in pleasant reflections, in complaisant admissions, and in a half willing, half reluctant and yet inevitable coming-closer: and all this was mutual. Long absence made for lengthy conversation. Now they were more enlightened they were even able to joke about their childhood unreasonableness, and it was as if they had to make good their former teasing and enmity by now being amiable and attentive, as if they now had expressly to recognize how ill they had recognized one another before.

For his part, all this stayed within sensible and desirable bounds. His position, his circumstances, his aspirations and ambitions occupied him so fully he complaisantly accepted the lovely young lady's friendship as a gratifying supplement without feeling himself involved with her in any way or begrudging her to her fiancé, with whom he was in any case on the best of terms.

With her, however, it was quite different. It seemed to her she had awakened from a dream. Her struggle against her young neighbour had been her life's first passion, and this violent struggle had in fact been, in the guise of hostility, only a violent, as it were inborn affection. When she looked back, indeed, it seemed to her she had always loved him. She smiled at the way she had gone after him armed; she wanted to remember what a supremely pleasant sensation it had been when he had disarmed her. She imagined she had felt the greatest bliss when he tied her up and everything she had done to injure and annoy him now appeared to her as no more than an innocent means of attracting his attention.

She cursed their separation, she bewailed the sleep into which she had fallen, she execrated dull and dreamy habit, which had wedded her to so unprepossessing a groom. She was transformed, doubly transformed, in her past and in her future.

If anyone could have unearthed these feelings of hers, which she kept entirely to herself, he could not have blamed her for them : for indeed, when you saw them together her future bridegroom could not endure comparison with her young neighbour. You could not help feeling a certain confidence in the one, but the other inspired the most unbounded trust; you would have enjoyed the company of the one, but desired the other for a companion; and if it came to higher interests, exceptional circumstances, you would have had doubts about the one, complete certainty as to the other. Women have an innate feeling for such things, and they have reason as well as occasion for developing it.

The more the fair bride-to-be nourished these thoughts in her heart and the more impossible it was for anyone to say anything in favour of the bridegroom-to-be, of what circumstances and duty advised and commanded, or indeed of what an unalterable necessity seemed irrevocably to demand, the more enamoured of its own partiality this heart became; and since she was on the one hand indissolubly bound by her world and her family, by her future bridegroom and her own agreement, and on the other the rising young man made no secret of his future prospects and plans, comported himself towards her simply as a loyal and not even fond brother, and there was now even talk of his immediate departure, it seemed as if the childish spirit of earlier days, with all its violence and spite, awoke again in her, and now, at a higher stage of life, indignantly prepared itself for more pernicious action. She resolved to die, so as to punish him she had formerly hated and now so passionately loved for his coldness towards her and, since she was not to possess him, to wed herself eternally to his imagination and remorse. Never should he be free of the image of her dead face, never should he cease to reproach himself that he had not recognized, had not fathomed, had not treasured her feelings towards him.

This strange madness went with her wherever she went. She concealed it in every way she could and, although people found her behaviour odd, no one was sufficiently attentive or astute to discover the true cause of it.

In the meantime, friends, relations and acquaintances had been putting themselves to no end of trouble to organize entertainments of all kinds. Hardly a day passed without there being arranged something new and unexpected. There was hardly a spot on the landscape that had not been adorned and prepared for the reception of merry guests. Our young arrival too wanted to play his part before his departure, and he invited the young couple and their immediate family for a pleasure trip on the river. They boarded a fine, well-appointed ship, a yacht of the sort that provides a small lounge and a number of cabins and seeks to transport the comforts of land on to the water.

They sailed down the great river to the accompaniment of music; in the heat of the day the company had assembled below to entertain themselves with games of chance and skill. The young host, who could never remain idle, had taken the tiller to relieve the aged ship's captain, who had fallen asleep at his side; and at this time he needed all his wits about him, for they were approaching a spot where a pair of islands narrowed the river bed and their flat, pebbly banks, extending out into the water, produced a dangerous channel. The alert and cautious helmsman was almost tempted to awaken the captain, but he resolved to rely on his own skill and steered for the narrows. At that moment his lovely foe appeared on deck with a wreath of flowers in her hair, which she took off and threw at the helmsman. 'This is to remember me by!' she cried. 'Don't disturb me!' he shouted back, taking up the wreath. 'I need all my strength and concentration.' 'I shall not disturb you again,' she cried, 'you shall see me no more!' And so saying, she hastened to the ship's prow and there leaped into the water. Voices cried: 'Help! Help! She's drowning!' He was thrown into the most agonizing dilemma. The noise awakens the old captain; he tries to take over the tiller and the young man tries to relinquish it to him; but there is no time to change control: the ship runs ashore, and at the same instant, throwing off the weightier of his clothes, the young man plunged into the water and swam after his fair foe.

Water is a friendly element for him who is familiar with it and knows how to manage it. It bore him up and, as a skilled swimmer, he was its master. Soon he had reached the girl being borne away in front of him; he grasped her round, he was able to lift her up and support her; and both were borne violently away by the river, until they had left the islands far behind and the stream again began to flow broad and smooth. Only now did he recover from the first sense of emergency, in which he had acted mechanically and without thought, and take stock of their situation. Raising his head with difficulty above the water, he looked around and steered as well as he could towards a flat, bush-covered spot which ran conveniently down into the river. There he brought his fair booty to dry land; but he could feel in her not a breath of life. He was seized by despair, but then a well-trodden path leading through the undergrowth met his eyes. He lifted up the dear burden again, he soon saw a solitary house, and when he reached it he found good people there, a young married couple to whom he quickly told his tale of misfortune and who brought him everything he asked for: a fire was soon blazing, woollen blankets were spread over a bed, pelts and furs and other warming garments were quickly fetched forth. The desire to revive the lovely, benumbed, naked body overbore every other thought, and nothing was left undone that might call it back to life. Their efforts succeeded. She opened her eyes, she beheld her friend, she embraced his neck with her ethereal arms. Long she held him, and a stream of tears poured from her eyes and completed her recovery. 'Can you leave me,' she cried, 'now that I have found you again like this!' 'Never,' he cried, 'never!' and knew not what he said or did. 'Only spare yourself,' he added 'spare yourself! Think of yourself, for your own sake and mine.'

She now regarded herself, and only now did she realize the state she was in. She could not feel shame before her darling, her rescuer; but she gladly released him so that he might look after himself, for everything he had on was still dripping wet.

The young married couple took counsel together and offered their wedding clothes, which were still hanging in the house complete and were sufficient to clothe two young people from head to foot. In a short time the two adventurers were not merely dressed but adorned. They looked delightful, gazed on one another in amazement when they met again and, although still half smiling at their fancy-dress, fell into one another's arms in a passionate embrace. The energy of youth and the agitations of love had in a few minutes altogether restored them, and but for the absence of music they would have begun to dance.

To have made their way from water to earth, from death to life, from the family circle to the wilderness, from despair to rapture, from indifference to passionate affection, and all in a moment – the head is inadequate to grasp it without bursting. Here the heart must take its place and do the best it can if such events are to be borne.

Utterly lost in one another, it was only after some time that they could think of the fears and worries of those they had left behind, and they themselves could hardly help worrying about how they were to meet them again. 'Shall we flee? Shall we hide away?' said the young man. 'Let us stay together,' she said, clinging to him.

The countryman, who had heard from them the story of the stranded ship, hurried without further ado down to the river bank. He saw the yacht come sailing happily along – it had, with considerable effort, been pushed loose. They were continuing uncertainly in hope of finding the two who were lost. So that when the countryman attracted their attention with shouts and gestures, ran to a spot where there appeared to be a good landing place, and continued to shout and gesture, the ship turned towards the bank, and what a scene there was when they landed! The parents of the bride- and bridegroom-to-be forced their way to the shore first; the loving bridegroom was almost out of his wits. Hardly had they learned that the dear children were safe when the latter emerged from behind a bush clad in their strange disguise. They did not recognize them until they had come right up. 'Who is this?' cried the mothers. 'What is this?' cried the fathers. The young people fell on their knees before them. 'Your children!' they exclaimed: 'A loving pair. Forgive us!' cried the girl. 'Give us your blessing!' cried the youth. 'Give us your blessing!' they both cried, as everyone around stood dumb with amazement. For a third time the words resounded: 'Your blessing!' And who could have had the heart to refuse them?

CHAPTER ELEVEN

THE narrator paused, or had rather already finished, before he noticed how agitated Charlotte had become; now, indeed, she rose and, excusing herself with a gesture, left the room: for the tale was already familiar to her. The event described had actually happened and had involved the Captain and a woman neighbour of his; it is true it had not happened exactly as the Englishman had told it, but its main features were intact and only individual details had been developed and embellished, as tends to happen with tales of this sort when they have passed firstly through mouths of the crowd and subsequently through the fantasy of an imaginative and stylish narrator. For the most part everything and nothing remains in the end as it was.

Ottilie followed Charlotte, as the two strangers themselves desired, and now it was the nobleman's turn to remark that perhaps another blunder had been made, something known to or even connected with the house spoken of. 'We must beware,' he went on, 'that we do not do any more harm. We seem to be making an ill return for the many good and pleasant things we have enjoyed here. Let us find a polite way of taking our leave.'

'I must confess,' his companion replied, 'that there is something else that detains me here, something I should like to have explained before I leave. When we took the *camera obscura* to the park yesterday you were too busy, my lord, in finding a truly picturesque view to have noticed what was going on otherwise. You turned aside from the main path so as to get to a little-visited spot beside the lake which offered you a charming prospect. Ottilie, who accompanied us, hesitated to follow, and asked to be allowed to go there in the boat. I sat with her and was delighted with the skilful way she handled it. I assured her I had not been so pleasantly rocked on the water since I was in Switzerland, where charming young ladies also play the role of ferryman, but I could not refrain from asking her why it really was she had refused to take that side path, for there had in fact been a kind of anxious embarrassment in her refusal. "So long as you won't laugh at me," she replied amicably, "I can tell you, although even for me there is a mystery about it. I have never taken that bypath without being seized by a quite peculiar feeling of dread which I never feel anywhere else and which I do not know how to explain. I therefore prefer to avoid laying myself open to such a sensation, especially as it is immediately followed by a headache on the left side which I suffer from now and again on other occasions." – We landed, you and Ottilie conversed, and I, in the meanwhile, examined the spot she had clearly pointed out to me from a distance. Imagine my astonishment when I discovered a very clear indication of the presence of coal, which convinced me that excavation there might well reveal a lucrative seam below.

'Forgive me, my lord : I see you smiling and know full well you condone my passionate interest in these things, in which you have no belief, only as a man of wisdom and as a friend; but it is impossible for me to depart from here without trying the pendulum experiment on Ottilie.'

When this subject came up for discussion the nobleman never failed to reiterate his arguments against it, which his companion always received with patience and discretion, but still persevered in his opinions and intentions. He likewise repeatedly maintained that the subject ought not to be abandoned because such experiments as this did not succeed with everyone; indeed, for that very reason it ought to be the more seriously and thoroughly investigated, since many connections and affinities between inorganic materials, between

246

inorganic and organic, and between organic and organic, which were at present concealed from us, would certainly be disclosed in the future.

He had already set out his apparatus of gold rings and pieces of iron and sulphur ore and other metallic substances which he always carried with him in a handsome little chest, and was now holding pieces of metal attached to thread over other pieces of metal. 'I do not begrudge you the pleasure I read on your face, my lord,' he said as he did so, 'when you think that nothing is going to move here for me. My operations are, however, only a subterfuge. When the ladies return I want them to be curious about the strange things we are engaged on.'

The women came back. Charlotte understood at once what was taking place. 'I have heard a great deal about these things,' she said, 'but I have never seen them work. As you have everything so nicely prepared, let me try and see if it will succeed with me.'

She grasped the thread in her hand, and as she was taking the matter seriously she held it steadily and without agitation: but not the slightest oscillation was to be observed. Then Ottilie was persuaded to do it. She held the pendulum even more quietly, composedly and unselfconsciously over the metals lying below. But in a moment the suspended object was agitated as if in a definite vortex and turned now to this side, now to that, now in circles, now in ellipses, or swung back and forth in a straight line, according to which metals were placed beneath it. Only the nobleman's companion could have expected this effect, and indeed even his expectations were surpassed.

The nobleman himself was somewhat taken aback, but his companion derived such pleasure from it he could not have enough and continued to ask for the experiments to be repeated and varied. Ottilie was kind enough to accede to his demands, until she finally had to beg him to release her be-

247

cause her headache had started again. Amazed, even delighted at this, he assured her enthusiastically he would completely cure her of this malady if she would entrust herself to his treatment. There was a moment's uncertainty; but Charlotte, who quickly grasped what was meant, refused this well-intentioned offer because she was not minded to allow something about which she had always felt strongly apprehensive.

The visitors had departed and, notwithstanding they had caused strange confusion in the house, left behind them the desire for a reunion. Charlotte now employed the fine days in completing her return visits in the neighbourhood and found she could hardly get through them, since throughout the whole region round everybody had, in part through genuine interest, in part through habit, been diligently concerned on her behalf. At home she was cheered by the sight of her child; he was indeed worthy of all the love and care you could give him. He was regarded as a little marvel, indeed a prodigy, and in size, proportions, strength and health a delight to behold; and what aroused even greater wonder and amazement was that twofold resemblance, which was growing ever more striking. In his features and figure he was coming ever more to resemble the Captain, his eyes were becoming ever less distinguishable from Ottilie's.

Under the influence of this strange affinity, and perhaps even more of the fine feeling of women who can embrace with tender affection the child of the man they love even when the child is not their own, Ottilie became as good as a mother to the growing little creature, or rather she became another kind of mother. When Charlotte was away Ottilie stayed alone with the child and his nurse. Nanni, jealous of the child, upon whom alone her mistress seemed to be lavishing her affection, had for some time been sulking and keeping away, and had now returned to her parents. Ottilie continued to carry the child out for his airing, and had grown accustomed to taking longer and longer walks. She took the feeding-bottle with her so as to feed the child if need be. She seldom neglected to take a book too; and thus, reading and walking, with the child on her arm, she made a wholly delightful *penserosa*.

CHAPTER TWELVE

THE main objective of the campaign had been achieved and Eduard decorated and honourably discharged. He at once betook himself to his little farm, where he found detailed news of his family, whom, without their knowing or noticing it, he had had closely watched. His quiet dwelling had a very welcoming appearance, for in his absence much had been arranged and improved according to his instructions, so that what the domain lacked in depth and breadth it made up for by what was immediately enjoyable within it.

Now become accustomed to greater decisiveness through a more impetuous mode of life, Eduard straightway resolved to put into effect a plan he had ample time to think over. Before all else he contacted the Major. Their joy at seeing one another again was great. Friendships of youth have, like affinities of blood, this considerable advantage, that errors and misunderstandings, of whatever kind they may be, can never do them any fundamental damage and after a certain time the old relationship is restored.

Eduard inquired how his friend was and learned how completely fortune had favoured his desires. With half-humorous familiarity Eduard then asked whether a happy marriage might not be in the offing. His friend denied it, and it was clear his denial was serious.

'I cannot and I must not keep back what I have to say,' Eduard went on : 'I must tell you at once what it is I have in mind. You know of my passion for Ottilie and you have long realized it was on her account I plunged into the late campaign. I do not deny that I wanted to be rid of a life which, without her, was of no further use to me; only at the same time I must confess I could not bring myself to despair utterly. To be happy with her was so fair, so desirable, it was impossible for me to renounce it altogether. So many comforting presentiments, so many happy omens had confirmed me in the belief, in the illusion, that Ottilie could become mine. A chalice inscribed with a monogram failed to be shattered when it was thrown into the air at the laying of the foundation-stone; it was caught up and was now again in my hands. "That is what shall happen to me too," I cried to myself after so many irresolute hours in this solitary place, "I myself will, in place of this glass, become an omen whether our marriage is possible or not. I shall go out and seek death, not as a madman but as one who hopes to live. Ottilie shall be the prize for which I fight; she it shall be whom I hope to win and to conquer behind every enemy battle-line, in every entrenchment, in every beleaguered fortress. I shall do wonders with the desire to be spared, that is to be spared losing Ottilie, but instead to win her. These feelings have inspired me and stood by me through every danger; but now too I feel as one who has achieved his goal, who has overcome every obstacle, who no longer has anything in his way. Ottilie is mine, and whatever still lies between this thought and its realization I can only regard as of no significance whatever.'

'You are wiping out with a few strokes everything that could and should be said against you,' the Major replied. 'And yet these things must be said. I leave it to you to recall the true value of your relationship with your wife; you owe it to her and to yourself not to remain in any doubt about it. But when I think that you have been given a son, how can I help saying that you belong to one another for ever, that you owe it to this little creature to live together, so that together you may care for his education and his future well-being.'

'It is a mere piece of parents' self-conceit to imagine that their presence is so necessary to their children,' Eduard replied. 'All that lives finds nourishment and succour, and if a

251

son does not have so comfortable and favoured a childhood when his father is dead, perhaps he may for that very reason learn more quickly how to live in the world, by recognizing betimes that he has to get on with others, which is what we all have to learn sooner or later. And here, in fact, there is no question of that: we are rich enough to provide for several children, and it is by no means a duty or a kindness to heap so many good things on to one head.'

As the Major was trying to make clear as briefly as he could how worthy Charlotte was and how long she had meant something to Eduard, the latter broke in impetuously: 'We committed an act of stupidity, and I can see all too well what it was. He who thinks to realize when he is older the hopes and desires of youth is always deceiving himself, for every decade of a man's life possesses its own kind of happiness, its own hopes and prospects. Woe to the man whom circumstances or delusion constrain to reach back into the past or forward into the future. We committed an act of stupidity, but do we have to go on committing it for the rest of our lives? Are there any scruples of any kind which can compel us to renounce that which the customs of the age do not forbid us? In how many things of life does a man not go back on his intentions or his acts, and is that to be impossible here, precisely here, where it is a question not of a part but of the whole, not of this or that condition of life but of the whole life-complex itself!'

The Major did not fail to delineate to Eduard, in a fashion as skilful as it was emphatic, his ties with and obligations towards his wife, his family, his properties: but he did fail to arouse any sympathetic response.

'All these things, my friend,' Eduard replied, 'passed before my soul in the midst of the tumult of battle, when the earth was trembling with continuous thunder, when the bullets were whistling about my ears, my comrades falling to left and right, when my horse was hit and my hat filled with holes; they hovered before my eyes as I lay beside the quiet fire by night beneath the starry vault of heaven. Then all my ties and obligations stepped before my soul; I have thought them through and felt them through; I have settled my accounts with them, again and again, and now for ever.

'At such moments – why should I not tell you this? – you too were present, you too are part of my life; and have we not both for so long been part of one another's life? If I have got into your debt, I am now in a position to repay you with interest; if you have ever got into my debt, you are now able to make it good to me. I know you love Charlotte, and she deserves your love; I know she is not indifferent to you, and why should she not recognize your worth! Receive her from my hand! Lead me to Ottilie! And we shall be the happiest human beings on earth.'

'It is just because the gifts you want to bribe me with are such great gifts that I must be the more cautious and the more severe,' the Major replied. 'This suggestion of yours, for which I have every respect, instead of making the thing easier only makes it more difficult. Formerly only you were involved, now I am involved too; and whereas it was your destiny that was in question, what is now also in question is the hitherto unblemished good name and honour of two men, who are now, as a consequence of this strange action – not to call it by any other name – in danger of appearing to the world in a very peculiar light.'

'It is just because our name and honour are unblemished,' Eduard replied, 'that we have the right to risk blemishing them for once. He who has proved himself a safe man all his life can safely perform an act which, if done by others, would appear dubious. As for me, I feel the recent trials I have imposed upon myself and the difficult and dangerous deeds I have done for others justify me in now doing something for myself. As for you and Charlotte, your fate is a thing for the future; but neither you nor anyone else is going to keep me from doing what I intend. If I am offered the hand of friendship, I am again ready to listen to any proposal; if I am left to my own devices, not to speak of being opposed, then there will be a crisis and I don't care what the nature of it is.'

The Major regarded it as his duty to oppose Eduard's proposal for as long as possible, and he now employed against his friend the shrewd tactic of pretending to acquiesce and speaking only of the formalities and routine by which this divorce and the subsequent unions were to be brought about. As he spoke of these things, so much that was unpleasant, difficult and unbecoming came to light that Eduard was put into the worst of moods.

'I can see well enough,' he exclaimed at last, 'that it is not only from enemies but from friends too that you have to take what you want by force. What I want, what I cannot do without, I shall keep firmly in view; I shall take it, and soon and surely. I know well enough that such relationships as these cannot be dissolved and created without much that is firm falling, and much that would like to persist having to give way. Such things cannot be dealt with by thinking about them; before the bar of reason all rights are equal, and a counterweight can always be found for the light end of the scales. So resolve, my friend, to act on my behalf and your own, and for my sake and your own to disentangle this situation. Let no consideration deter you; we have already given the world something to talk about, we shall now give it something else to talk about, but then it will forget us as it forgets everything when it has ceased to be a novelty, and will let us go our way as best we can without taking any further interest in us.'

The Major now had no other recourse but to let Eduard treat the matter as something that was definitely going to happen, and allow him to discuss in detail how it was all going to be arranged and launch forth on the future in the merriest and even bantering fashion.

Then, serious and thoughtful again, Eduard went on: 'If we were to recline in the hope and expectation that everything will work out of its own accord, that chance is going to favour and direct us, that would be criminal self-deception. That would certainly not be the way to save ourselves and restore us all to our peace of mind; and how could I ever console myself if we failed, since I am innocently to blame for it all! It was at my insistence that Charlotte took you into our house, and it was only as a result of this change that Ottilie too joined us. We are no longer in control of what has come of all this, but we are still capable of rendering it harmless and directing it to our own good. Even if you would like to turn your eyes away from the fair and friendly prospect I have opened up for us, if you would like to offer me, offer us all a sad renunciation, so far as you think that possible, so far as it would be possible, would there not also be much that is unbecoming, uncomfortable, annoying to endure if we proposed returning to our old way of life, without anything good or happy resulting from it? Would the happy position in which you find yourself at present give you any pleasure if you were prevented from visiting me, from joining your life to mine? And after what has happened it would always be painful. For all our wealth, Charlotte and I would be in a very sad situation. And if, with other men of the world, you like to think that separation and the passing years will dull these feelings and wipe away these lines so deep-engraven, well, these years of which you are thinking are precisely those we should like to spend, not in grief and renunciation, but in joy and comfort. And, to speak last of the most important consideration of all: even if we were able to bide our time and put up with all of this – what is to become of Ottilie, who would have to leave our house, do without our care, and drift about miserably in the infamously cold world! Paint for me a situation in which Ottilie could be happy without me, without us, and you will have uttered an argument stronger than any other and one which, though I cannot believe it can be produced, I am quite ready to take into consideration.'

This task was not so easy to accomplish, at least no adequate answer occurred to the Major, and there was nothing left for him to do but to impress on Eduard again how weighty, how doubtful and in many respects dangerous the whole undertaking was, and that they had at least to think very seriously how it was to be tackled. Eduard acquiesced, but only on condition his friend would not desert him until they had come to a complete agreement on the matter and the first steps had been taken.

CHAPTER THIRTEEN

If people who are complete strangers and indifferent to one another live for a time in company they will bare their hearts to one another and a certain intimacy must arise. It was thus all the more to be expected that our two friends, now they were once more side by side and going about together daily and hourly, would have no secrets from one another. They revived memories of earlier times and the Major did not conceal that when Eduard had returned from his travels Charlotte had intended Ottilie should be his, that she had had in mind that they should marry. Eduard, delighted to the point of derangement by this revelation, spoke without restraint of the affection between Charlotte and the Major which, since it was in his immediate interest to do so, he painted in the liveliest colours.

The Major could not entirely deny what he said, yet he could not entirely admit it either; but Eduard only insisted on it the more strongly. He thought of it all, not as merely possible, but as having already happened. All parties had only to consent to what they desired; a divorce could certainly be procured; an early marriage was to follow, and Eduard would travel away with Ottilie.

Of all things the imagination can picture, there is perhaps nothing more entrancing than young lovers, a young married couple, looking to enjoy their new relationship in a new world and to test and confirm the durability of their union against so many different scenes and circumstances. While Eduard and Ottilie were away, Charlotte and the Major were to have unlimited authority to regulate everything pertaining to their property, fortune and material arrangements, and to manage them justly and fairly, so that all parties could be satisfied. But what Eduard seemed to build on most of all, and to expect the greatest advantage from, was this: since the child was to stay with his mother, the Major would be able to bring him up, guide him according to his own outlook, and develop his capacities. Then it would not have been in vain that they had given him in baptism their common name of Otto.

All this had become so firmly complete in Eduard's mind that he wanted to wait not a single day before beginning to put it into practice. On their way to the estate they came to a little town in which Eduard owned a house; here he intended to stay and await the Major's return. But he could not bring himself to dismount at the house immediately and he accompanied his friend to the town's end. They were both on horseback and they rode on together sunk in earnest conversation.

All at once they beheld in the distance the new pavilion on the hill; it was the first time they had seen its red tiles glittering in the sunlight. Eduard is seized by an irresistible longing; everything is to be settled this very evening. He will conceal himself in a village close by; the Major shall put the whole matter urgently before Charlotte, take her unawares and by the unexpectedness of the proposal oblige her freely to disclose what she thinks of it. For Eduard had transferred his desires to Charlotte, and believed that all he was doing was meeting her own desires halfway: he looked for so immediate a consent from her because he himself would have given his consent at once.

He saw the happy outcome joyfully in his mind's eye and, so that this outcome should be quickly announced to him as he impatiently waited, a number of cannon-shots were to be fired or, if it had already become night, a number of rockets sent up.

The Major rode on to the mansion. He did not find Charlotte, he learned instead that she was at present living in the new building on the hill but was at that moment away on a visit in the neighbourhood, from which she would probably not be getting back until quite late. He returned to the inn where he had installed his horse.

In the meanwhile, Eduard, driven by uncontrollable impatience, had crept out of his hiding place and, by solitary paths known only to hunters and fishermen, had come to his own park, where towards evening he found himself in the undergrowth close by the lake, whose new enlarged expanse he then saw for the first time.

Ottilie had that afternoon gone for a walk beside the lake. As was her custom she carried the child and read as she walked, and thus reading and walking she reached the oak-trees beside the mooring place. The boy had fallen asleep; she sat herself down, laid him beside her, and went on reading. The book was one of those which draw a tender heart to it and refused to let it go. She forgot the time and that she still had a long way to go around the lake back to the new pavilion; she sat lost in her book and in herself, so lovely a sight that the trees and bushes around her should have come alive and been given eyes so as to admire and take delight in her. And at that moment a ruddy shaft of light fell upon her from the setting sun and turned her cheek and shoulder to gold.

Eduard, who had so far succeeded in advancing undetected and who found his park deserted and the whole region empty, ventured further and further in, until at length he broke through the undergrowth beside the oak-trees. He saw Ottilie and she him; he flew towards her and threw himself at her feet. After a long silence in which both sought to compose themselves, he explained in few words why and how he had come. He had sent the Major to Charlotte and their common destiny was perhaps being decided at that very moment. He had never doubted her love, and she had certainly never doubted his. He begged her to consent. She hesitated, he entreated; he made to assert his former rights and embrace her in his arms; she motioned towards the child.

Eduard saw it and was astonished. 'Great God!' he exclaimed, 'if I had reason to doubt my wife and my friend this little form would be a terrible witness against them. Are these not the Major's features? Such a likeness I have never seen.'

'But no!' Ottilie replied. 'Everyone says he resembles me.' 'Is that possible?' Eduard said, and at that moment the child opened his eyes, two big, black, penetrating eyes, deep and friendly. The boy already regarded the world with so steady a gaze, and it was as if he knew the two who were standing before him. Eduard dropped down beside the child and was kneeling a second time before Ottilie. 'It is you!' he exclaimed: 'they are your eyes. Oh, but let me look only into yours. Let me draw a veil over the fatal hour that gave this little creature existence. Am I to frighten your spotless soul with the unhappy thought that man and wife can, though estranged, embrace together and a lawful bond be profaned by the vehemence of desire! Or yes, since we have come so far, since Charlotte and I must part, since you are to be mine, why should I not say it! Why should I not utter the harsh words: this child was begotten in twofold adultery! It sunders me from my wife and my wife from me as it should have united us. May it bear witness against me, may these lovely eyes say to yours that in the arms of another I belonged to you; may you feel, Ottilie, feel truly, that I can atone for that error, for that crime, only in your arms!'

'Listen!' he cried, leaping up. He thought he heard a shot, the signal the Major was to give. But the shot came from a huntsman in the neighbouring hills. Nothing further followed, and Eduard grew impatient.

Only now did Ottilie notice that the sun had sunk behind the mountains. Its last rays were reflected from the windows of the building on the hill. 'You must go, Eduard!' she cried. 'We have waited so long, we have been patient so long. Consider what we both owe Charlotte. She must decide our fate; let us not anticipate her decision. I am yours if she consents;

if she does not, I must renounce you. Since you believe the decision to be so near, let us await it. Go back to the village where the Major thinks you still are. How much can happen that may require explaining. Is it likely that he will announce the success of his mission with a bare cannon-shot? Perhaps he is looking for you at this moment. He has not met Charlotte, that I know: he may have gone after her, for they knew where she had gone. How many different things may have happened! Leave me! She must be coming now. She is expecting me up there with the child.'

Ottilie spoke in haste. All that might happen passed through her mind. She was happy to have Eduard near her and she felt she now had to send him away. 'I beg, I beseech you, beloved!' she cried, 'go back and wait for the Major!' 'I shall obey your command,' Eduard replied, gazing on her passionately and then clasping her tightly in his arms. She embraced him and drew him with the utmost tenderness to her breast. Hope soared away over their heads like a star falling from the sky. They fancied, they believed they belonged to one another; for the first time they exchanged firm, frank kisses, and when they parted they had to tear themselves away from one another.

The sun had set, and already twilight and mist were settling on the lake. Ottilie stood agitated and confused; she gazed over to the pavilion on the hill and thought she saw Charlotte's white dress on the balcony. The way back around the lake was long; she knew Charlotte would be waiting impatiently for the child. She sees the plane-trees standing on the other side of the lake; only a sheet of water divides her from the path leading straight up to the pavilion. As with her eyes, so in her mind she has already reached it. The doubtfulness of venturing on to the water with the child is forgotten in this sense of urgency. She hurries to the boat, she pays no heed to her beating heart, to her trembling feet, to the signs that she is near to swooning.

261

She leaps into the boat, seizes the oar, and pushes off from the shore. She has to push hard, she pushes a second time, the boat sways and glides a little distance out into the lake. With the child on her left arm, her book in her left hand, and the oar in her right hand, she too sways and falls into the boat. The oar slips out of her hand to one side of the boat, and as she is trying to steady herself the child and book slip out to the other side, all into the water. She still has hold of the child's dress, but the awkward position she is in makes it difficult for her to get up. With only one free hand, she cannot push herself upright. At length she succeeds, she pulls the child from the water, but his eyes are closed and he has ceased to breathe.

At that moment she is restored to her full senses, but her grief is for that reason all the greater. The boat is drifting almost into the middle of the lake, the oar is floating off, she can see no one on the bank, and how would it help her if she could! Cut off from everyone, she is gliding across the faithless intractable element.

She tries to render aid herself. She had heard so often about how to save the drowning and she had seen it done on the evening of her birthday. She undresses the child and dries it with her muslin frock. She tears open her clothes and for the first time bares her breast to the open sky; for the first time she presses a living creature to her pure naked breast – alas, a living creature no longer. The unhappy child's cold limbs chill her bosom down to her innermost heart. An unending stream of tears pours from her eyes and imparts to the numb body an appearance of warmth and life. She persists, she covers the body with her shawl, and she thinks to make good with stroking, embracing, warming and kissing the child, and drenching it with her tears, those aids which, cut off as she is, she cannot bring him.

All in vain! The child lies motionless in her arms, the boat floats motionless on the water; but even here her spirit does not desert her. She turns to Heaven for aid. She sinks to her knees in the boat and with both hands raises the benumbed body over her guiltless breast, as white as marble and, alas, as cold. She gazes on high with tear-filled eyes and calls for help from that place where a tender heart looks to find abundant aid when there is none elsewhere.

Nor does she turn in vain to the stars which are beginning to show here and there in the sky. A gentle wind arises and drives the boat towards the plane-trees.

CHAPTER FOURTEEN

SHE hastens to the new pavilion, she calls for the doctor, she gives him the child. Calm in any emergency, he treats the tender body according to the prescribed formula. Ottilie assists in every way she can: she fetches and carries, but she does it all as if walking in a dream, for, like great good fortune, great misfortune alters the aspect of everything; and only when, after he has gone through all the procedures for reviving the drowned, the good man shakes his head and to her hopeful questions replies at first with silence and then a gentle No, does she leave Charlotte's bedroom, where all this has been taking place, and has hardly reached the living-room when she falls exhausted on her face on to the carpet before she can gain the sofa.

At that moment Charlotte is heard driving up. The doctor entreats those present to stay where they are: he will go to meet and prepare her; but she is already entering the room. She finds Ottilie lying on the floor, and one of the maids runs towards her crying and weeping. The doctor comes in behind her and she learns everything at once. But how can he ask her to abandon all hope in an instant! An experienced and prudent man, he asks her only not to go and see the child; he departs, to deceive her that there is more to be done. She has seated herself on her sofa, Ottilie still lies on the floor, but her lovely head has been raised on to Charlotte's knees and there it now lies. Their physician friend comes and goes; he appears to be attending to the child, he is really attending to the women. Thus midnight comes on, the deathly stillness grows ever deeper. Charlotte no longer conceals from herself that the child will never come back to life; she demands to see him. He has been washed and wrapped in warm woollen blankets

264

and laid in a basket, which is placed beside her on the sofa; only the little face is uncovered; it lies there serene and lovely.

The village had soon been aroused by the accident and news of it had at once reached the inn. The Major had gone up to the pavilion by the familiar paths; he walked around it, and when he stopped a servant who was running to a side-building to fetch something he learned what had happened in greater detail and asked for the doctor to come out and see him. The doctor did so, astonished at the sudden appearance of his former benefactor, and told him what the situation was and undertook to prepare Charlotte for his arrival. He went back inside and spoke with her, leading her mind from one thing to another, until he brought up the subject of her friend the Major, and how certain she could be of his sympathy, how close to her he was in spirit, in mind and, as he was now soon able to reveal, in body, in reality. It was enough: she understood her friend was at the door, that he knew everything, and wanted to be admitted.

The Major came in; Charlotte greeted him with a sad smile. He stood before her. She raised the green silk coverlet which concealed the body, and by the dim light of a candle he beheld, not without a shudder of horror, his own dead likeness. Charlotte gestured towards a chair, and thus they sat facing one another in silence the whole night through. Ottilie was still lying peacefully with her head on Charlotte's knee; she breathed gently, she slept or seemed to be sleeping.

The grey of day appeared, the light went out, and the two friends seemed to awaken from a vague and torpid dream. Charlotte looked at the Major and said composedly: 'Tell me, my friend, what fate brings you here to share this scene of death?'

'This is not,' replied the Major softly, as softly as she had asked the question – it was as if they did not wish to awaken Ottilie – 'this is not the time or place for concealment, for preambles, for treading gently. The situation in which I find you is so dreadful that even the weighty matter for the sake of which I have come here loses its importance beside it.'

He thereupon confessed, quietly and simply, the purpose of his mission in so far as he was an emissary of Eduard, the purpose of his coming in so far as his own free will and interest were involved. He laid both before her very delicately but with candour; Charlotte listened with composure and seemed to be neither surprised nor vexed.

When the Major had finished, Charlotte replied very softly, so that he had to draw his chair closer: 'I have never before found myself in circumstances like these, but in comparable circumstances I have always asked myself: How will it be tomorrow? I feel clearly enough that the destiny of more than one person now lies in my hands, and what I have to do admits of no doubt and is soon told. I agree to the divorce. I ought to have agreed to it earlier; through my hesitation and opposition I have killed my child. There are certain things which fate is obstinately determined upon. Reason and virtue, duty and all that is sacred, oppose it in vain; something is to happen that seems right to fate, even if it does not seem right to us; and so, do what we will, fate at last prevails.

'But what am I saying! In reality, what fate is now doing is fulfilling my own desire, my own intention, which I have been thoughtlessly trying to thwart. Did I myself not once think Ottilie and Eduard would make a most suitable match? Did I not try to bring them together? Did you yourself not know of this plan, my friend? And why was I incapable of distinguishing between a man's obstinacy and true love? Why did I accept his hand when, as a friend, I could have made him happy with another wife? And just look at this unhappy girl asleep here! I tremble to think of the moment when she awakens from this trancelike slumber. How can she live, how can she find solace, if she cannot look to restore to Eduard through her love what she has taken from him as an agent of the strangest fortune? And through her affection,

266

through the passion with which she loves him, she can do so, she can give him back everything. If love is able to endure all things, it is able even more to repair all things. At this moment there should be no thought of me.

'Go quietly away, my dear Major. Tell Eduard I agree to the divorce, that I leave it to him, to you and to Mittler to see to the whole business, that I am not worried about my future, and have no need to be worried in any sense. I will sign anything put in front of me; only do not ask me to participate or to think about it or to talk about it.'

The Major stood up. She reached out her hand to him over Ottilie's body. He pressed his lips to this dear hand. 'And I, what may I hope for?' he whispered.

'Let me leave that question unanswered,' Charlotte replied. 'We have not deserved to be unhappy, but neither have we deserved to be happy together.'

The Major went away, deeply sorry for Charlotte yet unable to regret the poor departed child. Such a sacrifice as this seemed to him necessary to their general happiness. He thought of Ottilie with a child of her own on her arm as the most perfect recompense for that of which she had deprived Eduard; he thought of a son of his own on his knee who would have more right than the departed child to bear his likeness.

Such caressing hopes and visions were passing through his soul as, on the road back to the inn, he encountered Eduard who, since there had been no fireworks or cannon-thunder to announce a successful mission, had been awaiting the Major all night in the open air. He already knew of the accident and he too, instead of pitying the poor little creature, saw it, without being quite willing to admit the fact to himself, as a dispensation which would at one blow remove every obstacle to his happiness. It was thus not very difficult for the Major, who quickly told him of Charlotte's decision, to persuade him to return to the village and thence to the little town, where they would consider what immediate steps should be taken.

After the Major had left her, Charlotte sat sunk in her thoughts for only a few minutes, for soon Ottilie raised her head and looked at her with wide eyes. She lifted herself from Charlotte's knee and then from the ground and stood before her.

'What once happened to me before' – thus the child began in an irresistibly sweet and solemn tone – 'what once happened to me before has now happened a second time. You once told me that similar things repeat themselves in people's lives and always at moments of significance. I now find that what you said is true, and now feel compelled to make a confession. It was soon after my mother's death, when I was a small child, and I had pulled my stool up close to you. You were sitting on the sofa as you are now; my head was lying on your knee, I was not asleep but I was not awake; I was dozing. I knew all that was going on around me, especially all that was being said, yet I could not move or speak or, even if I had wanted to, give any sign I was conscious. You were talking about me to a friend of yours: you said how sad you were that it was my fate to be left in the world as a poor orphan, you described how dependent I was and how ill things would go with me unless I had a special lucky star watching over me. I grasped precisely, perhaps too strictly, what you seemed to want for me and of me. According to my limited understanding I made rules for myself in this matter; for long I lived in accordance with these rules, I regulated by them what I did and did not do, in the days when you loved me and looked after me and took me into your house, and also for some time afterwards.

'But I have deserted my rightful path, I have broken my rules, I have even lost my instinct for them, and after a terrible event you again enlighten me as to the case I am in, which is even more wretched than my former situation. Resting on your lap, half benumbed, I hear once more, as if from another world, your gentle voice above me; I learn how I appear to others; I shudder at myself; but as once before, so now in my trancelike slumber I have marked out my new path.

'I have decided, as I decided once before, and what I have decided you must now know. I shall never be Eduard's! God has opened my eyes in a terrible way to the crime I am committing. I am going to atone for it, and let no one think of preventing me! Take what measures you have to take, my dear and best friend, in the light of that decision. Have the Major come back; write to him that nothing is to be done. What anguish it was that I could not move or stir when he went. I wanted to leap up and cry that you should not send him away with such sinful expectations.'

Charlotte saw the state Ottilie was in and felt it, but she thought that with time and persuasion she might bring her to a different frame of mind. But when she uttered a few words hinting at a future, at the alleviation of grief, at hope – 'No!' Ottilie cried exultingly, 'do not try to move me or deceive me! The moment I learn you have agreed to a divorce I shall atone for my crime and transgression in that same lake.'

CHAPTER FIFTEEN

IF, living together in happy and peaceful companionship, relations, friends, members of a household discuss their affairs more than is necessary or reasonable and repeatedly tell one another of their plans, undertakings, activities and, without exactly taking advice from one another, treat the whole of life as, so to speak, something for mutual deliberation, you find on the other hand that at moments of crisis, when it would seem he needed the support and encouragement of others most of all, the individual draws back into himself, each strives to act alone and after his own fashion and, in as much as each conceals from the others what he is doing, only the result, the outcome, the achievement is once more common property.

After so many strange and unhappy events, a certain quiet seriousness, which expressed itself as an affectionate forbearance, had thus also descended upon the two women. Charlotte had quite quietly had the child removed to the chapel, and he now lay there, the first victim of an ominous fate.

So far as she could, Charlotte turned back towards life, and she found firstly that Ottilie needed her support. She concerned herself chiefly with her, but without letting the fact become obvious. She knew how much the ethereal child was in love with Eduard: piece by piece, partly from Ottilie herself, partly from letters from the Major, she had learned every circumstance of the scene which had preceded the calamity.

On her side, Ottilie greatly alleviated Charlotte's day-to-day existence. She was open, indeed talkative, but she never talked about their present situation or the events of the immediate past. She had always been observant, always noticed what was going on, she knew a great deal: all this now became apparent. She entertained and amused Charlotte, who continued to nourish the silent hope of seeing united together a pair so dear to her.

Only Ottilie did not see the future in that light. She had revealed to her friend the secret of her life, and she was absolved from her former servitude and self-limitation. Through her repentance, through her decision, she also felt relieved of the burden of her guilt and misfortune. She no longer needed to impose any constraint on herself; she had in the depths of her heart forgiven herself, but only on condition of complete renunciation, and this condition applied for all the future.

Thus time passed, and Charlotte felt how the house and the park, the lakes, rocks and trees served only to renew their sorrow day by day. That they would have to have a change was only too evident, but how they were to manage it was less easy to decide.

Ought the two women to remain together? Eduard's former desire seemed to demand it, his threat to compel it: but it was plainly apparent that, with all their good will, their reasonableness, their efforts, the women were finding their situation a painful one. Their conversation was evasive. Sometimes remarks were intentionally ignored, but often an expression was misunderstood, if not by the mind, at any rate by the feelings. They were afraid of wounding one another, but it was precisely this fear which was most easily wounded and most capable of wounding.

If they wanted a change and at the same time to separate, at least for a time, the old question again arose: where was Ottilie to go? That great and wealthy house had sought in vain for entertaining and emulous playfellows for its promising daughter and heiress. Charlotte had been invited, during the visit of the Baroness and more recently by letter, to send Ottilie there; now she again mentioned it. But Ottilie expressly declined to go where she would find what is commonly called high society.

'Allow me, dear aunt,' she said, 'so that I may not seem narrow and obstinate, to speak of something which in any other circumstances it would be my duty to conceal and keep quiet about. Anyone who has been uncommonly unfortunate, even if he is innocent, is marked out in a fearful fashion. His presence arouses a kind of terror in all who see him, in all who become aware of him. It is as if the dreadful burden laid upon him were visible, and everyone is at once curious to see him and fearful of doing so. A house, a town in which some dreadful deed has been done retains an aura of horror for anyone who enters it. The light of day is not so bright there, and the stars seem to lose their lustre.

'How great, yet perhaps excusable, is the indiscretion of people, their foolish importunity and clumsy good-naturedness, towards such unfortunates. Forgive me for speaking like this, but I suffered unspeakably with that poor young girl when Luciane brought her out of the private rooms of the house, fussed over her and, with the best of intentions, wanted to make her join in the dancing and games. When the poor child, growing more and more afraid, at last fled and sank unconscious, when I took her in my arms, when the company, at first frightened and excited, then became curious about her, I did not think a similar fate awaited me. But my feelings of pity, always so sure and lively, are still alive, and now I can turn them towards myself and take care that I myself do not give rise to such scenes.'

'But, my dear child,' Charlotte replied, 'you will nowhere be able to avoid being seen by people. We have no convents where in former times such feelings could find sanctuary.'

'Solitude is no sanctuary, dear aunt,' Ottilie replied. 'The sanctuary we should prize the most is to be found where we can be active. No atonement or self-denial will help us to

272

elude fate if it has resolved to pursue us. Only if I have to stand as an idle spectacle to the world do I fear it or find it hateful. But if I am found cheerfully working, unwearying in my duty, I can endure to be seen by anyone, because I have no reason to fear being seen by God.'

'Unless I am very much mistaken,' said Charlotte, 'you feel drawn back to the boarding-school.'

'Yes,' Ottilie replied, 'I do not deny it. It seems to me a happy vocation to teach others in the normal way when we ourselves have been taught in the strangest. And do we not see from history that people who, because of great moral misfortunes, withdrew into the wilderness, were quite unable to remain hidden and concealed there as they had hoped? They were summoned into the world again to lead those who had gone astray back on to the right path, and who could do that better than those already initiated into the sins and errors of life! They were called to aid the unfortunate, and who could do that better than those beyond all further earthly misfortune!'

'You are choosing a strange vocation,' Charlotte replied. 'I shall not stand in your way: let it be so, even if, as I hope, it will be for only a short time.'

'How grateful I am,' said Ottilie, 'that you are willing to allow me this experiment, this experience. Unless I flatter myself too much, I think I shall be successful. When I am there I shall remember how many trials I endured, and how small and petty they were compared with those I had to endure afterwards. How cheerfully I shall regard the embarrassments of the young budding creatures, smile at their childish troubles and, with gentle hand, lead them out of all their little errors. The fortunate are not suited to be in charge of the fortunate; it is in human nature to demand more and more from oneself and from others the more one has received. Only the unfortunate who are recovering from their misfortune know how to foster in themselves and in others the feeling that even a moderate good should be received with joy.'

'Let me raise one more objection to your proposal,' said Charlotte at length, after some hesitation. 'It seems to me the most important. It concerns, not you, but a third party. You are aware of the feelings of our good, sensible schoolmaster; if you follow the path you propose, you will become daily more valuable and indispensable to him. Since he already dislikes living without you, once he has grown accustomed to having you with him he will no longer be capable of carrying on with his work if you leave him. You will start by assisting him in it, only to end by spoiling it for him.'

'Fate has not dealt gently with me,' Ottilie replied, 'and anyone who loves me ought perhaps to expect little better. This friend of ours is a good and understanding man, and thus I may hope that his relations with me will also develop according to sentiments of pure friendship; he will behold in me a person set apart who is perhaps able to atone for a dreadful evil, in her own eyes and in those of others, only if she dedicates herself to that holy spirit which, invisibly encompassing us, alone can protect us from the daemonic powers which press upon us.'

Charlotte quietly reflected on what the dear child had declared so warmly. She had inquired on occasion, though in the gentlest possible way, whether there was not some faint prospect of Ottilie's approaching Eduard, but even the gentlest hint, the slightest expression of hope, the slightest suspicion of prompting in that direction seemed to have the profoundest effect on Ottilie; indeed, on one occasion, when she could not avoid the subject, she expressed herself quite plainly.

'If your resolve to renounce Eduard is so firm and unalterable,' Charlotte replied, 'beware of the danger of seeing him again. When we are separated from the object of our love, the more lively our affection is, the more we seem to be in control of ourselves, because the whole force of the passion formerly directed outwards is now turned inwards; but how soon we are wrenched out of this error when the one we thought ourselves capable of doing without all at once stands before us again, and we see we cannot do without him. Do now what you think most fitting; test yourself, indeed even alter your present resolve, but of your own free will, out of a free heart. Do not let yourself be drawn back again into the old state of affairs by chance or surprise: it is this which makes that schism in the heart which is unbearable. As I have said, before you take this step, before you leave me and begin a new life which will take you who knows where, consider once more whether you can renounce Eduard for all future time. If, however, you have determined on this, we will come to an agreement that you will not admit him, that you will not even speak to him, if he should seek you out, if he should force his way to you.' Ottilie did not hesitate for as much as a moment: she made to Charlotte the promise she had already made to herself.

Yet still there hovered before Charlotte's mind that threat of Eduard's that he would renounce Ottilie only so long as she did not separate from Charlotte. It was true that circumstances had so changed, so much had happened, that that threat wrung from him in the heat of the moment could be regarded as annulled by subsequent events; yet she did not want to venture or undertake anything remotely likely to offend him, so Mittler was to go and discover Eduard's present attitude.

Mittler had, since the child's death, often visited Charlotte, though his visits had been brief. The accident, which made a reunion of husband and wife seem to him highly unlikely, had affected him powerfully; but, hopeful and energetic as ever, he now secretly rejoiced over Ottilie's decision. He trusted in the alleviating effect of the passage of time, continued to believe he might keep husband and wife together, and regarded these passions as no more than tests of marital love and fidelity.

As soon as Ottilie had first revealed her feelings, Charlotte had written to the Major informing him of what had happened and begging him most particularly to influence Eduard not to take any further steps, to keep calm, and to wait and see whether the child would be restored to her former frame of mind. She had also communicated the essentials of subsequent events and intentions, and now Mittler was charged with the admittedly difficult task of preparing Eduard for a change in the situation. Mittler, however, knowing well that a *fait accompli* is accepted more readily than a proposition is agreed to, persuaded Charlotte that the best thing to do would be to send Ottilie back to the school straight away.

As a result, preparations were made for the journey as soon as he had left. Ottilie packed her luggage, but Charlotte noted she made no move to take with her either the pretty little chest or any of its contents. Charlotte said nothing and let Ottilie do as she wished. The day of departure dawned; Charlotte's carriage was, on the first day, to take Ottilie to quarters where she would be lodged for the night, and, on the second, on to the school; Nanni was to accompany her and remain in her service. The passionate girl had found her way back to Ottilie immediately after the child's death and clung to her again as she had before; indeed, she seemed to want to make up for her previous absence by constant merry chatter and to dedicate herself wholly to her beloved mistress. Now, since she had never yet been away from her birthplace, she was quite beside herself with joy at the prospect of travelling and seeing strange places, and she ran from the mansion down to the village to tell her parents and relatives of her good fortune and to take her leave of them. Unhappily she also encountered a case of the measles and it was at once apparent that she had contracted the disease. There was no desire to postpone the journey. Ottilie herself insisted on it. She already knew the way, she knew the people who ran the inn where she was to stay, the coachman would drive her there. There was nothing to worry about.

Charlotte did not resist. In her mind she too was hastening away from these surroundings, only she still wanted to arrange for Eduard the rooms Ottilie had occupied in the mansion and to restore them to exactly what they were before the Captain's arrival. The hope of resurrecting old happy times refuses to die down in the human heart, and Charlotte was entitled, indeed compelled, to nourish such a hope.

CHAPTER SIXTEEN

WHEN Mittler arrived to discuss the situation with Eduard, he found him alone with his head on his right hand and his arm propped on the table. He seemed to be in great suffering. 'Is it your headache again?' Mittler asked. 'It is my headache,' Eduard replied; 'and yet I cannot hate it, for it reminds me of Ottilie. I think she too may be suffering at this moment, leaning on her left arm and perhaps suffering more than I am. Why should I not endure it, as she does? These pains are salutary pains, I might almost say I desire them: for they only make me picture her patience and all her other good qualities more clearly and vividly; only when we suffer are we really conscious of all those great qualities we need to endure suffering.'

Finding his friend resigned to this degree, Mittler did not hesitate to reveal why he had come, although he did present it in historical sequence, recounting step by step how the idea had been born in the women and how it had gradually matured into an intention. Eduard hardly spoke or objected. From what little he did say it appeared that he was willing to leave everything to them; his present pain seemed to have rendered him indifferent to everything else.

Scarcely was he alone, however, when he rose and paced up and down the room. He felt the pain no longer, he was altogether occupied with other things. The lover's imagination had been kindled into violent activity even as Mittler was talking. He saw Ottilie alone, or as good as alone, on the familiar roadway, in the familiar inn whose rooms he had so often frequented; he thought, he reflected, or rather he thought without reflecting, he only longed and desired. He had to see her and speak with her. Why or wherefore or what was to come of it was of no consequence. He merely succumbed to his desires : he had to do it.

He took his valet into his confidence and his valet at once discovered the day and hour of Ottilie's departure. The morning dawned; Eduard did not delay, but took horse alone to the place where Ottilie was to spend the night. He arrived there all too punctually; the innkeeper's wife, taken by surprise, received him joyfully. She was obligated to him for a piece of great good fortune : he had procured her son a medal. The young man, who had borne himself very bravely as a soldier, had performed a deed which Eduard, who alone had witnessed it, had broadcast abroad, commending it to his superiors up as high as the general and overcoming the impediments placed in the way by a few who begrudged the young man his decoration. His mother could hardly do enough to express her gratitude. She quickly tidied up as well as she could in her best room, which was, to be sure, also cloakroom and storeroom, but Eduard informed her a lady would be arriving who would use this room and had her fix up a backroom off the corridor with the minimum requirements for his own use. The innkeeper's wife scented a mystery in the affair and found pleasure in doing something to oblige her benefactor, who showed great interest in how the rooms were being arranged and himself lent a hand. And then with what sensations he spent the age that passed until evening ! He gazed around the room in which he was to see her : it seemed, with its unwonted air of domesticity, a heavenly abode. What thoughts did not pass through his head ! Ought he to surprise Ottilie or ought he to prepare her? The latter alternative finally gained the upper hand; he sat down and wrote. She should be met by this note :

Eduard to Ottilie

As you read this letter, my best beloved, I am near you. You must not be frightened : you have nothing to fear from me. I shall not force myself upon you. You shall not see me before you give me permission to come to you.

Consider first your situation, and mine. How grateful I am that you are not proposing to take any decisive step; but the step you are proposing to take is sufficiently grave. Do not take it! Here, at a sort of crossroads, consider once more : can you be mine, will you be mine? Oh you would be conferring a great blessing on us all, and on me an immeasurable one.

Let me see you again, and let it be with joy. Let me ask you this glorious question with my own lips, and let your reply be yourself, yourself in my arms, Ottilie! in the arms where more than once you have reposed and where you belong for evermore!

As he wrote he was seized by the feeling that what he longed for so ardently was approaching, would very soon be there. 'She will come in at this door, she will read this letter, she whom I have so often summoned up in longing will again stand before me in reality. Will she still be the same? Will she look different, will she feel differently?' He still had the pen in his hand, he was about to write what he was thinking, but the carriage came rumbling into the courtyard. With hasty pen he added : 'I hear you coming. For a moment farewell!'

He folded the letter and addressed it to Ottilie : there was no time to seal it. He ran off into a room through which he knew he could gain the corridor, and instantly remembered he had left his watch and signet behind on the table. She must not come in and see these; he ran back and managed to retrieve them. He could already hear the innkeeper's wife in the entrance hall making for the room to show it to her newly-arrived guest. He hurried back to the door but it had shut.

He had knocked the key from the lock as he had rushed in and it now lay outside; the lock had snapped shut and he was unable to get out. He pushed hard against the door but it did not yield. Oh how he would have liked to change into a ghost and slip through the cracks! In vain! He hid his face against the doorpost. Ottilie came in; when the innkeeper's wife saw he was there she went out again. Ottilie too could not fail to see him. He turned towards her, and thus the lovers were once more brought face to face in the strangest manner. She looked at him with grave tranquillity, not moving from where she stood, and when he made a move to approach her she stepped back a few paces to the table. He too stepped back again. 'Ottilie,' he exclaimed, 'let me break this dreadful silence. Are we no more than shadows facing one another? But before all, let me tell you it is by chance that you discover me here now in this room. There is lying beside you a letter which was meant to prepare you. Read it, I beg of you, read it! And then come to whatever decision you can.'

She looked down at the letter and, after some hesitation, picked it up, tore it open and read it. She read it without changing her expression, and without changing her expression she laid it gently down; then she pressed the palms of her hands together, and, raising them in the air, carried them to her breast, at the same time bowing very slightly and bestowing on him who had made this urgent request such a glance that he was glad to desist. The gesture tore at his heart. He could not bear to watch her as she stood there. It seemed as if she would sink to her knees before him if he persisted. He rushed from the room in despair and sent the innkeeper's wife in to the solitary figure he had left behind.

He paced up and down the entrance hall. Night had come on and it was still quiet in the room. Eventually the innkeeper's wife appeared and removed the key. The good lady was disturbed and embarrassed and did not know what she ought to do. Finally, as she was moving off she proffered the key to Eduard, who refused it. She left the light burning and went away.

In the profoundest misery Eduard threw himself down on Ottilie's threshold and dissolved into tears. Seldom have a loving couple passed so woeful a night so close together.

Day dawned; the coachman wanted to be off, the innkeeper's wife unlocked the door and went into the room. She found Ottilie asleep in her clothes; she came back and beckoned Eduard with a tender smile. They both went in and stood looking down at the sleeping girl, but Eduard was unable to bear even this sight. The innkeeper's wife would not venture to waken her but sat down close to where she was lying. Eventually Ottilie opened her lovely eyes and rose to her feet. She refuses breakfast, and then Eduard comes in to her. He implores her to speak but one word, to say what it is she wants; he swears he desires to do only what she wants; but she does not speak. Again he asks her, tenderly and insistently, if she will be his. With downcast eyes she gently shakes her head. He asks if she wants to go on to school. She shakes her head indifferently. But when he asks whether he may take her back to Charlotte, she replies with a confident affirmative nod. He hastens to the window to instruct the coachman but she is away, out of the room like the wind, down the stairs, into the carriage. The coachman takes the road back to the mansion; Eduard follows on horseback some distance behind.

CHAPTER SEVENTEEN

CHARLOTTE was astounded to see Ottilie come driving and Eduard come riding into the courtyard at the same time. She hastened to the entry: Ottilie dismounts from the carriage and approaches with Eduard. With fervour she forcibly seizes the hands of Eduard and Charlotte, presses them together and hastens to her room. Eduard falls upon his wife's neck and bursts into tears. He cannot explain, he asks her to be patient with him, to stand by Ottilie, to help her. Charlotte hastens to Ottilie's room and shudders as she goes in, for it had already been cleared and only the bare walls remained. It looked as enormous as it seemed cheerless. The servants had removed everything: only the little chest had been left in the middle of the room, since they had been uncertain where to put it. Ottilie lay on the floor, her head on the casket and her arms thrown over it. Charlotte kneels down beside her, asks what has happened and receives no answer.

She leaves her maid with Ottilie and hastens to Eduard. She finds him in the drawing-room; he too tells her nothing. He throws himself on the floor before her, he bathes her hands with his tears, he flees to his room, and when she makes to follow him she is met by his valet, who enlightens her as far as he is able. She pieces the rest together for herself, and then at once quickly resolves on what must immediately be done. Ottilie's room is restored as quickly as it can be. Eduard had found his own rooms exactly as he left them, down to the last scrap of paper.

The three appear to resume their former life together; but Ottilie continues to keep silence and Eduard can do nothing but beg his wife to show that patience which he himself appears to lack. Charlotte sends messengers to Mittler and the

Major. The former was not to be found; the latter arrives. To him Eduard pours out his heart, he confesses every last detail, and thus Charlotte learns what has happened, what has changed the situation so remarkably, the cause of all the emotion.

She speaks most lovingly to her husband. She does not know what else to ask but that he should for the present leave Ottilie alone. Eduard is sensible of his wife's love and good sense, but he is exclusively dominated by his passion. Charlotte offers him hope and promises to agree to the divorce. He places no confidence in her words. He is in so morbid a condition that hope and belief alternately desert him; he urges Charlotte to offer her hand to the Major; he is in the grip of a sort of frantic ill-humour. Charlotte, to soothe and sustain him, does what he demands. She offers the Major her hand, provided Ottilie is willing to be united with Eduard and on the express condition the two men go away together for the time being. The Major has some foreign business to transact for his court and Eduard promises to accompany him. Arrangements are made and, since at any rate something is being done, a certain calm is achieved.

Meanwhile, it is apparent that Ottilie is taking hardly any food or drink, while she is continuing to persist in her silence. They speak to her, but this makes her distressed and they forbear. For have not most of us the weakness that we would not gladly torment anyone even for his own good? Charlotte pondered every possible way of assisting her and at length she lit upon the idea of summoning the young schoolmaster, who had great influence over Ottilie and who had made very friendly inquiries about her unexpected failure to arrive, which inquiries had not yet received a reply.

So as not to present her with a surprise they discuss this proposal in Ottilie's presence. She seems not to be in agreement; she deliberates; at length a resolve seems to mature within her; she hastens to her room, and before they have assembled together for the evening she sends down the following epistle:

Ottilie to her Friends

What need have I, my dear friends, to say that which speaks for itself? I have deserted my rightful path and I am not to return to it. Even if I could become at one with myself again, it seems that a malign demon has gained power over me to bar my way from without.

My intention to renounce Eduard and to go far away from him was quite sincere. I hoped never to meet him again. It has turned out otherwise: he stood before me even against his own will. Perhaps I took too literally my promise not to speak with him. As my feelings and conscience prompted me at that moment I stood silent before him, and now I have nothing more to say. On an impulse of feeling I chanced to impose on myself a vow which, to sober consideration, might seem hazardous. Let me persist in it so long as my heart commands me. Do not call in any mediator! Do not urge me to speak or to take more food and drink than I absolutely need. Help me through this time by your patience and consideration. I am young, and youth recovers unawares. Suffer me in your company, gladden me with your love, instruct me with your conversation: but leave my soul to me!

The long-prepared departure of the men did not take place because that foreign business of the Major's was delayed: much to Eduard's delight! Excited now by Ottilie's note, encouraged anew by her comforting, hope-giving words and feeling justified in continuing to hold out, he all at once declared he would not go. 'How foolish,' he cried, 'deliberately and precipitately to throw away what we most need and can least do without, and, even if we are threatened with losing it, might still hold on to! And for why! Merely so it may seem that man is capable of willing and choosing. Possessed by such foolish self-conceit I have often in the past torn myself away from my friends hours, indeed days, before

I had to, merely so as not to be compelled to leave when the final unavoidable hour arrived. But this time I will stay. Why should I go, why should I leave her? Has she not already left me? I have no intention of touching her, of taking her hand, of pressing her to my heart: I even dare not think of it, I shudder at the thought. She has not gone away from me, she has risen above me.'

And so he stayed, as he wanted to, as he had to. And he had never felt anything to compare with the sense of well-being he felt when he and she were together, a sensation which she too still retained: she too could not forsake this blissful feeling which had become for them both a necessity. They exerted, as before, an indescribable, almost magical attraction upon one another. They lived beneath one roof, but even when they were not actually thinking about one another, when they were involved with other things, driven hither and thither by society, they still drew closer together. If they found themselves in the same room, it was not long before they were standing or sitting side-by-side. Only the closest proximity to one another could make them tranquil and calm of mind, but then they were altogether tranquil, and this proximity was sufficient: no glance, no word, no gesture, no touch was needed, but only this pure togetherness. Then they were not two people, they were one person, one in unreflecting perfect well-being, contented with themselves and with the universe. Indeed, if one of them had been imprisoned at the far end of the house, the other would gradually and without any conscious intention have moved across in that direction. Life was an enigma to them whose solution they could discover only with one another.

Ottilie was altogether cheerful and relaxed, so that the others began to feel quite at ease about her. She rarely absented herself from their company, though she had persuaded them to let her eat alone. She was served by no one except Nanni.

Typical experiences are repeated more frequently than one thinks, because their immediate cause is the nature of him who experiences them. His character, personality, inclinations, tendencies, the locality in which he lives, his environment and habits, together form a whole in which he lives as in his own element, his own atmosphere, and in which alone he can be comfortable. And thus we are astonished to find that human beings, about whose changeableness so much complaint is heard, are after a lapse of many years unchanged and, in spite of subjection to an endless number of inner and outer influences, unchangeable.

And so too almost everything in our friends' daily life together was back again on its old lines. Ottilie continued to give silent proof of her obliging nature by many acts of kindness, and the others too behaved normally, each according to his own nature. In this way the domestic circle appeared to be a replica of their former life and they could be forgiven the illusion that everything was still as it had been.

The autumn days, of a like length to those earlier spring days, called the company back into the house at the self-same hour. The adornment of fruit and flower which this season owns gave them to imagine it must be the autumn of that first spring: the time between had fallen into oblivion. For now there bloomed such flowers as they had planted in those first days too; now those trees bore fruit which then they had seen in blossom.

The Major came and went, and Mittler too was often to be seen. Their evening gatherings were usually of the routine sort. Eduard usually read to them, more vivaciously, with more feeling, better, indeed more cheerfully than before. It was as if he sought to thaw out Ottilie's numbness through gaiety as well as through warmth of feeling. As before, he sat so that she could see his book, indeed he grew restless and distracted if she did not read over his shoulder, if he could not be certain she was following his words with her eyes.

The joyless troubled feelings of the time between had gone. No longer did anyone bear resentment against anyone else: all bitterness had faded away. The Major accompanied on the violin Charlotte's piano-playing, as Eduard's flute again kept time with Ottilie's. And thus they drew closer to Eduard's birthday, which had not been celebrated the year before.

This time, they had half tacitly, half explicitly agreed, it was to be celebrated quietly, without festivity. Yet the nearer it approached, the more solemn Ottilie became, with a solemnity which the others had hitherto sensed rather than expressly noticed. She often seemed to be inspecting the flowers in the garden; she had hinted to the gardener that he should preserve as they were as many of the summer plants as he could, and she had lingered in particular before the asters, which that year were blossoming in exceptionally great profusion.

CHAPTER EIGHTEEN

THE most significant thing the friends quietly observed, however, was that Ottilie had for the first time unpacked the casket and selected various materials from it and cut up sufficient to make a single complete set of clothes. When she tried with Nanni's help to pack it away again she could hardly manage it: the casket was over-full, even though part of its contents had been removed. The girl stared covetously at the clothes, especially when she saw that all the smaller accessories had also been provided. There were shoes, stockings, embroidered garters, gloves and many other things. She begged Ottilie to give her just a few of them. Ottilie declined to do so, but straightway opened a chest of drawers and let the child have her choice. Nanni made a quick grab and at once ran off with her booty to exhibit it and announce her good fortune to the other members of the household.

Ottilie eventually succeeded in arranging everything carefully back in the chest, whereupon she opened a concealed compartment fitted into the lid. There she had hidden a number of notes and letters from Eduard, various dried flowers culled on their walks together, a lock of her beloved's hair, and other things. She added one more object – it was her father's portrait – and closed it all up, after which she hung the little key on the gold chain back around her neck.

Sundry hopes had in the meanwhile begun to stir in our friends' hearts. Charlotte was convinced that Ottilie would start to speak again on that coming day, for she now seemed to be secretly occupied and she wore an air of cheerful self-content, a smile such as appears on the face of one who is concealing something good and gratifying from those he loves. No one knew that Ottilie passed many hours in a state of great debility from which she roused herself by will-power only when she appeared outside her room.

During this time Mittler had been calling more frequently and staying longer than had been his custom. The obstinate gentleman knew only too well that you must wait till the iron is hot before striking. He interpreted Ottilie's silence and abstinence in a sense favourable to his own notions. Up to now no steps had been taken towards a divorce, and he hoped to be able to steer Ottilie's fate in some other propitious direction. He listened, he yielded, he demurred, and, in his own fashion, behaved as prudently as might be desired.

Only, when opportunity arose for arguing about matters which he regarded as being of great weight, then he was always carried away. He was much given to introspection, and when he associated with others it was usually in the sense of actively assisting them. But if he once started talking among his friends, his loquacity would, as we have seen, go rolling heedlessly on, wounding or healing, harming or help-ing, just as it might turn out.

On the evening before Eduard's birthday Charlotte and the Major were sitting together waiting for Eduard, who had gone out riding; Mittler was pacing up and down the room; Ottilie had stayed in her own room laying out her finery for the morrow and giving various silent instructions to Nanni, which the girl understood quite well and carried out very ably.

Mittler had just got on to one of his favourite topics. He was fond of asserting that nothing was more inept or barbaric, in the education of children or the government of peoples, than prohibitions, than prohibitive laws and regulations. 'Man is by nature active,' he said, 'and if you know how to command him he will get on with whatever you will tell him to do. Speaking for myself, I prefer to tolerate crimes and errors in my own circle until such time as I am able to suggest a better alternative, rather than abolish the error without having anything to put in its place. Man likes to do what is good and purposeful if only he can discover what it is; he does it so as to have something to do, and thinks no more about it than he does about the follies he commits through idleness and boredom.

'How often it puts me out of humour to hear the way the Ten Commandments are repeated in Sunday school. The fifth is quite a nice, reasonable, positive commandment: Honour thy father and thy mother. If children inscribe that on their minds they can practise it the whole day long. But what is one to say of the sixth? Thou shalt not kill. As if anyone had the remotest desire to kill anyone else! You may hate someone, you may grow angry, you may act rashly, and as a consequence of this and of much else it may occasionally happen that you kill someone. But is it not a barbaric custom to forbid children to kill and murder? If it said: Care for thy neighbour's life, remove what may be harmful to him, save him even at risk to thyself, if thou harmest him think thou harmest thyself – these are commandments that have a place among cultivated, rational peoples, yet when they are dragged into the catechism, it is only as a wretched footnote.

'And as for the seventh, that one I find quite repulsive! What! Are we to stimulate children's curiosity about dangerous mysteries of which they already have an inkling and excite their imaginations to strange ideas and images which are likely violently to precipitate precisely that which we want to keep from them? It would be far better for such things to be arbitrarily punished by a secret tribunal than for them to be blabbed about before church and congregation.'

At that moment Ottilie came in. – 'Thou shalt not commit adultery,' Mittler went on: 'How coarse, how improper! Would it not sound far different if it said: Thou shalt reverence the marriage bond; where thou seest a loving husband and wife thou shalt rejoice thereat and be glad as at the happiness of a bright day. Should anything trouble their relationship, thou shalt seek to rectify it: thou shalt seek to bring them to peace with one another, to make clear to them their mutual advantages, and with fine selflessness further their well-being by letting them feel what happiness lies in every duty and especially in that duty which binds man and wife indissolubly together.'

Charlotte was in an agony of apprehension. The situation was all the more dreadful for her in that she was convinced Mittler had no idea what he was saying or where he was saying it, and before she could interrupt him she saw Ottilie leave the room, her face and aspect transformed.

'Perhaps you will spare us the eighth commandment,' she said with a forced smile. 'All the others,' Mittler replied, 'provided I can save that upon which they all rest.'

Rushing in with a shriek of horror, Nanni cried: 'She's dying! The lady's dying! Come quick!'

When Ottilie had returned fainting to her room all the finery for the following day lay spread out over the chairs, and Nanni, who had been running about gazing upon it with wonder and admiration, cried out triumphantly: 'Just look at it, miss! Clothes for a bride really worthy of you!'

Ottilie heard these words and sank down on the sofa. Nanni sees her mistress turn pale and motionless: she runs to Charlotte and they come along to the room. Their friendly physician comes hurrying up; it seems to him only a case of exhaustion. He has some strong broth prepared; Ottilie refuses it with a gesture of revulsion, indeed she is almost convulsed when they take the spoon to her mouth. He asks earnestly and urgently what Ottilie has had to eat that day. The girl falters; he repeats the question, and the girl confesses that Ottilie has had nothing to eat.

Nanni seems to him more frightened than she ought to be. He pulls her into a neighbouring room, Charlotte follows, the girl falls to her knees and confesses that for a long time now Ottilie has had as good as nothing to eat. At Ottilie's insistence she has eaten the food instead; she has kept silent about it because of her mistress's silent entreaties and threats, and also, she added innocently, because it tasted so good.

Mittler and the Major came in and found Charlotte and the doctor busy with Ottilie. The beautiful child sat, pale and apparently conscious, in the corner of the sofa. They beg her to lie down; she refuses, but gestures to them to bring over the little chest. She places her feet upon it and finds this semi-recumbent position comfortable. She seems to be wanting to take her leave, her gestures seem to be expressing the tenderest attachment to those standing about her – love, gratitude, appeal for pardon, and the most heartfelt farewell.

Eduard returns and learns what has happened, he rushes into the room, he throws himself down beside her, clasps her hand and bathes it with silent tears. For long he remains thus, without moving. At last he cries: 'Shall I never hear your voice again? Will you never return to this life with a word for me? Very well! I shall follow you across: there we shall speak together in another tongue!'

She grips his hand tightly, she gazes upon him with eyes full of life and love, and after drawing a deep breath, after an ethereal silent movement of the lips, 'Promise me you will live!' she cries with gentle exertion, and at once sinks back. 'I promise!' he cried to her – yet he only cried it after her, for she had already departed.

After a night of tears it fell to Charlotte to care for the interment of the dear remains. Mittler and the Major stood by her. Eduard's condition was pitiable. As soon as he was able to emerge from his despair and come at all to his senses, he insisted that Ottilie should not be removed from the mansion but waited on and attended, and treated as a living person, for she was not dead, she could not be dead. They did as he wished, in as much as they did not do what he had forbidden. He did not ask to see her.

Yet another dreadful event now came to plague our friends. Nanni, whom the doctor had sternly reprimanded, forced to a confession by threats, and after the confession heaped with reproaches, had run away. After a long search she was found again; she seemed distracted. Her parents took her back into their care. No treatment, however kind, seemed to have any effect upon her and, since she threatened to run away again, she had to be locked in the house.

Gradually they succeeded in banishing the black despair into which Eduard was sunk, but it was only to transport him to a worse condition; for he now perceived, he was now convinced, that his life's happiness was gone from him for ever. They ventured to suggest to him that if Ottilie were laid in the chapel she would still be among the living and would not lack a quiet friendly dwelling-place. It was hard to obtain his consent, and only on condition that she was carried there in an open coffin and the coffin was laid in the vault covered only by a glass lid and that an ever-burning lamp was set before it did he finally agree and seem to resign himself to everything.

They dressed the gentle body in the finery she herself had prepared; they set on her head a wreath of asters, which glittered strangely like melancholy stars. To decorate the bier, the church, the chapel, all the gardens were plundered. They lay deserted as if winter had already come and blotted out all their joy. In the early morning she was borne out of the mansion in an open coffin and the rising sun again brought a glow of red to her ethereal features. The mourners crowded about the pall-bearers: no one wanted to go on ahead or follow behind, they all wanted to press close to her and again, and for the last time still be with her. The boys, the men, the women: none was left unmoved. The girls, who felt their loss most immediately, were inconsolable.

Nanni was not there. They had kept her away, or rather concealed from her the day and hour of the funeral. She was being kept at home with her parents in a room looking on to the garden. But when she heard the bells she soon realized what was going on, and when the woman who had been left to look after her slipped away to watch the *cortège* she climbed out of the window into a passageway and, since she found all the doors locked, up into the garret.

The *cortège* was just winding its way along the road through the village, which had been swept clean and then strewn with leaves. Nanni saw clearly her mistress below her, more clearly, more completely, more beautifully than any who were following. In an unearthly way, as if borne on clouds or the waves of the sea, she seemed to beckon to her servant, and Nanni, confused, trembling and giddy, fell down to the ground.

With a cry of horror the crowd scattered in all directions. The confusion and pressure compelled the bearers to set down the bier. The child lay quite close to it: she seemed to be shattered in every limb. They lifted her up and, either by chance or a dispensation of providence, they rested her over the corpse, indeed she herself seemed to be trying with her last remaining spark of life to reach her beloved mistress. But hardly had her lifeless limbs touched Ottilie's dress, her powerless fingers touched Ottilie's folded hands, than the girl sprang up, first raised her eyes and hands to heaven, then fell on her knees before the coffin and gazed up at her mistress in an ecstasy of amazement and devotion.

At length she sprang up as if inspired and exclaimed in tones of solemn joy: 'Yes, she has forgiven me! What no man could forgive, what I could not forgive myself, God has forgiven through her glance, through her gestures, through her mouth. Now again she reposes so still and gentle: but you saw how she raised herself and blessed me with her hands, how she gazed on me with such friendly eyes! You all heard, you are witnesses, how she said to me: Thou art forgiven! – Now I am no longer a murderess among you; she has pardoned me, God has pardoned me, and now no one can hold anything against me.'

The crowd stood pressing round her; lost in astonishment, they listened and gazed about them and hardly knew what to do next. 'Now carry her to rest!' said the girl: 'she has done what it was hers to do and suffered what it was hers to suffer, and she can no longer dwell among us.' The bier moved on, Nanni followed it at the head of the crowd, and they came to the church and the chapel.

And thus Ottilie's coffin now stood enclosed in an oaken shrine, the dead child's coffin at its head and her little casket at its foot. They had engaged a woman to keep watch over the body lying so fair under its glass cover, but Nanni insisted on performing this office herself: she wanted to stay there alone, without any companion, and tend the lamp now lit for the first time. So passionately and persistently did she demand it, they let her have her way for fear her mind might grow more unhinged if they refused.

But she was not alone for long: for as night was falling and the flickering light, now coming into its own, began to spread around a brighter glow, the door opened and the architect came into the chapel; and the chapel, with its piously decorated walls bathed in so gentle a light, seemed to him more ancient and mysterious than he had ever believed possible.

Nanni sat at one side of the coffin. She recognized him at once, but in silence she indicated her dead mistress. And so he stood on the other side, in the strength and charm of his youth, sunk in his own thoughts, motionless with drooping arms and piteously wringing his hands, his head bowed towards the inanimate form.

Once before he had stood thus, in the tableau of Belisarius. Now he involuntarily adopted the same posture, and as the posture had then been a natural one, so it was now. Here too something immeasurably fine had fallen from its heights;

and if, in the case of Belisarius, bravery, prudence, power, rank and wealth combined in one man was mourned as irretrievably lost, if qualities indispensable to the nation and its prince in times of crisis had, instead of being valued, been thrown aside and banished, so in the case of Ottilie many other quiet virtues not long since called forth by nature out of its capacious depths had quickly been obliterated again by its own indifferent hand: rare, beautiful virtues, whose peaceful influence the needy world in every age embraces with joy and satisfaction and longingly mourns for when it is gone.

The young man stood in silence, and the girl too stayed silent for a time; but when she saw tears flowing copiously from his eyes, when he seemed to be dissolving utterly in grief, she addressed him with such truth and force, with such kindness and certainty, that, astonished at her flow of speech, he was able to pull himself together, and in imagination he saw his fair friend alive and active in a higher region. His tears were dried, his grief was assuaged; on his knees he took his farewell of Ottilie, he pressed Nanni's hand warmly in farewell, and that same night he rode away without having seen anyone else.

Without the girl's knowledge the physician had stayed in the church throughout the night, and when he came to see her in the morning he found her cheerful and in good heart. He was prepared for all sorts of aberrations: he thought she would talk of nocturnal colloquies with Ottilie and other such phenomena, but she acted naturally and was tranquil and altogether self-possessed. She recalled her earlier life and circumstances perfectly well and with great exactitude, and nothing she said departed from the sphere of normal truth and reality except the episode at the funeral, which she was often joyfully to reiterate: how Ottilie had raised herself up, blessed her, forgiven her, and thereby brought peace to her heart for evermore.

Ottilie's continuing beauty, and the state resembling rather sleep than death in which she lay, attracted people to the chapel. The villagers and those living in the neighbourhood around wanted to see her once more and each was eager to hear the unbelievable event from Nanni's lips: some to mock, most to doubt, a few to believe.

Every need to which reality denies satisfaction compels to belief. Nanni, who in front of the eyes of all the world had been shattered in every limb, had been made whole again by touching the hallowed body: why should a similar good fortune not be available here for others too? At first fond mothers brought their ailing children in secret and believed they perceived a sudden improvement. Faith and confidence increased, until at length there was no one so old or weak but he had sought refreshment and relief at this shrine. More and more came to visit it, and it was found necessary to close the chapel and indeed the church outside the hours of divine service.

Eduard did not venture to go to his departed beloved again. He lived on unheeding, he seemed to have no more tears to shed, to be incapable of further grief. His participation in social life, his enjoyment of food and drink decline with every passing day. The only solace remaining to him seems to be that which he imbibes from that chalice which had indeed been no true prophet to him. He is still fond of contemplating the intertwined initials, and his soulful mien as he does so seems to suggest he has still not lost all hope of a reunion. And just as every circumstance seems to favour and every chance event uplift a happy man, so the pettiest things like to combine to mortify and undo an unhappy one. For one day, as Eduard was taking the beloved chalice to his lips, he started with horror and put it down again: there was something different about it, a little distinguishing mark is missing. The valet is interrogated and constrained to confess that the genuine chalice has not long ago been broken and a similar one, also dating from Eduard's youth, substituted. Eduard is incapable of anger: his fate has been enunciated by events, why should he be troubled by a symbol? Yet he is nonetheless profoundly impressed by it. From then on drink seems to be repugnant to him and he seems to be deliberately abstaining from food and from speech.

But from time to time he is seized by a feeling of restlessness. He again asks for something to eat, he again begins to speak. 'Alas!' he said on one occasion to the Major, who was seldom far from his side, 'how unfortunate I am that all my endeavours have ever been no more than an imitation, a counterfeit! What was bliss to her is grief and pain to me; and yet for the sake of that bliss I am compelled to take this grief and pain upon me. I must go after her, and by this path: but my nature holds me back, and my promise. It is a terrible task to imitate the inimitable. I well perceive, my dear friend, there can be genius in anything, even in martyrdom.'

What need, in face of this hopeless condition, to dwell upon the wifely, friendly and medical exertions to which Eduard's nearest and dearest put themselves for a little time yet? Eventually he was found dead. It was Mittler who made the sad discovery. He called the doctor who, with his usual composure, observed with exactitude the circumstances in which the deceased had been found. Charlotte came running up: a suspicion of suicide crossed her mind; she was about to accuse herself and others of unpardonable lack of foresight. But the doctor and Mittler were soon able to convince her – the doctor on natural grounds, Mittler on moral – that this could not be the case. It was quite clear that Eduard had not been expecting his death. He had taken out of a chest and a portfolio and spread out before him what remained to him of Ottilie – a practice he had hitherto succeeded in keeping secret: a lock of hair, flowers gathered in a happy hour, every little note she had written him back to that first note which his wife had by ominous chance picked up and handed to him.

He could not have wanted to expose all this to fortuitous discovery. And so this heart too, not long since roused to boundless agitation, lay in imperturbable peace; and as he had fallen asleep in thoughts of the blessed saint, he too might be called blessed. Charlotte laid him beside Ottilie where he belonged, and decreed that no one else was to be buried in this vault. With this condition she made large bequests to the church and the school, to the clergy and the teachers.

And thus the lovers lie side by side. Peace hovers about their abode, smiling angelic figures (with whom too they have affinity) look down upon them from the vault above, and what a happy moment it will be when one day they awaken again together.

READ MORE IN PENGUIN

In every corner of the world, on every subject under the sun, Penguin represents quality and variety – the very best in publishing today.

For complete information about books available from Penguin – including Puffins, Penguin Classics and Arkana – and how to order them, write to us at the appropriate address below. Please note that for copyright reasons the selection of books varies from country to country.

In the United Kingdom: Please write to *Dept. JC, Penguin Books Ltd, FREEPOST, West Drayton, Middlesex UB7 OBR*

If you have any difficulty in obtaining a title, please send your order with the correct money, plus ten per cent for postage and packaging, to *PO Box No. 11, West Drayton, Middlesex UB7 OBR*

In the United States: Please write to *Penguin USA Inc., 375 Hudson Street, New York, NY 10014*

In Canada: Please write to *Penguin Books Canada Ltd, 10 Alcorn Avenue, Suite 300, Toronto, Ontario M4V 3B2*

In Australia: Please write to *Penguin Books Australia Ltd, 487 Maroondah Highway, Ringwood, Victoria 3134*

In New Zealand: Please write to *Penguin Books (NZ) Ltd,182–190 Wairau Road, Private Bag, Takapuna, Auckland 9*

In India: Please write to *Penguin Books India Pvt Ltd, 706 Eros Apartments, 56 Nehru Place, New Delhi 110 019*

In the Netherlands: Please write to *Penguin Books Netherlands B.V., Keizersgracht 231 NL–1016 DV Amsterdam*

In Germany: Please write to *Penguin Books Deutschland GmbH, Friedrichstrasse 10–12, W–6000 Frankfurt/Main 1*

In Spain: Please write to *Penguin Books S. A., C. San Bernardo 117–6° E–28015 Madrid*

In Italy: Please write to *Penguin Italia s.r.l., Via Felice Casati 20, I–20124 Milano*

In France: Please write to *Penguin France S. A., 17 rue Lejeune, F–31000 Toulouse*

In Japan: Please write to *Penguin Books Japan, Ishikiribashi Building, 2–5–4, Suido, Bunkyo-ku, Tokyo 112*

In Greece: Please write to *Penguin Hellas Ltd, Dimocritou 3, GR–106 71 Athens*

In South Africa: Please write to *Longman Penguin Southern Africa (Pty) Ltd, Private Bag X08, Bertsham 2013*

READ MORE IN PENGUIN

A CHOICE OF CLASSICS

READ MORE IN PENGUIN

A CHOICE OF CLASSICS